SEE NO EVIL

Evelyn, Gay and Margaret are sisters. When their widowed mother dies, the caring Evelyn is thrust into looking after Margaret, who was born blind. Gay, always pursuing her own interests, is happy to be taken out by the rich Gordon de Verriland, leaving Evelyn wondering if she will ever meet someone herself. Then, when Nicky March comes into Evelyn's life, could he be the one for her? Or will Gay's selfishness ruin her hope of love?

PATRICIA ROBINS

SEE NO EVIL

Complete and Unabridged

LINFORD
Leicester

First published in Great Britain in 1945

First Linford Edition
published 2010

British Library CIP Data

Robins, Patricia, *1921 –*
  See no evil. - -
  (Linford romance library)
  1. Sisters- -Fiction. 2. Blind women- -
  Care- -Fiction. 3. Women caregivers- -
  Fiction. 4. Love stories.
  5. Large type books.
  I. Title II. Series
  823.9'14–dc22

  ISBN 978–1–44480–454–6

20292668
Published by
F. A. Thorpe (Publishing)
Anstey, Leicestershire

Set by Words & Graphics Ltd.
Anstey, Leicestershire
Printed and bound in Great Britain by
T. J. International Ltd., Padstow, Cornwall

FOR MY GRANDMOTHER

for whom Yeats must have written these
words:

> Time can but make her beauty
>   over again:
> Because of that great nobleness
>   of hers
> The fire that stirs about her, when
>   she stirs,
> Burns but more clearly.

1

Evelyn and Gay Challis knew they were going to have a third sister because they had heard Nanny and Cook talking about it.

'It will be here by August,' Nanny had said, and:

'The Missus don't want it!' Cook had replied in a voice which made twelve-year-old Evelyn look up from her pastry cutting and say in the soft serious tone of voice which so resembled her father's:

'Not want the baby, Cook? But Mummy *must* want it!'

'There's no must about it!' Cook answered caustically. But a glance from Nanny silenced any further comments on the subject.

Evelyn, tactful even at that age, did not persist in her questioning as she would have liked to do. She continued cutting little rounds of pastry for Cook's jam tartlets, but her mind was busy with thoughts about the baby.

It could not be true that Mummy did not want it! Why, she, Evelyn, was so looking forward to having another sister that she wanted to shout and sing and tell everyone she knew how pleased and happy she was. It wasn't that she did not love Gay. She did love her — passionately and selflessly. But her eight-year-old sister was as self-sufficient as she was clever. Dependence was unknown to her and she needed no one — least of all Evelyn, to help her live her life.

'I can do it!' she would say resentfully if anyone offered to help her.

And, usually, this was true. She could do almost anything she put her young mind to, and in some ways, she was already far older than Evelyn.

'Them two's as unalike as sisters could be,' Cook had remarked often enough.

Evelyn knew it was true. She and Gay were different in looks as well as in character. Where Gay was all golden curls and sparkling, flashing, blue-grey eyes, she, Evelyn, was pale-skinned, had dark, smooth hair and serious, thoughtful brown eyes. Where Gay was a creature of sudden tempers and spells of infectious good spirits, her sister knew herself to be quiet, even-tempered and reliable.

True to her name, Gay could be sunshine and quicksilver. She could be as generous as at times she was selfish, and there was only one person who really mattered to her — herself.

Evelyn, always easy to manage, always willing to give way to others, was thought by Cook and most people who knew her, to be 'a dear little thing' but rather weak and stupid. Actually, Evelyn had all Gay's strength of character, but it had not yet come to light since she was only to be strong when her strength was needed for others. She loved everything small and helpless, her capacity for giving sympathy and understanding being apparent even at her age. Evelyn admired her sister and wished she were more like her. But she was very much an individual in a class of her own and the very qualities which distinguished her from Gay were to be the chains which kept her shackled. The first link in that chain was forged when Cook said:

'The Missus don't want it!'

Well, if Mummy didn't, she, Evelyn, did! She would take care of it and love it so much that it would not need a mother's love. And Gay — yes, she, too, must love it because anyone Gay loved would have to be happy. Just to be with her made one realize what a good world it was.

Evelyn finished her pastry rounds and went up to the nursery.

'Gay!' she called. 'Gay!'

'What is it, Evie? I'm under the table.'

'What are you doing?' Evelyn asked curiously.

'I've been Robinson Crusoe,' Gay said, emerging from under the nursery

4

table with a cloth thrown round her shoulders and her fair hair ruffled. 'But I'm tired of it now. It's no fun without a Man Friday.'

'I'll be Man Friday for you,' Evelyn offered hopefully, but Gay shook her head vigorously.

'You wouldn't know what to do!' she said, oblivious to the sudden hurt in her sister's eyes.

But Evelyn said nothing of her disappointment and returned to the subject foremost in her mind.

'Gay, *you* want our baby sister, don't you?'

Gay looked up in surprise.

'Gosh, no!' she said flatly. 'Why, we will have to share all our toys and the pony and, anyway, how do you know it will be a girl?'

'I don't *know*,' Evelyn said carefully. 'But I kind of feel sure . . . Gay, you will love it — *do* love it! You see, Cook says Mummy doesn't want it.'

'Nor do I!' said Gay, turning away petulantly. 'Anyway, it isn't here yet, so don't let's bother about it. I'm going to ride Jeremy!'

Evelyn watched her stride out of the nursery, knowing better than to try and detain her. Gay would feel differently when the baby came. She was sure of it.

But Evelyn, precocious though she was in an understanding of other people, was blind where her emotions were involved. And she loved Gay. Therefore Gay could do no wrong, and if she did, Evelyn usually found an excuse for her. When she had come upon Gay severely thrashing the pony in one of her fits of temper, she had, before condemning her, asked in her gentle voice:

'But why were you doing it, Gay? It didn't kick you, did it?'

Gay, staring at her sister with flushed cheeks and bright eyes, said furiously:

'He wouldn't jump.'

'But you didn't just hit him because of that, did you, Gay?'

The child avoided Evelyn's steady gaze and said:

'Yes! He's got to learn to do what I want.'

Evelyn, explaining aloud that it was the wrong way to treat a dumb animal, excused her sister's cruelty to herself with the thought:

'She was only trying to teach Jeremy a lesson.'

In the same way, she excused her mother to herself and Gay.

Ella Challis was a spoilt, hard, selfish product of society. She had no love or use for her children and her dealings with them were both unjust and thoughtless.

'Mummy's a beastly pig!' Gay had cried when they had not been allowed to go to a children's party on Nanny's afternoon off because their mother wanted to go to a cocktail party. 'If she couldn't take us, she could have let us go alone.'

'No, she couldn't, Gay,' Evelyn had said. 'She would be afraid all the time that we would get lost or something.'

'But why couldn't she come to *our*

party?' Gay had challenged.

'She told you why,' Evelyn answered. 'She didn't want to disappoint Daddy.'

'Rot!' Gay retorted rudely. 'You know Daddy doesn't like parties.'

Evelyn knew this was true.

'Then Mummy must think he likes them,' she answered.

Gay was not convinced. Like a bright, inquisitive squirrel, she had observed the differences between her mother and father and knew instinctively that they did not love each other. She knew, too, that her father saw through her own wiles and respected him even while she was thwarted by him. She passionately wanted his love because she knew he did not care for her or pay her the attention she could usually get from grown-ups, and was frantically jealous of Evelyn because she seemed to inspire their father's affection with no apparent effort. She had to study the things which pleased him; Evelyn did them naturally.

For her mother she had neither love

nor respect, and would have been considerably put out to know her father considered her to be her mother's daughter — selfish, spoilt, temperamental, difficult. But he also pitied her because there was good in her — a gay simple side to her nature and a desire to be happy which he thought could not triumph over that other side.

Had he lived, he might have helped her, but he died before he knew he was going to have a third child.

Mrs. Challis made no pretence of being heartbroken inside her own home when her husband died suddenly of pneumonia. She had never ceased to regret the day she married him, and she was relieved to be free of him. He left her and the children a considerable sum of money, and at thirty-five, she was a very attractive woman and knew it. She grieved for her husband to the outside world, and in her own home, she gloried in her freedom.

When she discovered she was going to have a baby, she quite lost control of herself in her rage at being frustrated in such a way. Cook, who had been with her eleven years and still stayed — not because of her faithfulness or devotion to the family, but because of the high wage she always received from them — locked her mistress in her room where she was powerless to do any harm to those around her.

Nanny, who had been Lionel Challis' nurse when he was a boy, hurried the children out of the house where they could no longer hear their mother's hysterical screams, thinking for the hundredth time since Mr. Lionel's death that if it were not for her love for little Miss Evelyn and her promise to look after Miss Gay, she would leave the house for good and all. That any lady — and Mr. Lionel's wife! — should have to be locked in her room to prevent her harming her own children . . .

But while her two daughters were watching the other children sail their boats on the pond in the park, their mother was throwing herself about the large, luxurious bedroom, trying in her rage to so harm herself that the coming child should never be born.

Cook was a moral, though unscrupulous woman, and such behaviour was intolerable to her righteous mind.

'If you do harm to the baby, it'll be murder,' she said with an outspokenness that surprised Ella Challis into momentary silence. Then she started to whimper like a child.

'I won't have it! I won't! I won't!' she cried.

But in spite of her violent treatment of herself in succeeding months, the child within her continued to grow, and Cook, with a smile of triumph, said:

'Nature will have her way, no matter what.'

Evelyn's quiet gentle ways and worried, concerned looks, reminded her mother too much of the husband she was so glad to be rid of, and she refused to allow the child near her. Gay, on the other hand, she asked for continually.

The months she spent as her mother's close companion influenced Gay's character for life. Nanny could do nothing with her because Mrs. Challis spoilt her and allowed her to stay up until all hours at night so that she would have someone to amuse her. She would not go out to parties because she did not wish her condition to be guessed by her friends.

'Mummy does not mean to spoil her,' Evelyn said to her nurse. 'It's just that she needs someone bright and sweet, and Gay is both.'

Nanny looked down at the pale, serious face and stooping suddenly, she caught the child fiercely to her.

'You come away with me, Miss Evie,' she cried in a low, urgent voice. 'You come away with me, dearie, and I'll take care of you.'

Evelyn drew away from the protection of the kind, plump arms about her, and looked up in surprise.

'But Nanny, I couldn't leave Gay — and Mummy. They may need me.'

'Your mother only wants Miss Gay!' the old woman cried, still swept away by her desire to save this child from a woman she was fast believing in her old-fashioned way to be a witch. She was too blinded by her own emotions to see how much she had hurt the child by referring to her mother's preference for Gay.

'Well, Gay needs *you*,' Evelyn said quietly. 'And perhaps if Mummy and Gay really don't want it, the baby will need me to love it.'

The old woman's face softened suddenly and she coughed and blew her nose and went bustling round the nursery doing nothing very much but making a big job of it.

'Of course, I didn't really mean it, dearie,' she said in her usual motherly voice. 'I just meant to go away for a little holiday.'

'Oh, a holiday!' exclaimed Evelyn, instantly credulous.

'Yes, but of course, we can't go now with the baby coming and all.'

'No,' said Evelyn. 'No, we can't go now.'

During the last month of her confinement, Ella Challis refused to leave her room or to allow anyone but Gay into it. Nanny did not like to think what state of filth and untidiness it would be in, and Gay's descriptions were not very lucid or encouraging.

'It's a fairy palace!' she told Evelyn. 'Mummy's the queen and I'm a royal princess.'

'How lovely!' Evelyn said. But Nanny only snorted.

'She ought to have the doctor,' she told Cook. But the one time they had sent for him on their own accord, Mrs. Challis had flatly refused to let him enter her room. She shouted through the door that it wasn't her first child and she could look after herself.

'She will call for me when the time comes,' the doctor had said calmly. 'Women often get these peculiar ideas if they are highly strung.'

Nanny would have liked to tell him

that this eccentricity was no mere nervous complaint and that she feared her mistress intended harm to the child, but her loyalty to Lionel Challis' wife kept her lips closed, and she did her best for her in her own way.

When Evelyn was out of earshot she would corner Gay and promise her extra sweet biscuits and chocolate if she would give any information of the 'Palace' and the 'Queen,' and in this way, found out that all seemed to be progressing well and normally, and reckoned that the baby was due to be born any day. She watched and waited anxiously.

Evelyn never forgot the night her second sister came into the world. It was not a wild, rainy night as so often colours such scenes in films. But it was a hot, sultry summer's night, with the air almost hollow in its stillness and any small sound doubling its volume in an uncanny way.

Lying in her little room, Evelyn looked at Gay's empty bed (Mrs.

Challis had had a camp bed put in her own room for the child) and wished that her sister were there with her. Her sensitive nature was alive to something unusual in the air . . . not just the weather, but something else she could neither define nor explain.

After an hour she fell asleep, and the fiery sky darkened and clouded, but without bringing any welcome breath of wind with it. The sudden slamming of a door downstairs started Evelyn into instant wakefulness so uneasy had been her sleeping, and she sat up in bed, listening to the footsteps running along the passage, up the stairs that led to her room.

'It's me, Gay!'

'Is anything wrong?' Evelyn asked, jumping out of bed to greet the small, pyjama-clad figure which had just broken into the room.

Gay burst into a sudden storm of tears, throwing herself face downwards on Evelyn's bed. Her crying was difficult and uncontrolled and there was no doubt about the genuineness of her tears. It was some minutes before the elder girl could make any sense of her gasped words. Then at last she understood her mother was in great pain and thought the baby was coming.

Evelyn hurriedly flung a dressing-gown round her shoulders, and with a last order to Gay to get into bed and keep warm, she went off to find Nanny.

From that minute onwards, it was all one long nightmare, punctuated at regular intervals by Ella Challis' screams and Cook's hysterics.

'You'll have to help,' Nanny said, turning to Evelyn in desperation. 'Telephone the doctor again. There must be someone there to answer, even if he's out.'

And she hurried back to Ella Challis' room.

Evelyn stood in the hall for ten minutes, shivering and frightened. She thought her mother was dying. But there was no reply from Dr. Wright's house, and she gave it up and went to find Nanny.

'It won't be the first baby I've delivered,' Nanny said, when Evelyn reported her failure to get hold of the doctor. 'Do you think you can bear the sight of blood, Miss Evie?'

'Yes, I think so,' Evelyn said.

'Then go and put the kettle on, and every saucepan you can find. We'll need hot water. Bring it straight up to me as soon as it's boiling . . . '

By morning the baby was born and Ella Challis would have nothing of it. Weak though she was, she was firm in this decision, and with tears in her eyes Nanny took the baby girl from Evelyn's arms and carried it into the nursery.

Evelyn ran upstairs to ascertain that Gay was asleep, then returned to the nursery. Nanny was trying to hush the baby's crying, but without much success.

'What's the matter with her?' Evelyn asked. 'Is she ill?'

'I don't know,' Nanny answered. She

stood up and put the child back into Evelyn's arms. 'I'm going to make a cup of tea.'

Evelyn didn't know much about babies, but she realized now that her mother wouldn't feed the baby and that it would have to be bottle-fed. In that moment, her heart went out to the small fragment of humanity in her arms, and her young heart was filled to the brim with loving and protective instincts. This was her sister, someone she would care for and cherish all her life. Mummy would learn to love her in time; Gay, too. And she, Evelyn, loved her already, with her whole heart.

She sat rocking the baby until Nanny returned with the tea. Then she climbed the stairs to her own little room and, rather than wake Gay, she made up the empty bed and more tired than she realized she dropped into it and was soon sound asleep.

Downstairs, Nanny took a cup of tea in to Cook. Then she fell thankfully into her rocking-chair by the nursery fire and rocked herself to and fro, her hands clutched together beneath her apron.

'Poor wee bairn. Poor little mite!' she said aloud.

Nanny meant the baby, but had she foreseen the future, her pity would have been for Evelyn, too.

Later when she took the infant along to her room, they slept — the old woman whose life was nearly over, and the baby whose life had just begun.

2

It was exactly one year before war broke out. Evelyn was now twenty-two, but most people mistook her for twenty-four or five. Two years previously Mrs. Challis had been killed in a motor accident and she, Evelyn, had taken up her position as head of the family.

Ella Challis' sister, their aunt Dorothy, had suggested the three girls should come and live with her, but Evelyn had politely refused this offer and announced her intention of staying exactly where she was, and of looking after Gay and the ten-year-old Margaret herself.

There was more than one objection raised by the other family relatives, but Evelyn had shown surprising strength in opposing them all, and had stuck to her guns, stating that she considered her plan to be better for all concerned.

Gay backed her up with floods of tears and pleadings to be allowed to remain in the house where 'Poor darling Mummy' had lived, and had succeeded in softening more than one heart in this way.

Evelyn had reproved her for this later, knowing full well that Gay had had very little love for their mother, and that her death, probably due to the fact that she was by no means sober when she had started out on that fatal car ride, was both a relief and a release for them all.

Mrs. Challis' bouts of drinking had grown increasingly worse as time went by. She had not married again, and attributed this to the fact that she had lost both her looks and her figure after Margaret's birth. Nanny had managed fairly successfully to hide from the children the fact that their mother was drinking, but she was herself growing very old and short-tempered, and it was not long before Mrs. Challis dismissed her from service.

Evelyn had been heartbroken.

'Never you mind, dearie,' Nanny had said with tears in her eyes. 'I've saved a bit these years and I'll do with a rest now. It's not myself I'm a-worrying over, but you and little Miss Margaret.'

'I shall be all right, Nanny,' Evelyn said, putting her arms round the old woman and hugging her tightly. 'And I shall take care of Margaret.'

'If ever you want help, or a friend, you must come to me,' Nanny said. 'There will always be a home and a welcome for you with me, dearie. Remember that.'

Evelyn had cried herself to sleep the night Nanny left, but Gay was dry-eyed and scornful.

'It's a jolly good thing she has gone,' she said. 'It was always 'Don't do this.' 'Do that,' and 'Do the other.' I'm sick and tired of Nanny telling me what to do. I'm nearly fifteen now and old enough to know what's good for me. I'm glad she's gone.'

'Oh, Gay!' Evelyn had cried aghast.

'How could you? You know how kind Nanny has always been, how much she has done for us.'

'You just liked her because you were her pet,' Gay said in a cold, hard voice. 'She always liked you better than me and let you do just what you wanted.'

'Gay, she didn't favour me any more than you and you know it.'

'She never did anything for *me*,' Gay retorted.

But she found this was not true some few days later. Her mother was wanted on the telephone and Gay went up to her room to find her asleep — as she thought — on her bed. She tried to wake her, but Mrs. Challis had not stirred for all Gay's shaking.

'Evie, Evie! I think Mummy's ill,' she had shouted, and Evelyn had come hurrying upstairs. As she came close to the bed, her foot knocked against something underneath it, and stooping to pick it up, she saw an empty whisky bottle.

'Why, she — she's drunk!' Gay had

whispered. 'Oh, how beastly!'

From then onwards it was Evelyn who took care of her mother following one of those bouts; Evelyn who tried to keep her from drinking by hiding bottles or emptying their contents down the drain. She lost her respect and with it her love for her mother, but pity took its place, and she never relaxed her vigilance or her attention until the day of her death.

Gay was as callous about her mother's death as she had been about Nanny's departure when she was alone with Evelyn.

'Now we'll be able to live our own lives and be happy,' she said. But she did not stop to think that, as house-keeper, it was Evelyn who made the sacrifices and did the work so that she could be happy.

Always a musical child, Evelyn had taken the best advantage of her expensive school piano lessons and soon passed higher grades of exams and took her teacher's certificate. Her ambition was to become a great pianist like Myra Hess and give recitals in different parts of the country.

Her mother's death soon put an end to any such dreams, and her ambitions faded into the reality of ordering meals and keeping house and looking after Gay during the holidays and Margaret all the time; struggling on the annuity left for the two elder girls by their father.

Mrs. Challis had bequeathed them nothing but a sheath of debts, and Evelyn, after a bitter struggle with her mathematical calculations, had discovered that she could only afford to keep Gay at school by strict economy at home.

She started to make a lot of their clothes — many for Gay and nearly all her own and Margaret's. Cook's wages had to be cut down and, soon afterwards, she left. Evelyn engaged a young girl with little or no experience because she required much smaller wages and was strong and healthy and, above all, willing. Between them they did all the housework.

Now Gay was eighteen and she had left school and was home, not just for the holidays but for good. She had blossomed into an amazingly attractive young girl with fair, curly hair, sparkling, vivacious eyes and a slim rounded figure which commanded most men's attention. Gay was by no means unaware of her charms and used them to the best advantage.

When Evelyn suggested she should find some kind of job to help out the family budget, Gay begged and pleaded to be allowed three months' liberty, as she called it.

'I have been working so very hard all this time at school, Evie,' she said persuasively. 'Let me have a good time for three months and then I'll settle down and work, I really will.'

Evelyn had been unable to resist Gay, as was always the case whenever Gay wanted anything.

'All right, darling,' she said. 'You shall

enjoy yourself all you can.'

And she made her some new, attractive dresses in grown-up styles which turned Gay from a pretty schoolgirl into a lovely young woman. She let her join the tennis club where she soon met a crowd of young people, and almost before Evelyn had had time to appreciate Gay's companionship, her younger sister was immersed in an exciting world of her own friends.

Evelyn, who had often felt lonely during the past years, and in need of company of her own age and intellect, felt vaguely disappointed. She had hoped so much to have Gay to herself, had looked forward so much to the day when she would leave school and come home. In an effort to see more of her, she said to Gay:

'Why not bring your friends home? Have them to tea, Gay. I'd like to meet them.'

'Oh, it's usually easier for me to go to them,' Gay had replied evasively. 'And it is so much cheaper.'

'But Gay, we aren't as hard up as all that . . .'

Gay had laughed, and putting her arms round her sister she planted a kiss on her forehead where a habitual little frown creased the smooth white skin.

'You work hard enough already, Evie,' she said.

But her real reason for keeping her friends from the house bore no connection with such unselfish thoughts for Evelyn's benefit. It was because of Margaret, Margaret whom she pitied and hated because of the drag on her which that pity entailed.

Margaret was blind.

Two days after her birth the doctor had broken the news to them that both the baby's optic nerves were quite dead, and that there was no hope that she would ever be able to see.

Mrs. Challis, believing herself to blame, did at first try to make up for her sin by being attentive and kind to the child. But she started drinking heavily and, in her less sober moments, the little girl's presence was intolerable to her — a constant reminder of her guilt. She would watch the child groping her way around the room and be forced to think:

'It's my fault! I did not want her! I tried not to have her.'

She would have another drink, hoping to drown such thoughts, and gradually her remorse would change to anger — anger against Margaret for upsetting her peace of mind.

Nanny had kept Margaret away from her as much as possible, and Evelyn, when Nanny left, did the same. The months before Mrs. Challis was killed she never saw her youngest daughter, and Margaret, now ten years old, could hardly remember her. Evelyn was the centre of her world — the person she held dearest and nearest to her heart. It was to Evelyn she took her childish troubles, in Evelyn she confided her baby hopes and secrets; to Evelyn she said her prayers, and on whom she depended for nearly everything — and her sight.

At first it had hurt Evelyn almost physically to see Margaret, as a toddler, tripping over obstacles and groping her way around where other children ran and laughed and fell and got up to run again. But gradually she trained herself to ignore this immense pity for the child, and gave herself up to describing the things she could see, trying to make it up to Margaret with explanations and detailed descriptions of everything around them.

Gay seldom had time to do this.

'It only makes her *want* to see,' she excused herself to Evelyn. 'Besides, she's so silly. She does not understand what you mean.'

'Can you explain sight to someone who had never seen?' Evelyn wondered.

But she continued telling Margaret colours and scenes, and the child gradually associated shapes and smells with the image pictures her sister conjured up in her mind.

Lately, she had taken to walking

31

round the garden by herself, touching things, mentally noting their size and shape and 'feel.' Then she would go back to the house and find Evelyn and say:

'Evie, it was small — just a little baby round thing; smooth, and it smelt of earth and wood. What does it *look* like?'

And Evelyn would stop whatever she was doing and think carefully for a moment, before replying:

'It sounds like a conker, darling. It's brown and has a soft green shell with prickles all over it. Conkers are really nuts, and they grow on horse-chestnut trees. If you collect a little pile of them I'll make some holes through the middle and you can thread them on a string and make a necklace.'

She would watch the little girl groping her way down the stairs, counting them carefully; feeling her way out through the garden door and down the path towards the trees. She would think for the hundredth time, how glad she was she had not had to give up the house. Margaret knew every nook and cranny of it and was almost as conversant with the big garden. Gay had tried to persuade her to go to a smaller house at the far end of the town.

'Just think of the money we would save,' she had said. 'And the work, Evie! Margaret would soon get used to it.'

But Evelyn had been determined in her refusal to move.

'We must not make things any harder for Margaret unless it is absolutely necessary,' she said gently. 'I don't mind the work, Gay.'

Gay had stormed out of the house in a temper, calling Evelyn selfish and silly, and accusing her of favouring Margaret.

Evelyn had been terribly upset by this scene, but she had not given way. For the first time in her life, Gay realized her sister was not as weak-willed as she had supposed, and being utterly dependent on her for everything she had no alternative but to do as Evelyn wished.

Sometimes, in her better moods, Gay would take her small sister for walks, describing all they saw with far greater volubility than Evelyn. Margaret, returning with flushed cheeks and bright eyes, would tell Evelyn all they had 'seen' and say with a little sigh of content:

'Oh, I love going out with Gay.'

Evelyn was not jealous for she realized of old how bright and amusing a companion Gay could be, and only wished she had more time to spend with Margaret.

But Gay's compassionate moods were few and far between.

'I don't seem to have a moment to spare,' she would say. 'There's so much to be done.'

And although this was true, the things to be done were chiefly for her own amusement. When she did take Margaret out she always avoided the town and the park, or any place where she might meet any of her friends. No one of them knew her sister was blind, and she did not intend that they should find out. She was desperately afraid they would be sorry for Margaret and pity her, and above all, Gay hated to be pitied. It never occurred to her that she was always pitying herself — because she had no mother and father to pet and spoil her and give her lovely, expensive presents; because she had not enough money to buy all the clothes she wanted; because she had not been to a finishing school abroad as had most of the girls she knew at the club; because of Margaret. Margaret always made her feel she ought to be more kind, more generous, more thoughtful. Sometimes Evelyn made her feel like that, too, but she was used to it now and had learned to squash those feelings of guilt before they were really there. Besides, she liked Evelyn . . . she always did things for one and listened to little grumbles with a sympathetic ear; she admired and loved Gay and admiration was food and drink to her. She thrived and blossomed on it and was always her most charming and her most attractive self to the people who liked her.

Gay, therefore, enjoyed Margaret's obvious hero-worship, and this was the chief reason she ever took her out. The little girl would say:

'Oh, it's much more fun with you than with Evie, Gay!'

And Gay would laugh and buy her some sweets.

At other times Margaret's devotion annoyed and irritated her.

'Gay, can I come and talk to you while you dress?'

Gay hated anyone to come into her room.

'No, I'm in a hurry, Margaret.'

'Oh, please, Gay! Evie's busy and I haven't anything to do.'

'Oh, go and play, Margaret, do!'

'But there's nobody to play with.'

'Then go and look at a book.'

The child would go slowly downstairs without a word, and Gay would suddenly realize what she had said and feel a moment's regret.

'I'll stop at the nursery on my way down and see if she's all right,' she would console herself. But more often than not, she would be in too much of a hurry and either forgot or else remembered too late. Then, to ease her conscience, she would bring some paper cap or toy trumpet back with her from the party, and Margaret would touch her and say:

'Oh, Gay, thank you! You are so nice to me!'

And later, she would come up to Gay's room with a little bunch of flowers which she had picked herself.

Gay, unable to square that irritating conscience of hers, would take them with an effort to be thankful, and silently wish to heaven that the child was rude or difficult or unpleasant instead of looking and behaving like a small angel. She always made one feel so boorish and unkind.

'Gay, can I come and talk to you?'

'Oh, Margaret, haven't you anything

else to do? I'm going to a dance tonight and I'm in a hurry.'

'Couldn't I help you? Oh, Gay, please let me. I'll pretend I am your maid. Evie lets me be maid sometimes. Gay, please!'

'Oh, all right. Do these hooks, then.'

In spite of her blindness, Margaret was nimble with her fingers. Evelyn had taught her to use her hands and fingers, and she was now learning to knit.

'I'm Hilda,' she chattered happily. 'Evie says maids are usually called Betty or Hilda and I like the name Hilda best. What's the smell?'

'It's perfume,' Gay told her, her good spirits suddenly returning. This was going to be a real party — a very special one that might make all the difference in the world to her. It was Joan de Verriland's twenty-first birthday and she was very very rich and important. (Anybody who was rich was important to Gay.)

And, more important still, Joan's second cousin, Gordon, was going to be there and Joan had said he was terribly good-looking and a 'catch' for any girl.

Gay had resolved to do the catching. Life as somebody's private secretary, or as a typist did not appeal to her, and she had already made up her mind to marry the first reasonably attractive man she met — provided he had plenty of money — and live her life as she really wanted it. She wanted lots of lovely clothes, and a car, and servants to order here, there and everywhere. She wanted her own maid, like Joan de Verriland's Miriam. She wanted . . .

'Here are your shoes, Miss Gay!'

Margaret's childish treble brought her back to the present. She slipped her feet into the white sandals, noting absently that they looked perfect with the white organdie frock Evelyn had made for her. Evelyn was certainly clever with her needle, and the dress looked expensive. Gay wanted to look expensive, and as she pinned a white rose into the top of her curls, she noted with satisfaction that she resembled a model from *Vogue*.

She picked up the black velvet evening cape which had been her mother's, and turned to Margaret with shining eyes.

'How do I look?' she asked.

As always when Gay forgot her blindness, the child remained silent, her head bent.

'Oh, I'm sorry, Margaret,' Gay said quickly, and with her quick imaginativeness, she added:

'You were such a good maid, I was really beginning to think you were Hilda.'

'Oh, Gay, did you really?'

Gay felt a stab of — was it pity? — at her heart. Then she heard the tonk-tonk of a car horn outside the window and thought:

'That's Mark. He said he would fetch me.'

Mark England had never left her side since the day they had met down at the tennis club, and although he was certainly the best-looking man there, he was studying to be a doctor, and as a medical student, had little or no money to spend. Nor would he ever be able to marry — not for years and years. Gay rejected him in her mind, but hung on to him with an occasional smile and a very occasional kiss, because he was useful to her. When Mark was in town, she was never without a partner. And he did have a car, however old and disreputable it was.

'Goodnight, Gay. I hope you enjoy the party.'

'Goodnight, Hilda. Don't wait up for me.'

'No, Madame. I won't!' cried Margaret, following her as quickly as she could down the stairs. Then excitement got the better of her and she cried: 'Oh, Gay, do come into my room when you come home and tell me all about it. Please do!'

'Well, maybe,' said Gay. 'I won't promise.'

Evelyn was in the sitting-room, bent over some sewing. She was making

41

Margaret a new cotton frock for the very hot weather.

'Gay! How lovely you look!' she cried as Gay sailed through the door and paused with an instinctive theatrical artistry on the threshold.

'Do I, Evie?'

'You look beautiful, Gay,' Evelyn said.

'It's the dress you made!' Gay said generously.

The horn sounded again, and she bent and kissed each of her sisters with an affection she did not often show them, and with a little whirl of her skirts which sent a cold wave of air round the room, she was gone into the hall.

Evelyn sat silently a moment or two, her eyes wistful and full of longing. She was twenty-two and young and pretty, and she would so much have liked to go to the party with Gay. It was such a long time since she had worn a lovely dress and danced in some young man's arms. There had been a party or two before her mother had died — very rare occasions when she had left Margaret in Cook's care, and, young, lovely, carefree, she had danced, laughed and been kissed on the terrace by her attentive escort. The young man had called several times to take her out; he had telephoned, too, asking her to go to his house for a party, for tea, for cocktails. But each time Fate had intervened and she had been unable to go. Firstly, her mother had been recovering from one of her bouts of drinking, and Evelyn had not dared leave Margaret alone in the house. The second time, Margaret had been ill and she had not left the child's bedside. The third time, she had promised Margaret faithfully to take her down to the farm where there were some baby kittens, and she had not wanted to disappoint her. Each time, she had said, No, she wasn't feeling very well; she had a headache, and soon he had stopped calling.

The same thing had happened after she had met some young man at the

Tennis Club. Once she had really been ill, and the next time he telephoned her, asking her to meet him that afternoon for tennis, it had been Cook's half day off, and she had had to stay behind to look after Margaret. He had not called again.

From then onwards Evelyn had refused any invitations, knowing that she would be sure to find friends whom she had not time to keep in with. She devoted her time to Margaret and had not really missed the bright, amusing parties and picnics and dances which should have been the lot of so pretty a girl as herself. She had not really thought about them until Gay, grown up and lovely, danced her way in and out of the house, a constant reminder of her own youth.

'Evie, Evie! You aren't listening to me!'

'Oh, Margaret! I'm so sorry, darling. I must have been dreaming.'

'Evie, tell me, what *did* Gay look like? You said she looked lovely. *How* did she look? What does lovely look like?'

Evelyn touched the child's dark wavy hair with her hand, then she smiled her soft, tender smile, and picked up her sewing, adjusting the light so that she could see better. Margaret settled herself down at her feet and waited in an eager, expectant way.

'Well?' she prompted.

'Well,' said Evelyn, frowning a little as she tried to find the right words. 'She was dressed in a white frock and she looked like the Snow Queen in that story I read to you yesterday — cool and soft and flowing . . . '

'Yes?' said the child. 'Yes?'

'And her hair . . . '

At that moment the front doorbell rang, startling the two girls into silence. It rang again, loudly and insistently, and Evelyn put down her sewing and said:

'That's strange. Now I wonder who that can be?'

And she went slowly into the hall to open the front door.

3

The tall young man standing on the front step blinked at the sudden glare of light as Evelyn opened the door.

'Oh, excuse me!' he said, taking off his soft felt hat. 'I wonder if you would be good enough to let me use your telephone. Ours is out of order and . . . '

'Won't you please come in?' Evelyn asked in her calm voice.

The young man smiled and stepped into the hall. Evelyn closed the door behind him and pointed to the tiny room under the stairs.

'The telephone is in there,' she said, and walked slowly back into the sitting-room.

The young man stared after her, noting the unusual grace of her movements, wondering a little at the extraordinary poise and calmness that she had portrayed in those first few moments of their meeting. It was unusual in a girl so young — at least, he supposed she was in her early twenties. He raised his eyebrows suddenly as a faint childish treble reached his ears.

'Oh, Evie, it's a man, isn't it? Who is he? What does he look like?'

Her daughter? No, surely not! She was too young to have a child old enough to ask such questions. Besides, she had called her 'Evie.' Eve? Eva? Evelyn?

He smiled at himself, suddenly realizing that he was standing where she had left him, lost in thought. He turned to the telephone and dialled the operator.

'It is strange we have not met before,' he said to Evelyn when he had finished his call and followed her into the sitting-room. 'You see, we are neighbours really . . . that is to say, your house is the nearest to ours, although that's two miles away! My name is Nicky March.'

Evelyn looked up from her sewing and held out her hand.

'Mrs. March's son?' she asked.

'Yes, the youngest one,' he explained, noting her surprise. He had been born twenty years after Rupert, and his mother, therefore, was quite an old woman now. He was used to being thought her grandchild. She had that authoritative, dictatorial air that belonged to another generation. 'It *is* strange we have not met before,' he said again.

'Perhaps we have, only you don't remember it,' Evelyn answered without coquetry.

'No!' he replied quickly. 'If we had I should certainly have remembered you!'

Evelyn felt the colour mounting to her cheeks. She was very conscious of him standing there and felt she should ask him to sit down. At the same time she wondered if this were the right gesture, seeing that he had just walked into her house and that they had never met before.

The silence became intolerable.

'I don't go out very much,' she said, saying the first thing that came into her head.

'What a loss for the world,' the young man replied with a smile.

'Do you learn all your compliments from books?' Evelyn countered.

The young man laughed.

'It was rather unoriginal, I know,' he said. 'But I meant it.'

Again Evelyn felt the colour mounting to her cheeks.

'Perhaps you have met my sister, Gay?' she said, sewing quickly as she spoke.

'Gay Challis? Is *she* your sister?'

His voice sounded incredulous.

'But is it possible? You are so different . . . ' he broke off.

'No, we are not very alike, are we?' Evelyn said with a smile. 'And Margaret, here, is different from us both.'

He had forgotten the child — had not observed her standing quietly by the window, her head lifted a little and turned in his direction.

'Margaret, say how-do-you-do!' Evelyn told her.

Margaret took a step or two towards him, saying:

'Are Evie and Gay so different? Why, I never even thought of that! Why? How are they different?'

Nicky March was frankly puzzled. Evelyn saw his expression and said quietly:

'Margaret is blind, Mr. March. Did Gay not tell you about us?'

'No, no, she didn't!' He nervously pulled the brim of his hat through his fingers. 'I'm so sorry!' he said awkwardly.

Evelyn looked up at him, meeting his gaze.

'Margaret is not sorry for herself, Mr. March,' she said gently.

'She has never known what it is to 'see' so she does not miss anything.'

'No!' said Margaret, nodding her dark head. 'Besides, if I want to see anything, I can use Evie's or Gay's eyes. They tell me how things look.'

Nicky March stared into the wide, gentian-blue eyes that were looking at him — no, past him. His embarrassment had gone and a quick smile flashed across his face.

'Well, Margaret,' he said, his eyes crossing quickly to Evelyn's face. 'I'll do some seeing for you. Firstly, you have two very attractive sisters. One of them is just pretty but the other one is lovely.'

Margaret nodded her head.

'Yes, Evie said Gay looked lovely,' she said.

'No, Gay is the pretty one,' Nicky corrected, his eyes never leaving Evelyn's face.

'What's the difference 'tween pretty and lovely, then?' Margaret asked curiously.

Nicky March did not care to elucidate. How could he say before Evelyn that her sister Gay's attraction was of the flesh only — a pretty face hiding a hard, selfish heart. That Evelyn's attraction was something from within — a spiritual loveliness . . . He turned to the child and said lightly:

'You know, you are very attractive, too!'

Margaret came a step nearer him.

'Oh, am I?' she asked eagerly. 'Why, how do I look? I never thought of that before! Do I look like Evie? Or Gay?'

'You look like Evie,' he said. 'Nice dark brown hair with red tints in it — chestnut coloured. She has hazel-green eyes, of course, whereas yours are the colour of gentians. But the expression is the same.'

'Oh, I 'spect our eyes is different 'cos of me being blind,' Margaret said cheerfully, oblivious of the hurt she caused Evelyn by such a remark. But Nicky March noted the shadow across her calm face and knew that he was now interested — deeply interested in this family . . . in this trio of sisters, and in Evelyn in particular. Was it Evelyn? Or Eve?

'I think I had better be going,' he said. 'Goodnight, Margaret! Goodnight, Miss . . . ?'

'Challis,' Evelyn supplemented.

So he still did not know.

'Goodnight, Miss Challis,' he said, holding out his hand. 'It was very good of you to let me use your 'phone.'

'That's quite all right.'

'I have put one and eightpence on the table by the telephone.'

'Oh, please! You shouldn't have bothered.'

She walked out into the hall with him.

'Of course!' he said.

Margaret was standing in the entrance to the sitting-room. Evelyn went over to her and put her arm round her shoulders.

'Hilda — would you show Mr. March to the door?' she said with her slow smile.

Margaret jumped up and down and cried:

'Oh, yes! I'm the maid!' she added for Nicky's benefit. 'It's great fun to pretend.'

'Perhaps I could pretend to be the

butler,' the young man said.

'Oh, yes! cried Margaret excitedly. 'And we will play house and help Evie!'

Evelyn smiled at her, thinking:

'He's so nice to Margaret. I like him. In spite of his compliments . . . '

'May I call again some time now that we have met?' he was saying.

'Oh, Evie, say yes!' Margaret said naïvely. 'Do say yes. I think he sounds nice!'

He was still looking at Evelyn questioningly.

'Margaret says 'yes,'' she answered.

He took her hand, holding it for a moment longer than was conventional.

'Then we will meet again soon,' he said, and releasing her hand, he went with Margaret to the door, and soon he had disappeared into the soft spring night.

Evelyn walked back into the sitting-room, her thoughts confused, her cheeks flushed. She was suddenly conscious of the fact that she was more than glad she had not gone to the party with Gay, and she found herself wondering whether Nicky March would call again as he had said he would. Remembering his steady gaze, his long handclasp as he had said goodbye, she thought perhaps he would. And she knew that she wanted him to — very much.

'Evie — Evie — you aren't listening! Tell me, what does he look like? Is he handsome, like the Prince in *Cinderella*?'

'It's past your bedtime, Margaret,' Evelyn said absently. But she allowed the child to settle down on the floor and lean her dark head against her lap.

'He was tall,' she said with a thoughtful little smile. 'He had light-brown hair and blue eyes. He . . . he looked nice . . . sort of sunburnt. And he wore a grey flannel suit . . . '

'He was nice, wasn't he?' Margaret stated. 'Do you think he will come and play houses with me, Evie? It would be much more fun to be housemaid if there were a butler, too. Oh, I do hope he comes!'

'Yes,' said Evelyn quietly. 'So do I.'

They sat in silence for a minute or two, Evelyn stroking the long silky hair of Margaret's head. They were very close together, these two, and the twelve years' difference in their ages made no difference to their companionship. Sometimes when she sat like this with her little sister leaning against her, Evelyn felt a great sense of peace and contentment, and thought perhaps that she required no more of life than this. Sometimes she had thought she would never marry but devote her life to the little girl, caring for her, loving her.

But tonight, she felt a queer restlessness in her heart — a soft stirring of something awakening within her that she associated with the coming of spring . . . and the tall young man who had walked into the house to disturb them in this strange, unaccustomed way.

'Margaret, dear, you really ought to go to bed. Why, I'm going myself, in a little while!'

'All right, Evie,' the child said sleepily. 'But it's so nice like this — just us two by ourselves.'

'Yes,' said Evelyn. But something was missing . . .

When the younger girl was tucked into bed Evelyn went back to the sitting-room and, drawing back the curtains, she leaned out of the window, staring into the night.

Outside in the garden, the grass was smelling sweet with a heavy fall of dew. The light from the reading lamp flickered on the drops of moisture like tiny glow-worms, making a sparkling oblong carpet on the shadowed lawn. The air was filled with the noise of crickets and frogs, and there seemed to Evelyn to be a magical charm about this June night which she had never known before.

She wondered idly if Nicky March were walking home, seeing in her mind's eye the solitary figure striding through the darkness. Then she blushed, realizing the trend her thoughts had taken once again, and she turned quickly back into the room, drawing the curtains across the window, shutting out the darkness and its unsettling influence. She picked up her sewing with a determined gesture, but soon she put it down again, leaning her head back and closing her eyes.

'I wonder where he is now,' she thought. 'I wonder where he is!'

★ ★ ★

Nicky March had not yet reached home. He had stopped at the 'Horse and Groom,' an old-world country inn, which he frequented, liking it more for its oak beams and tiny, low-ceilinged rooms than for its renowned good beer! He was sitting at a small table by the diamond-pane window overlooking the trout stream, and for once, he took no part in the local gossiping of the farmers and labourers who adjourned there at evening.

He wanted to be alone — to try and

sort out the variety of emotions that assailed him.

Above all other sentiments, he felt surprised — completely and utterly bemused. Why, he wondered, had Gay Challis kept her family so dark, seldom mentioning her elder sister, never the youngster? What motive could be behind her reticence?

Knowing Gay for what she was — a pleasure-loving, spoilt, selfish young girl, he was sure there *was* a motive. Did she fear competition from her elder sister?

This did not seem at all probable to Nicky. Lovely as 'Evie' was, Gay also had her charms together with an extra sparkle about her that gathered the men around her in handfuls. He, himself, had been mildly attracted the first time he had met her. Conversation with her, however, had soon satisfied him that she was not 'his type,' but she was popular enough with a certain set, and had a steady stream of followers.

Enough, anyway, to be able to spare a

few to Evelyn even had she not been able to find her own friends.

Then what was her motive? Surely, he thought, she was not ashamed of her younger sister's defect? Why, it could be scarcely called that. Margaret was lovely, and the large, cornflower eyes were by no means the least attractive feature she possessed. To meet her — just to see her, one would never know she was blind. There was nothing noticeable until you spoke to her and she looked in your direction but yet not quite at you. But defect — no, it could not be called that!

Was there, then, something in the family history — a skeleton in the Challis' cupboard which they did not want brought out in the daylight? Somehow he had not had the impression that 'Evie' was hiding something from him. In fact she had seemed surprised that Gay had not mentioned her sisters. A good actress, perhaps? But he put this thought from him immediately. The girl had not even been actress enough to hide her blushes from him.

Nicky emptied his tankard, giving up the puzzle . . . but only temporarily. His curiosity was aroused and he was determined to find out more about the Challis family.

'I will ask Mother,' he thought. 'She is sure to know if there was any scandal attached to the name.'

Mrs. March, however, knew very little.

'Their father was a great friend of mine at one time,' she told him. 'But after he was married, he ceased coming to see me. I never liked his wife, of course. She was a hard, selfish woman from all accounts. I only met her twice and what I saw I did not like. Quite the wrong wife for Lionel who was a quiet, serious-minded boy. She was killed in a car crash while you were studying in Munich.'

'Oh, yes! I remember now. You wrote and told me about it. Wasn't there some scandal attached?'

'Some said she had been drinking,'

Mrs. March said sourly. 'I shouldn't be surprised. But if that were so, it was all hushed up. Why do you ask, Nicholas?'

'Oh, I just wondered,' said Nicky vaguely. 'I used their telephone this evening and met the girls.'

'Used their telephone?' his mother repeated. 'What's the matter with our own?'

'Nothing, Mamma dear,' Nicky said, smiling. 'My innate journalist's curiosity was aroused as to the identity of our neighbours. So instead of paying a formal call — something I could never do! — I rang the front-door bell and asked if I could use their telephone because ours was out of order.'

'Nicholas!' said his mother.

'Mama!' he mimicked her.

Her face softened, and she drew him close to her, thinking as she so often did nowadays what a tall, handsome boy her son was; how deeply she loved him and how little she understood him. He was so casual, so easy-going, and yet he must be clever to make all the money he did just by freelance journalism. And how different from her good, pompous Rupert! It was not very often that she admitted to herself that Nicholas was her favourite, but tonight as she sensed a new 'something' about him which she could not understand, she wished she were younger, that they were closer to each other and able to share their deepest emotions. But Nicholas had a way of shutting himself away from her, always hiding from her that secret self she knew existed but could not bring to light or possess.

She touched his brown wavy hair and gave a little sigh of resignation.

'Well, and what did the sleuth discover?' she said with a smile.

Nicky drew away from her and went over to the door.

'Oh, nothing of interest!' he replied vaguely. 'Goodnight, Mother darling. I'm going to turn in early.'

She watched him go with sad, inscrutable eyes. The child of her old age! Once she, too, had been young, at the start of her life as Nicholas was now, curious about everybody, everything; eager, expectant, vigorous . . . She sighed, and settled down again to her book, but her thoughts remained with her son.

In the sanctity of his room, Nicky was sitting down on his bed, puffing methodically at his pipe.

'Now what in the world possessed me to tell a blatant lie like that,' he asked himself. 'Not interested, my foot! I'm interested in that little minx Gay, and I'm interested in the little kid. I suppose I might as well admit that I'm also more than interested in this 'Evie.' And I still don't know if it's Eve, Eva, Evelyn or just plain 'Evie'!'

He scowled heavily for a moment or two, then he undressed slowly and climbed into bed.

'I'll call on the Challis family formally,' he told himself with a smile. 'And as soon as convention decently allows.'

As he switched out the light, he added softly:

'Perhaps sooner!'

And he fell into a sound, dreamless sleep.

4

Gay collected the black evening wrap from the maid, added a touch of powder to her nose, and hurried back to the hall where Gordon was waiting for her.

As she approached him, he called out to her:

'Stop there a moment, Gay!'

She stood quite still, watching him with a small puzzled frown crinkling her brow. He came over to her then, saying in his low, lazy voice:

'You looked lovely just then, my sweet!'

Gay smiled up at him from beneath her lashes.

'Did I?' she asked softly.

He did not answer, but took her arm and led her out through the big studded oak door, and across the gravel drive to his parked car.

'I never said goodbye to Joan,' Gay said, as she slipped into the seat beside him.

'Never mind! I'll make your apologies in the morning,' Gordon said confidently. He found a rug in the back seat and tucked it round her knees. She snuggled down, peeping up at him with a gaze he found childish and sweet.

'He really is quite good-looking,' she was thinking. 'His chin is a bit weak, but I suppose I shan't have to mind that! I wonder how he kisses!'

There was no doubt about the fact that he would kiss her. He had held her quite unnecessarily tight while they had danced, and he had dropped a light playful kiss on her forehead when the lights went out for a moment while they had been sitting on the stairs. All the evening, ever since she had first been introduced to him, he had been very attentive and obviously attracted to her.

'So he should be,' Gay thought. 'I've been my nicest self.'

This was true. Gay had put herself

out to charm Gordon de Verriland, and she had succeeded. As he sat beside her, driving steadily along the main road out of the town, he wondered just how experienced she was — how many men she had kissed before. She was such a weird mixture — childishly naïve and then suddenly sharp, astute, mistress of the situation. Was she a child pretending to be an experienced woman, or a woman pretending to be an inexperienced child?

He laughed suddenly, resolving to find out the answer now. A kiss would tell him. He pulled the car in against the side of the road and switched off the engine.

'What's the matter?' Gay asked. 'There's nothing wrong, is there?'

He laughed again, and with sure, expert arms, he held her tightly to him and kissed her soft, willing lips.

The kiss was a long one, and Gay, forgetting her intention of pretending she had never been kissed properly before, allowed herself to enjoy the moment, returning his embrace with equal passion.

As he released her, Gordon's face was covered by a faint, inscrutable smile.

'What's so funny?' Gay asked, child enough to be piqued by his lack of . . . of emotion.

'Nothing at all, my pet!' Gordon said, staring straight at her. 'In fact I think I'd like to do that again.'

'Well I don't want you to,' Gay said, remembering the part she was playing. 'Why, I've only met you tonight. We're strangers.'

Gordon did not seem in the least put out by this answer.

'My dear girl,' he replied caustically. 'We are two of the same type, and we understand each other. In fact I think if you will call off the bluff and show up in your true colours, we shall get along very well indeed. Now suppose you kiss me again!'

Gay stared at him, wondering if she had understood him. Then she laughed and, watching him carefully as she did so, she leant slowly towards him and brushed his lips with her own.

She was still smiling as he caught her roughly to him and bruised her mouth with a hard, savage kiss.

'You little witch!' he said, when he let her go. 'And once or twice tonight I thought you were sweet seventeen and at your first party.'

Gay snuggled up against him, raising her eyebrows a little.

'I am only eighteen,' she said. 'But I suppose I've grown up more quickly than most girls. I'm an orphan, you know.'

She thought that sounded feminine and pathetic.

Gordon looked down at her, a new expression in his eyes.

'Do you know, I might marry you,' he said, half serious, half playfully. 'Just think of a girl without any in-laws. None at all?'

'None at all!' Gay said, smiling. 'But *I* wouldn't marry *you*.'

'Oh, and why not?'

She followed up her advantage quickly.

'I'm not in love with you,' she said.

'I'll soon make you fall in love with me,' Gordon said confidently, but Gay stopped him from putting his arms round her again.

'Besides,' she went on. 'I don't think Evie would approve.'

'Evie?'

'Yes, my elder sister. She would choose someone more steady, more reliable.'

'My dear girl,' Gordon said loftily. 'If your sister raises any objections, you can tell her my net income runs into five figures. There isn't anything much more reliable than that!'

'But I shan't marry for money!' Gay cried quickly. 'I shall have to care.'

This time she did not stop him as he put his arms round her, kissing her again and again, murmuring against her lips.

'You're damned attractive, Gay . . . I think I really mean that about marrying you . . . you're so sweet, so very sweet.'

No, thought Gay silently. I'm not sweet. I'm cold and calculating. I want this man and I'm going to get him. I shall never know what it is to fall in love and have someone really care for me.

'Gordon,' she whispered. 'Love me! Please love me!'

She put her arms round his neck, drawing his face down to hers, trying to believe that this could also be love, this vague, exciting, exhilarating sensation.

But deep in her heart, she knew it was not so; knew enough to know physical attraction even if she had never been in love, and when he said softly, urgently:

'I do love you, Gay. I've never felt like this about any girl before,' she drew away from him straightening her dress, tucking the rug around her, and said:

'Please take me home now, Gordon. I'm tired.'

Gordon studied her face, pale and shadowed in the half-light. Then he pulled out his cigarette case and held it out to her. Gay took one, thinking how quickly she had fallen into the habit of smoking. Incredible to imagine herself as a schoolgirl. After all, this time three months ago, she had still been at Beaumont's. Not that they hadn't smoked there, of course, whenever lights were out, or in the bathrooms and cloakrooms where there was small risk of being found out.

She had hated school. She hated the discipline that school life entailed, and had always been more trouble than anyone else to her teachers. It wasn't that she could not do the work. When she chose she could be top of the class, and, now and again, just to prove to some teacher or other who accused her of being no good that she could do it, she would write the best essay, or learn the most Shakespeare or draw the neatest map. She enjoyed doing that — seeing their puzzled faces and hearing them say:

'Well, Gay, there's no doubt about

the fact that you can when you want to!'

But she had been popular with the girls. They flocked to her waiting for her to set a lead, attracted by her gaiety, her imaginativeness, her ability to have a good time. Even the dullest lecture could be amusing if Gay were seated beside one, making soft sarcastic remarks under her breath, drawing little caricatures of the lecturer on her notebook, writing funny rhymes about them.

'We flock to his lecture in herds
To hear his short talk on wild birds.
But we ought to have brought
A book of some sort
For the lecture's too boring for words!'

But, still, games had been fun. The only part of school she had really enjoyed. Even as a junior she had been in the hockey eleven and in the second tennis six. Later she had been in the first six and captained the hockey team.

She had loved to hear the onlookers shouting:

'*Play up Beaumont's. Come on Beaumont's. Come on, Gay! Shoot! Shoot, Gay! Oh, well done! . . .*'

She had loved the handshakes afterwards, the juniors clambering round her saying:

'Oh, Gay, you were marvellous! Gay, you saved the situation. It was two to one against and you shot that last beauty! Gay, can I carry your stick?'

Admiration, praise, excitement, she had craved them all her life.

'Gay!'

'Yes, Gordon?'

'I'm going to speak to Mother tomorrow — break the news that I want to get engaged.'

Gay looked at him quickly.

'Will it be such a shock?'

'Well, yes, I suppose it will,' Gordon said thoughtfully. 'You see, Mother's always been scared stiff I would dash off and marry some actress or something. You see, I'm the last of the male de Verrilands and Mother's out to see that I carry on the good name. She has produced any amount of suitable girls, but I haven't liked any of them.'

'Do you think I'd make a suitable mother for the future de Verrilands?' Gay asked carefully, watching his face.

'Oh, lord, yes!' Gordon said carelessly. 'For one thing, you haven't any difficult relatives. For a second, you speak the King's English and are obviously well educated (an essential in Mother's eyes!) and for a third, there isn't any insanity in your past family history, or any black sheep died in gaol from excessive drinking!'

Gay sat very still, twirling the cigarette stump round and round in her fingers. Margaret, she was thinking. He mustn't find out about Margaret! That would lead to reverse enquiries about her parents, about her mother . . .

'Well, you're very quiet suddenly,' Gordon said. 'There's no need to be frightened, Gay. Mother isn't such a tartar as she sounds. I think she's really just afraid some scheming little minx will marry me for my money. Gay, you aren't listening. What is the matter?'

Gay pulled herself together with an effort.

'I . . . I was just thinking,' Gay said in a voice studiedly casual.

'I know we have only just met,' Gordon was saying. 'In fact we have only known each other about five hours, but it doesn't really take five minutes to know one cares, does it? And I knew right away about you. You're different, darling — not like the usual girls I've met. You — you do like me, too, Gay?'

'Yes,' Gay said quietly.

'Then we'll see lots of each other from now on,' Gordon said masterfully. 'We won't rush anything, darling. When I mentioned marriage, an engagement, just now, I was only half-serious. But the more I think about it, the more I like the idea. Mother keeps fussing me to get married and now I've met you, I'm not at all sure I'm averse to the idea

77

myself. Does it strike any chord in your little heart?'

He was smiling again, but there was no doubt about the sincerity of his words.

'It seems extraordinary to be saying so to a stranger and of course I would like to know you better before we fix anything definitely,' Gay said slowly. 'But I think I feel as you do, Gordon. Marriage with you should be fun.'

He did not even notice the flippancy of such a remark. The girls he went about with all married 'for a good time,' and that Gay should be contemplating the same seemed natural enough. After all, he was doing, or thinking of doing, the same thing.

'You break the news gently to this elder sister of yours,' Gordon said eagerly. 'And I'll drop a few broad hints to Mother when I go back next week.'

'Go back?' Gay repeated.

Gordon laughed and touched her cheek with his hand.

'Only for a day or two, my sweet,' he

said. 'Then I shall wangle another invitation from young Joan. You didn't think I was going to leave you here alone to be carried off by one of your many other admirers, did you?'

Gay gave a little sigh of relief.

'Is this sister of yours your guardian?' Gordon asked.

Gay nodded her head.

'I don't think she will raise any objections if my mind is made up,' she said. 'How — how about your mother, Gordon?'

'Well, I hope to heaven she doesn't raise any,' Gordon said with a frown. 'She holds the purse strings as far as I am concerned, so her word goes.'

'How — how do you mean?'

'Well, when Father died, he left me a lot of money but Mother controls it until I'm thirty.'

'Thirty!' Gay cried aghast. 'How old are you now?'

'Twenty-five. But don't look so worried, precious! Mother gives me a pretty large allowance, you know. And I shall want a lot of money to spend on you, you lovely thing.'

Gay allowed him to put an arm round her shoulders.

'Mother must approve,' Gordon went on. 'I'm not trained to do any job, for one thing, and you and I will want a lot of money, Gay. I'm used to it, and I shall have a lot of fun dressing you. I'd love to see you in a Schapparelli model. You've got a first-class figure!'

'Gordon!'

He laughed and dropped a kiss on her fair hair.

'Don't pretend you're shocked,' he said. 'There must be no pretence between us, Gay, if we're going to make a success of 'us.' I don't want to marry a sweet little innocent babe. I prefer the sophisticated you — the little witch in you! You know, you are a little witch, my poppet!'

She looked up at him smiling.

'I brought my spells to the party,' she said.

She was teasing him, but when he

leant close to her and whispered, 'The love potion worked, Gay!' he was more than half serious. His lips when they found hers, were sure, compelling, experienced, and Gay did not push him away but let herself go limp in his embrace.

'We *are* suited,' she thought, only half conscious of his kisses on her eyes, her lips; on her neck and shoulders; of his hands discovering the slim, firm lines of her body.

'Gay! Gay, kiss me!' he whispered.

But as she obeyed his passionate command, she was thinking furiously:

'He mustn't find out about Mother. Evie must take Margaret away. She *must* take Margaret away!'

★ ★ ★

It was nearly three o'clock when Gay let herself into the house and climbed the stairs leading to Evelyn's room. She was tired, exhausted physically, but still mentally alert and she knew she would not be able to sleep until she had spoken to her sister.

Evelyn was sleeping deeply, her dark hair spread about her, her hand tucked up under her chin like a child.

She looked very young — and rather lovely. Gay noticed it with surprise. She had never really thought of Evie as being pretty — attractive to men.

She watched her for a moment and then stooped and shook her roughly.

'Evie! Evie!'

Evelyn sat up, rubbing her eyes, not at all cross at being woken when she saw who it was.

'Oh, Gay!' she said. 'Did you have a good time, darling?'

Gay sat down on the bed and nodded her head.

'Well, tell me about it!' Evelyn said, slipping an arm through her sister's, drawing her closer.

Gay did not speak for a moment, then she turned suddenly, burying her face in the pillow and burst into tears.

'Why, Gay! Whatever is the matter, darling?'

Gay allowed herself to cry a little longer. Then she looked up at her sister from tear-drenched eyes, and said:

'Oh, Evie! I've fallen in love! . . . And it's all so difficult.'

'Fallen in love?' Evelyn echoed. 'But, Gay, there's nothing to worry about in that. He — he isn't married, is he, darling?'

'No!'

Gay gave a little sob and Evelyn hugged her and stroked the fair hair.

'Then what is it, darling? Tell me!' she said softly.

'It's — it's Margaret! . . . And Mother!' Gay said, her voice suddenly growing firm and convincing. 'Evelyn, you must take Margaret away!'

'Take Margaret away!' Evelyn said, astounded.

'Yes!' Gay cried vehemently. 'Unless you want to ruin my whole life — my only chance of happiness.'

'Gay, what *is* all this about?'

Gay turned to Evelyn and gripped her arm.

'I want to marry Gordon de Verriland,' she said urgently. 'He — he loves me, and . . . oh, I know it's sudden, Evie, but it was love at first sight. Evie, he's the last of an old aristocratic family and his mother is watching like a hawk to see he doesn't marry the wrong type of girl.'

'But, Gay, I don't see that you . . . '

'It isn't me!' Gay broke in. 'It's Mother. You know as well as I do, Evie, that she . . . she wasn't sober when she was killed; that she was slowly drinking herself to death anyway. She should have gone to a sanatorium ages ago, before it was too late. Suppose Gordon's mother gets to hear about it.'

'But that was all so long ago now, darling,' Evie said with difficulty. 'How can Mrs. de Verriland find out?'

'Oh, Evie, wake up!' Gay cried in an exasperated tone. 'Through Margaret, of course. If she knows Margaret's blind, she will be certain to make sure it is not a hereditary complaint . . . she'll check up on Father and — and Mother, and then it will all come out. You must take Margaret away, before anyone knows about her. Joan is the only one of my friends who has met her, who knows about it, and she won't tell. Evie, please — before it is too late . . . before you ruin my only chance of happiness.'

Evelyn remained silent as the full force of Gay's words penetrated into her mind. Her eyes darkened as their import struck her heart. That she had never thought of such a thing before! It simply had not occurred to her that either Gay's or her own marriage or lives could be affected in any way by their mother now that she was dead. But Gay was right! Of all things — insobriety in a woman was a taint to be avoided — and at all costs. How would one know that she or Gay or Margaret might not end up the same way? Oh — it was horrible!

'Gay, it can't be as serious as all that!' she said, trying to keep her voice reasonable, her thoughts controlled.

'But it is!' Gay cried. 'His mother is bound to visit us and when she sees Margaret, she'll start making enquiries. Evie, she will stop him marrying me!'

'That's nonsense, Gay!' Evelyn said calmly. 'If he really loves you, he will marry you anyway.'

'But Evie, you don't understand,' Gay cried. 'He hasn't a penny other than what his mother allows him. The money is really his but his father left it in trust and his mother controls it until he is thirty. If she did not approve of me, it would mean either we waited until then — five whole years! — or that Gordon should earn his own living, and he isn't trained to do that. I couldn't ask him to throw up five thousand a year for me!'

'Five thousand pounds!'

The enormity of the sum amazed Evelyn who had been struggling along on little over five hundred.

'Oh, Evie, please!' Gay said, softening her voice to a low persuasive note. 'If you will just go away for a little while — until we are married. It shouldn't be more than three months at the most, and . . . '

Go away! Evelyn was thinking. But I can't — not now that I have met *him*.

She recalled with sharp vividness Nicky March's bright, compelling eyes, his sudden wide smile, and soft wavy brown hair. She heard him saying, 'May I call again sometime now that we have met?' . . . Perhaps when he called she would be away somewhere . . .

'No, I can't go, Gay,' she said aloud.

Gay looked quickly at her.

'Margaret will soon get used to a new place,' she said, mistaking the reason for Evelyn's remark. 'She can't spend all her life here, Evie. A change would do her good, and you could go and stay with Nanny in Sussex. You know how much she would love to have you.'

'No, it isn't Margaret,' Evelyn said quietly, suddenly ashamed of herself for thinking only now of her little sister.

'I'm afraid it is a more selfish reason, Gay. You see, tonight — last night, I mean — I met someone.'

'Met someone?' Gay repeated, not understanding.

'Yes! Someone I want very much to see again.'

'Evelyn!' Gay's voice was more surprised than annoyed. Evelyn — with a boyfriend! It must be a boyfriend, she was sure. Curiosity replaced surprise.

'Who was it?' she asked blandly.

'Somebody you know — a man called Nicky March,' Evelyn said. 'Oh, Gay, don't ask me to go just yet. I meet so few people . . . and he — he is so different! . . . Give me a chance to meet him again. Mrs. de Verriland — '

'Lady de Verriland!' Gay corrected.

'Lady de Verriland won't start paying calls just yet. You and Gordon could keep it secret for a little while and maybe by then I shall have seen him again. And when I know — I'll go away with Margaret.'

She was speaking quickly, urgently,

pleading with Gay who so short a while ago was pleading with her.

'Nicky March!' Gay said. 'Why, I don't believe it! He's supposed to be a woman-hater, or so our crowd thought. How — how far has it gone?'

'Oh, no way,' Evelyn said with a half-apologetic smile. 'It is just that he came in to use the telephone and then — he stayed a little while . . . and said he would call again.'

Gay mentally compared this account with her first meeting with Gordon, and a wry smile twisted the corners of her mouth. Dear, old-fashioned Evie, she thought. Oh, well! Let her have her fling. A few weeks would not make much difference to her and Gordon. In fact it might be better, seeing how recently they had met. And this way, she could get a promise out of Evie to go away eventually. Once out of the way, her own road was clear. Evelyn could go up to town and meet Lady de Verriland by herself, and they could say Margaret was at school.

'Of course, Evie! There's no desperate hurry. We will have to know each other at least a month before we get engaged, anyway.'

'Oh, Gay, you are an unselfish darling! I do hope Margaret won't mind the change. I have always tried so hard to stay here where she knows her way. But perhaps the change would do her good. She likes Nanny so much . . . Gay, are you sure about — about your feelings for Gordon? I mean, it is rather sudden, isn't it? Are you quite certain?'

'As certain as you are that you want to see Nicky March again,' Gay said, and saw her shot go home. Evelyn gave a little sigh and lay back against the pillow, her eyes soft and dreamy.

'Yes,' she said. 'Yes, I want to see him again.'

Gay kissed her lightly and went quickly out of the door and along to her own room.

'It is going to be all right,' she thought as she undressed and climbed into bed. 'Evelyn just isn't Nicky March's type. She is not nearly clever or witty enough for him. Why, I don't even suppose he will bother to call again. It was probably only politeness that induced him to suggest it!'

She snuggled down contentedly under the clothes and her mind gradually relaxed. Soon she was sleeping deeply like a very young child.

Her dreams, however, would have been less sweet had she known how wrongly she had judged Nicky March — how wrong she had been about Evelyn. Because, for a quick, clever, vital person like Nicky, Evelyn, with her gentleness, her poise, her charm, was *just* the right type . . . In fact, just the kind of girl with whom he was destined to fall in love — and to marry.

5

'Evie, can I wear my new dress?'

Evelyn packed the thermos into the picnic basket and called her assent upstairs to Margaret as she did so.

'Hurry up, darling! We have quite a long way to walk before lunch.'

'All right, Evie. I'm hurrying!'

Presently Margaret's coltish figure came slowly down the stairs, reminding Evelyn for the hundredth time that any other child of ten would be jumping them two at a time.

'I can't do the fastening,' Margaret announced, standing for Evelyn to do up the little buttons at the back of the neck.

In the middle of this operation, the telephone bell rang.

'Can I answer it? Oh, please, can I, Evie?'

It was not very often the 'phone rang,

and whenever it did, Gay usually managed to reach the hall first. The calls, unless they were tradespeople, were always for her and she did not want Margaret to answer them. But this morning Gay had gone driving with Gordon and Evelyn was only too pleased to grant her little sister's whim.

'If it is for Gay, take the name of the caller carefully,' she called after Margaret's retreating figure.

'Hullo! Who is it?'

Evelyn smiled at Margaret's telephone voice, and returned to her sandwich-cutting for their picnic lunch.

'No, it is Margaret here! ... Yes, Evie's in the kitchen ... No, we are going out for a picnic ... Oh, would you really like to? ... Oh, yes, do! Please do! I'll go and ask Evie if it is all right.'

Evelyn heard Margaret's slow stumbling steps as she felt her way through the hall and into the kitchen. She went on slicing the loaf, but with her heart beating so swiftly and her hands trembling, the result was not as good as it should have been and the sandwiches were undoubtedly going to be door-steps.

'There are so few people Margaret knows,' she was thinking. 'Could it be . . . ?'

'Evie, it is that nice man — the one who used our telephone the other night and said he would be a butler with me! He wants to come to our picnic. He can come, can't he?'

Evelyn cleared her throat.

'Did he ask if he could come, or did you invite him, Margaret?'

'He asked to speak to you and I said you were in the kitchen, so he asked if you were cooking lunch and I said no, you were cutting sandwiches for our picnic and he asked if he could come . . . '

Margaret stopped to draw breath, and Evelyn laughed suddenly, feeling happy. He had asked if he could come!

'You speak to him, Evie,' Margaret said persuasively.

Evelyn was glad Margaret could not see the colour she knew to be in her cheeks.

'No, you go back and tell him we would love him to come if he will undertake to carry the picnic basket for us,' she said.

Margaret hurried back into the hall and soon she heard her voice talking to Nicky, repeating her message.

'Evie says you must carry the picnic basket, but you don't really have to, so you will come, won't you?' Margaret pleaded.

'I had better put in another cup,' Evelyn thought. 'And cut some more sandwiches and another slice of cake . . . I wonder if he will drink tea! We haven't any beer . . . I will wear my blue cotton frock. It is much more becoming than the green.'

'He is coming to call for us in half an hour,' Margaret broke in on her thoughts. 'Evie, won't it be fun? A picnic party! Do you suppose he will tell us a story? Evie, you do want him to come, don't you? You don't sound a bit excited! You're not cross, are you, because I asked? . . . '

'No, darling,' Evelyn said quickly. 'I am pleased he is coming — very pleased.'

She had kept her voice as natural as possible, trying not to appear too enthusiastic, but Margaret's sense of hearing was unusually acute, this sense being over-developed in place of her sight, and as Evelyn went upstairs to change, she sat down on one of the kitchen chairs and said aloud:

'That's funny! Evelyn didn't say that at all as if she meant it. I wonder if she doesn't really want him after all.'

But when Nicky arrived, complete with a bottle of beer for himself and ginger beer for Margaret, Evelyn's voice was undoubtedly pleased as she greeted him, and all Margaret's fears vanished.

'And I hope you don't mind this intrusion,' Nicky said formally, his quick glance taking in Evelyn's neat, slim figure, her bright, happy eyes as they met his for one short second.

'I am afraid you will be bored. There are only Margaret and myself on this 'party'!'

'I consider myself fortunate to have two such beautiful ladies to escort!' Nicky said, his eyes twinkling.

Margaret looked up at him suspiciously.

'I believe you are teasing!' she said.

Nicky laughed, and lifted the picnic basket as easily as if it were empty.

'Ladies,' he said, 'I await your pleasure!'

'Here, take my hand, Margaret,' Evelyn said. 'I'll tell you if there are any steps. Otherwise you can go straight ahead.'

'Where are we bound for?' Nicky asked as they went out through the front door and into the road.

'I thought we would go up to the forest,' Evelyn said. 'There's rather a nice spot up there which Margaret and I used to go to last summer. We call it 'Goblin's Hill.''

'But there aren't any goblins there really,' Margaret supplemented cheerfully.

'How do you know?' Nicky questioned. 'Just because you have never seen' — he corrected himself quickly — 'heard any suspicious noises, it does not necessarily mean there aren't any weird little people there. I dare say there are quite a number.'

'What, real live ones?' Margaret asked incredulously.

'Yes,' said Nicky. 'Little old grey-bearded elves with spectacles, and pointed caps. And funny little baby ones perched on the tops of toadstools.'

Margaret gave a little sigh of pleasure.

'Go on!' she begged. 'Tell me some more!'

Evelyn walked in silence — her mind gradually ceasing to absorb Nicky's stories and centring on the man himself. She was not looking at him now, but a quick shy glance earlier had taken in his whole appearance — the brown hair curling over his head like a small boy's; the grey flannel trousers and white sports shirt opened at the neck; the blue silk scarf knotted at his brown, sunburnt throat; the rough tweedy jacket slung over one muscular sunburnt arm. She could see the outline of the other one, the muscles strained to take the weight of the picnic basket.

'We are going to climb a fairly steep hill now, Margaret,' she said automatically.

Margaret nodded her head and turned back eagerly to Nicky.

'And do they all dance?' she asked. 'Or only the wood sprites.'

'I don't want to go away,' Evelyn thought suddenly and intensely.

'Oh, I wish Gay had not met Gordon — at least not just now. I wish . . . '

As if aware of the trend her thoughts had taken, Nicky broke in:

'Where's Gay? Didn't she want to come to the picnic?'

'Oh, she has gone for a car ride,'

Evelyn said, and: 'Mr. March, do you know any people called de Verriland?'

'Why, yes,' Nicky said, looking at her with sudden interest. 'There is one part of the family here, but the better-known relations live in London. I used to be up at Oxford with the son and heir, Gordon de Verriland. Not that we were ever very great friends. I was studying English seriously and he was taking History just for the fun of it. He used to spend most of his time roaring round in his Bentley.'

'Are they very rich?' Evelyn enquired.

'Goodness, yes!' Nicky said with a wry smile. 'Simply rolling in it! But most of the cash is in trust. Gordon doesn't come into it until he is thirty. Papa had a good idea what his son was like and left it in trust.'

'Is he unreliable?' Evelyn asked anxiously.

Nicky shot another quick look at her.

'Well, I don't know about now,' he said. 'Of course he was in those days. Who wouldn't be with his allowance and his looks! He may have changed, of course.'

'You don't see them now, then?' Evelyn pursued.

'Not really,' Nicky answered. 'Actually I had to interview the family once. You see, I've been a journalist for some years and I used to do a society page write-up for the *Readyman's News*. It was my business to tell the public who was who, why, where and how. The de Verrilands are celebrities, so they were news. Why do you ask?'

'I can smell bracken!' Margaret broke in excitedly. 'We must be nearly there: Are we going by the lake, Evie?'

Evelyn was glad to change the subject.

'Unless Mr. March has any other suggestions,' she said, smiling.

'Well, I have one,' Nicky temporized. 'And that is that you should call me Nicky. Mr. March is very formal for a picnic, isn't it?'

'Oh, yes!' said Margaret, before Evelyn had time to speak.

'And you must stop calling Evie 'Miss Challis.' It sounds so funny!'

Nicky looked at Evelyn and she smiled suddenly.

'Yes, it would be nicer if you called me Evelyn,' she said simply.

'Evelyn!' So at last he knew!

'You don't like the name?'

'Yes, very much. It was simply that I had been wondering if you were Eve, Eva, or Evelyn, and now at last, like the cat, my curiosity has been satisfied.'

'What cat?' Margaret asked.

'There is a rhyme that says, 'Curiosity killed the cat; satisfaction brought it back,'' Nicky explained.

'How can it be brought back if it was killed?'

'Oh, Margaret! So many questions!' Evelyn broke in half-apologetically. But Nicky did not seem to mind them.

'Cats have nine lives!' he said ingeniously. 'And I hope I have as many.'

'Why?' Margaret asked.

'Because I am always dying of

curiosity,' Nicky said with a smile.

'Are you?' Margaret enquired, taking his words seriously. 'Are you really dying now? It doesn't sound like it,'

Nicky and Evelyn laughed, but Nicky's voice as he looked at the tall girl beside him, was more than half serious.

'Yes,' he said slowly, 'I am! I want to know all sorts of things, and I shall go on dying until I find out.'

'What sort of things?'

Nicky looked hard at Evelyn and saw the colour deepen her cheeks before she turned her face away from him, saying quickly:

'We're there, Margaret! Don't fall over the tree stump. It is two paces in front of you.'

Nicky put down the picnic basket and stretched his arms above his head. Margaret sat down on the carpet of young green ferns, and said persistently:

'Please, Nicky, tell me. What are you dying of?'

Nicky gave a low, lazy laugh and settled himself down beside the little girl, prodding her playfully in the middle.

'Of hunger!' he said evasively. 'It must be lunch time.' An answer which satisfied Margaret but which left Evelyn with a lot to think about and, not a little of it, to be feared.

'Suppose he finds out that Gay is seeing a lot of Gordon de Verriland,' she thought. 'Suppose he decides to see Gordon again and mentions Margaret!'

But she pushed the idea from her. It was none of Nicky's business and it was not very likely that he would suddenly decide to renew his acquaintance with Gordon after all these years.

'But do journalists mind their own business?' Evelyn asked herself. 'Suppose he thinks it is a good story for his society page. Gordon de Verriland's wedding or engagement is bound to be news!' He would want more details of Gay's family; would mention Margaret . . .

'Do you write much now?' she asked Nicky carefully.

'Well, quite a bit,' Nicky answered. 'To tell the truth, I've rather let the journalism slip. I want to write a book. It has always been an ambition of mine, which was one of the reasons I went to Oxford to take English. But occasionally when I come across something that would make a good story, the old habits persist and I do an odd article or write-up.'

'Oh!'

Nicky looked at her curiously.

'Did you think I was trying to get some copy today?' He asked lightly but with an undercurrent of seriousness.

Evelyn said in a voice she did not mean to sound quite so vehement:

'I sincerely hope not!'

'Now is that just maidenly pride that prompted that remark, or The Mystery again?' Nicky asked himself. 'I'd give a lot to know more about the Challis family!'

But Evelyn had already changed the

subject and was talking busily to Margaret as she spread out their lunch before them. He gave up trying to solve the puzzle and prepared to enjoy the moment, so unexpected and so very nice. Enough for the time being that he was here, with Evelyn, with the quaint little blind child.

'I'll open the ginger pop!' he said, and reached for the bottles and the opener which Evelyn handed to him. As their fingers touched, he looked straight into her eyes, and for one moment before the dark lashes hid them from his view, he thought he saw the colour deepen, darken, as if she, too, had felt the same little thrill of excitement by the light contact of their hands. But when next he looked into them, her eyes were the same hazel-green, reminding him of some still, woodland lake, and he felt he must have imagined that moment.

'Wishful thinking!' he chided himself, and turned his attention to the little girl.

When lunch was over, Margaret clamoured for Evelyn to take her down to the lake.

'Please, Evie!' she begged. 'We can take off our shoes and paddle like we did last summer.'

'Would you like to come?' Evelyn asked Nicky with a shy little smile.

Nicky shook his head.

'I would far rather lie here in the sun,' he said.

'Lazybones!'

He laughed and settled himself more comfortably in the fern, and watched the two girls as they walked down to the edge of the lake. Their two cotton frocks — Evelyn's bright blue and Margaret's pink — made a splash of colour against the grey-green water and dark background of pine trees. He wished he had remembered his camera.

It was very beautiful up there in the forest. He wondered how he could have lived so many years in one district and yet never have found this spot before. Not, of course, that he had spent much time at home. Only school holidays and weekends off from work.

The little lake lay quiet and peaceful, surrounded by tall, shadowy pines which were yet sparse enough to allow the sunlight to glint on the water and encourage the kingcups to grow in abundance.

Evelyn was bending over Margaret, undoing her shoes. Then, as he watched, they waded into the water, holding their dresses above their knees. Margaret was shouting, laughing, but she was too far away for him to hear her words, and although he could only see Evelyn's slim, straight back, he could imagine the soft smile on her face.

A dragon-fly skimmed over his head, and the sun was very hot and sleepifying. He turned over and buried his face in his arm, and was soon fast asleep.

Perhaps half an hour later, still drowsy and only half awake, he heard the two girls talking as they drew near.

Then a pause, and Evelyn's voice saying:

'Hush, Margaret! He is asleep.'

'Oh!' cried Margaret in a subdued squeak. 'What a waste of a nice afternoon!'

He did not move, but lay with closed eyes, listening to their soft whispers.

'He is probably tired,' Evelyn was saying. 'He's certainly sleeping very soundly.'

'He isn't snoring!' came Margaret's whispered treble. 'Evie, what does he look like?'

Nicky knew he should 'wake' up now, but he was too curious to hear Evelyn's reply.

'Oh, Margaret, the questions you ask!' she said, but she furthered her reply with, 'He is lying on one side with his head on his arm, and there is a piece of fern in his hair which is curling all over his head so that he looks like Pan.'

'Peter Pan?'

'No, darling! The great god Pan.'

'Who's he?'

'He was half man, half goat,' Evelyn explained. 'And was the god of . . . '

'Does he look like a goat?' Margaret broke in. 'I thought you said goats had horns and funny little tails!'

Nicky felt it was time he 'woke' up.

'Hullo!' he said, sitting up and looking round at the girls. 'What time is it?'

'It's three o'clock,' Evelyn said, busying herself with Margaret's sandals. But the little girl was not so willing to drop the subject.

'Evelyn says you look like a goat when you are asleep,' she announced.

'Oh, Margaret, I did nothing of the sort!'

The colour rushed into her cheeks, and Nicky bit his lip, trying to keep from smiling.

'You know you are blushing, Evelyn!' he said. 'I do believe you are guilty!'

'No, I'm not!' Evelyn cried, still not meeting his gaze. 'If — if I am blushing, it is only because it sounded so rude. I — I said you looked like Pan, who was

half goat, half man. But I meant your —
your curly hair.'

'In that case you are forgiven,' Nicky
said, trying to smooth his head with his
hand, but soon giving up the job as
hopeless. He lit his pipe and leaned
back on one elbow, puffing contentedly.

Was it possible, he wondered, that
this girl who must be quite twenty at
least, was really so shy, so unused to the
company of men that even to meet his
gaze made her blush? If so, why? Surely
she must have dozens of admirers,
boyfriends, with her face, her figure, her
soft gentle voice and smile, and
altogether feminine ways.

'Evie, can I go and pick some of
those flowers you told me about?'

'Do you think you'll be all right
alone?'

Margaret nodded her head.

'I'll be careful,' she said. 'You can call
me if I go too near the lake, can't you?
But I don't suppose I will. The ground
smells different when you get near

111

water, so I shall know.'

'All right, darling.'

Nicky and Evelyn watched the little girl feeling her way step by step down towards the lake.

'She is wonderfully self-sufficient — no, that's not quite the right word. I think I mean active,' Nicky said, half to himself. He turned to Evelyn. 'Isn't there any hope of a cure?' he asked. 'Surely there must be some operation that could be performed?'

Evelyn played with a piece of dried lantern grass, shedding it of its seeds, one by one.

'No, I'm afraid not,' she said. 'Both the optic nerves are dead.'

'Do you look after her yourself?'

'Yes. I teach her lessons, too.'

'Braille?'

'Well, no, I haven't done anything about that yet. I thought I would leave it another year or two,' Evelyn replied. 'Don't you think that is best for her?'

'Frankly, no! There must be so much she could learn from books,' Nicky answered carefully. 'Besides, it is a form of escape — reading; something you can do when you have to be alone.'

'Margaret is never by herself,' Evelyn said. 'And she has no need of an escape, as you put it. She is really quite happy, you know. As to the learning, I want her to learn all she can by herself — to make use of her own faculties before she has to resort to other people's observations. If she can use her own imagination as well, that, too, must be better for her than any amount of story books.'

'Oh, I agree with you in a way,' Nicky said thoughtfully. 'But think what she misses. Remember how you enjoyed *Peter Pan* and the *Water Babies*, and *Alice in Wonderland*?'

'I have read them all to Margaret, and *Black Beauty* and the Pooh books — oh, and all the others!'

Nicky smiled.

'You must devote a lot of your time to her,' he said. 'You love her very much, don't you?'

'Yes,' said Evelyn simply. 'Her happiness means more to me than my own.'

'But your own is important, too!' Nicky countered swiftly. 'Margaret loves you, too, Evelyn, and being so sensitive, she is probably more aware of your moods than you are yourself. If you are not happy, she would not be either.'

'I don't think that occurred to me before,' Evelyn answered. Then she smiled. 'But I am happy. I have everything I want.'

'Everything?'

She looked round at him quickly and again the tell-tale blush deepened the colour in her cheeks.

'Are you happy *now*, this minute?' Nicky persisted.

She met his gaze steadily.

'Yes,' she said quietly. 'I am.'

'Then we — we must do this again,' Nicky said quickly, eagerly. 'At least, not quite the same thing, because such moments are never as beautiful if you try to repeat them. But other things —

together. You and Margaret and I. You would like that, wouldn't you?'

'Yes,' she said. 'Yes, I would. But . . . '

'There are no buts,' he answered. 'You must not let there be any.'

'But, Nicky . . . '

'No!' he broke in smiling. 'Not one! Promise?'

'I can't promise,' Evelyn answered, remembering with a deep sinking in her heart that other promise — to Gay — to leave at the end of next month. 'But I would like there to be another day — like this,' she added shyly.

There was the puzzle again! But Nicky did not allow it to spoil his happiness in this moment.

'Let's have tea,' he said, changing the subject.

'I am sure it must be tea-time!'

He saw the little frown disappear and Evelyn's charming smile take its place.

6

'Gay, will you be going out this evening, darling?'

Gay looked over the top of her novel.

'No,' she said. 'I want an early night. Gordon's gone up to London to see his mother and won't be back until the weekend.'

'Then would you mind very much if — if I went out?' Evelyn said. 'Nicky wanted me to go to a dance at some road-house he knows. I told him I thought you would be out and I couldn't leave Margaret, but if you are staying in, I'll go and telephone him. He may not have got another partner yet.'

Gay's eyes narrowed.

'You are making headway, aren't you, Evie?' she said shrewdly.

'I — I like him very much,' Evelyn said inadequately.

'And how does he feel?' Gay enquired carefully.

'I — I don't know!'

'Oh, well, I don't mind looking after Margaret. You go ahead and enjoy yourself. Did you have a reply from Nanny?'

'Yes! She is expecting us on the fifteenth of August. Gay, will you be all right here alone? Do you think you ought . . . '

'Oh, yes, Evie!' Gay broke in. 'Don't fuss so! Joan de Verriland says she will come and stay for a week or two, and Betsy knows how to manage the house now.'

'Yes, but . . . '

'It's sweet of you to bother, but there's no need,' Gay said, forcing herself to keep calm. 'You go and telephone Nicky.'

Evelyn put the sewing basket away and went out to the hall. Presently she returned with shining eyes and said:

'Gay, it is all right. He had not asked anyone else. He's calling for me at seven. What shall I wear?'

Gay gave her sister an amused look. This young, breathless creature — was it really the old-fashioned, motherly Evie? With a sudden rush of pity caused by the knowledge that Evelyn's gay times were soon coming to an end, she said:

'You had better wear my new green taffeta. It'll suit you with your green eyes and dark hair.'

'Oh, Gay, may I? You are a darling!'

Gay allowed herself to be kissed but she did not really like her sister's demonstrativeness.

'Where's Margaret?' she asked, changing the subject.

'She's making something in the kitchen,' Evelyn said. 'Shall I call her for you, Gay?'

'No!' said Gay, picking up the novel. 'It can wait until later.'

Later was after supper when she and her small sister were sitting on the veranda enjoying the last warm rays of the July sun.

'Margaret!'

'Yes, Gay?'

'Have you and Evie and Nicky seen a lot of each other?'

'Oh yes, Gay! Nearly every day since our picnic.'

'Do you like Nicky?' Gay asked casually.

'Oh, yes! He's ever so nice! He likes me, too! He said so!'

'And Evie?'

'He likes her better'n me. At least, he hasn't said so, but I can tell. His voice goes different when he speaks to her.'

Gay bit her lip.

'Did you or Evie tell him you were going to stay with Nanny?' she asked.

'Oh, no, Gay! Evie said it was to be a secret. She said it would spoil everything so we haven't told him. Not until the day 'fore we go, Evie says.'

'Does Nicky go out much?' Gay asked then. 'I mean with other people?'

'I — I don't know, Gay! How do you mean?'

Gay chose her words more carefully.

'Well, who does he talk about all the time?' she asked. 'Surely he mentions his friends.'

'Well, not very much,' Margaret answered. 'Once he told us about some people called de Verri-something-or-other. But I can't remember the name properly.'

'De Verriland?' Gay asked quickly.

'Yes!' said the little girl. 'That's right. He used to go to school with the little boy.'

'What little boy? Gordon de Verriland? Try and remember, Margaret. It's important.'

'Yes, that's who it was,' Margaret said. 'Why, Gay? Is anything wrong?'

Her quick hearing had caught the different intonation of Gay's voice.

Gay forced herself to speak lightly.

'Oh, I just wondered,' she said casually. 'I know someone by that name, too. Does Nicky ever see this Gordon de Verriland now?'

'I don't know, Gay! I can't remember if he ever said so or not.'

'Oh, never mind! It doesn't matter,' her sister said.

But it did matter! If Gordon and Nicky were friends it would soon be out that she and Evelyn had a blind child for a sister and then . . .

'Oh, damn!' she said under her breath. 'If this affair between Nicky and Evelyn really is serious after all, I shall have to do something about it. Stop them seeing each other until Gordon and I are safely married — something that will part them temporarily — just for a month or two . . . '

She sent Margaret off to bed, and herself sat down to try and find a solution to her problem.

Suppose Evie were to tell Nicky the whole truth, she thought. Then he could be asked to keep quiet for all their sakes until she and Gordon were married. But she rejected the idea almost immediately. Obviously if Evie did care for Nicky, she would not want to risk losing him by revealing their family history any more than she, Gay, was going to risk losing Gordon.

Suppose, then, that Nicky and Evelyn continued to write to each other while Evie was at Nanny's — that he went down to see her sometimes, imagining she was there for Nanny's sake, or some such thing? And that he should either accidentally or purposefully run into Gordon some day and they started to talk about mutual friends. Nicky would be bound to mention Evelyn and then . . .

No! Gay saw in a flash what that would lead to. There was only one way to silence Nicky and that would be by seeing that he lost all interest in Evelyn. From the short fund of experience she had gathered, Gay knew that no man cared to mention past love affairs — not unless they had been successful ones which he could brag about.

Then how could she disinterest Nicky in Evelyn? Say Evelyn had another boyfriend? But that would only increase his interest. Say then that she was married? How could she explain this to Evie should Nicky question her about it? Say that she believed Nicky was married and that she was trying to safeguard her sister from a man she had believed to be a blackguard. As soon as she, Gay, and Gordon, were married, she would explain to Evie, that she had mistaken Nicky's name for that of his married brother, Rupert, and she could make it up again, explain to him . . .

The telephone rang, cutting into the silence of the room; the medley of her thoughts.

'A personal call for Miss Gay Challis, from London.'

'This is Gay Challis.'

'Hold on a minute . . . You're through!'

'Hullo! Hullo! Gay? It's Gordon here! How are you, sweet?'

'Fine, darling. And you?'

'Well, a bit anxious,' came Gordon's voice. 'You see, darling, Mother's decided to come down with me tomorrow. I think she wants to give you the once-over. She will probably want to meet this sister of yours, too. Will that be O.K., darling?'

Gay gripped the receiver hard.

'Gay, are you there? Can you hear me?'

'Yes, Gordon, I heard! Actually Evie won't be here. She is going away tomorrow.'

'Oh, well, never mind! But put on your glad rags, darling! Mother's awfully fussy about clothes and a first impression with her is all-important. She will just have to meet your sister some other time.'

'Yes!' said Gay. 'Perhaps in town one day. What time will you be down, Gordon?'

'About four-ish,' Gordon said. 'Will you be at Joan's for tea?'

'Yes, I'll be there,' Gay answered.

'Then I'll say goodbye for now, my sweet? Do you love me?'

Today Gay found the question irritating, but she controlled her voice, saying:

'Of course, darling!'

'I've got a present for you, sweet,' came Gordon's reply. 'I noticed you hadn't got one, so it should be useful.'

'Oh, Gordon, what is it?'

Gay's interest was not feigned this time.

'It's a wrist watch, my sweet. Rather a pretty gold one I saw at Asprey's yesterday.'

'Oh, Gordon! How lovely! Do you think I ought . . . '

'Of course,' he broke in. 'Why, we will be officially engaged next week — if all goes well with Mother. See you tomorrow, then, Gay.'

'Yes!' said Gay. 'Goodbye, darling!'

''Bye, sweet!' said Gordon, and Gay, still automatically clasping the receiver to her ear, heard the line go dead.

She replaced it carefully and went slowly upstairs to her room — the room that had once belonged to her mother.

'Oh, lord!' she said aloud. 'Now what! And how am I going to get rid of

Evie and Margaret by tomorrow?'

As if in answer to her problem, the telephone rang again — this time with a telegram for Evelyn.

'NANNY ILL. IF POSSIBLE
COME IMMEDIATELY'

It had been sent by the district nurse.

It was characteristic of Gay that she gave no thought to Nanny — or to how serious her illness might be. All that mattered to her was that this was a heaven-sent opportunity for her to get rid of Evie and Margaret. They could be packed off first thing in the morning — even before Evie could telephone Nicky of her new address. She, Gay, would promise to give him a ring and from then on, it would be plain sailing.

She telephoned a reply to the district nurse saying:

'COMING TOMORROW'

She had no doubt at all that if Evelyn

were needed she would go without question.

Gay wondered once or twice after the telegram had been sent, if it were all worthwhile. Was she ruining Evie's life in order that she could marry Gordon whom she did not even love?

She comforted herself with the thought that although breaking up Nicky's and Evelyn's little affair, it would only be temporarily. As soon as she and Gordon were married, she would tell Evie what she had done — explain that Joan had said Rupert March was married and she had understood it to be Nicky. Then Evie would write to Nicky and explain and the whole 'mistake' would be forgiven and forgotten.

If Gay's conscience troubled, it did not do so very severely. As she went back to the sitting-room to find her book, she comforted those few qualms with the thought of all the things she would do for her two sisters when she was Gordon's rich wife. Evie need no longer do the housework, and she, Gay, would send both her and Margaret on a long cruise — safely out of the way.

But in all her planning, Gay had forgotten one thing. Even as Gordon's wife, she would have no right to the de Verriland fortune. That would still be controlled by his mother. She had not stopped to think that if Lady de Verriland found any reason to disapprove of her daughter-in-law after their marriage, she could still stop Gordon's allowance.

Gay had yet to learn that there is a flaw in every jewel.

* * *

'Evelyn, would you care to come to tea tomorrow — to meet my mother?'

Nicky leant across the little table and looked eagerly into Evelyn's shining eyes. 'Margaret, too, of course!' he added, smiling.

'Have — have you told her about us

128

— about Margaret and me?' she asked a little shyly.

'No,' Nicky answered. 'I am keeping you as a surprise!'

'Oh, Nicky!'

'You will like Mother,' he said, 'once you know her. And I know she will like you — that is, as long as she is not jealous of you.'

'Jealous?' Evelyn repeated. 'But why should she feel like that? There's nothing to be jealous of.'

'Oh, but there is!' Nicky said. 'My feelings for you, for instance, would be guaranteed to make even the most indifferent mother think twice.'

Evelyn looked quickly down at the table-cloth, tracing the pattern with the edge of her fork.

'Evelyn, look at me!'

Still she would not raise her eyes.

'Evelyn, please! Don't you want me to tell you . . .'

'Nicky, I'm going away!' she broke in then.

'Going away!'

'Yes! Just for a little while. I'm going to visit Nanny. She is old now, and I thought I would take Margaret down to see her before she dies. She has a lovely little cottage in Sussex and . . . '

'Evelyn!'

She looked up at him, startled, and the colour rushed into her cheeks as it seemed to do so often nowadays when she met his gaze. Her eyes dropped and she nervously fingered the edge of the table-cloth.

'Evelyn, that is not the real reason you are going away, is it? You weren't speaking the truth!'

'N-no!'

'Can't you tell me?'

Evelyn looked up again, and this time her eyes were calm, steady,

'No!' she said. 'No, I can't! Please don't ask me to explain, Nicky. You must just trust me.'

'Of course!' he said immediately. 'Can you tell me, Evelyn, if it has anything to do with — with me?'

'No! . . . Yes! . . . Well, in a way!'

Evelyn faltered. 'Oh, Nicky, please don't ask me to explain. It — it involves other people than myself. If it were for myself alone — this situation would never have arisen. One day, I will tell you all about it.'

'All right, my dear!'

Nicky laid his hand on top of hers for a moment, then stood up, saying lightly:

'Shall we go?'

She nodded her head and went to fetch her wrap while he called the waiter and paid the bill.

Outside, the sky was brilliantly bejewelled with stars, and the air, though cooler and more fresh than it had been indoors, was still warm and sweet-smelling. Nicky tucked Evelyn into his car, and they drove home in silence, each wrapt in thought.

When they reached the front door, Nicky turned off the engine and helped Evelyn out of the car.

'It's been a heavenly evening,' she said. 'Thank you so much, Nicky.'

'It is always wonderful being with you!' Nicky said quietly. 'Evelyn . . . '

She turned towards him and suddenly she was in his arms and his lips were pressed against her mouth. For one moment, Evelyn forgot everything but the beauty, the excitement, the utter contentment of that kiss, knowing then that she loved him with her whole heart, her whole body, her whole soul. She felt as if she had been on a very long journey, and that here, held tightly in his arms, she had at last come home.

'Evelyn! I love you! I love you! Tell me that you care just a bit for me, too?'

'I do, Nicky! I love you!'

He did not kiss her again, but held her more tightly in his arms so that her head was pressed against his shoulder and the curve of her smooth, white forehead brushed his chin.

'I have so much I want to say to you — to ask you,' he said quietly. 'But it will wait since you wish it so, my dear. Nothing really matters very much except that you should love me.

Darling, tell me again that you do.'

'There will never be anyone else but you,' Evelyn said simply. 'I love you with all my heart, Nicky.'

She allowed him to kiss her once more, then she drew away from him, afraid that if she did not soon go in, she would never have the strength to leave him.

'Goodnight, dearest Nicky,' she said, and by the light of the stars he saw her face, smiling at him with that tender, inscrutable smile that was so peculiarly her own and which he found the most attractive of her many charms.

When she closed the door, he turned and climbed into his car, and Evelyn, listening in the silence of the dark hall, heard the throb of the engine fade rapidly into the distance.

'Evie! Evie, is that you?'

'Why, Gay! You'll catch your death of cold! Where is your dressing-gown?'

Gay glanced unseeingly at her slim body, clad only in a thin white nightdress which clung to her, revealing

133

the outline of her small virginal breasts, the long straight legs and rounded thighs. She was unconscious even of the picture she made, standing on the landing at the top of the stairs like a mythical ghost.

Evelyn went quickly up to her, hurrying her back into her room, into bed.

'For goodness' sake!' she said. 'You must be mad!'

'Oh, it's quite warm!' Gay said petulantly. 'Evie, there has been a telegram for you from Nanny. She is ill and you are to go down right away. I've looked up a train and it goes about twelve tomorrow morning. That should just give you time to get packed.'

'Tomorrow morning!'

'Yes! Nanny needs you, Evie!'

'Oh, poor Nanny! I hope it's nothing serious!'

It was the old pull and, as Gay had known, it went straight to Evelyn's heart.

'We'll go first thing,' Evelyn went on.

134

'I wonder, though, if I ought to take Margaret. Maybe Nanny has something catching . . . '

'Nonsense, Evie!' Gay broke in sharply. 'At her age! No, it is probably her heart. She had an attack this time last summer. Besides, what would Margaret do here without you!'

Once again Evelyn felt the ties of her own unselfishness.

'You had better get to sleep right away,' Gay said persuasively. 'You'll have to be up early to get packed.'

'Yes,' said Evelyn. 'Goodnight, Gay! I'm so sorry you had to wait up.'

She kissed her sister and went along to her room. But although she was soon in bed, it was over an hour before she slept, and then it was only fitfully, and her dreams were all of Nicky.

The next morning, however, she had little or no time to think of him, or day-dream about the wonderful end to their evening, and she readily agreed to Gay's suggestion that she should leave her to telephone Nicky at lunch time and give him Nanny's address.

Apart from being in such a hurry, Evelyn still felt a little breathless and shy, and thought she would rather wait to hear from him before she spoke to him again. Besides which, a telephone can be most impersonal and it had been so indescribably perfect last night, that she did not want to spoil the memory of it with explanations and addresses. So she kissed Gay goodbye and with an excited, curious, talkative Margaret, she caught the midday train to Sussex.

Gay telephoned Nicky after she had had her own lunch. Mistaking her for Evelyn, Nicky said:

'Darling, I am so glad you 'phoned. I was just going to ring you. Last night . . . '

'Mr. March, it is not Evelyn. This is Gay Challis speaking . . . '

'Oh!' There was disappointment, anxiety in even so short an exclamation. 'Is anything wrong?'

'Well, yes!' Gay said carefully, trying to make her voice sound hesitant, distressed, doubtful. 'Evelyn asked me to ring you to tell you she had gone away.'

'Gone away? But I thought she wasn't going until the end of next week!'

'She — she changed her mind,' Gay said, feeling her way. 'After last night.'

'Last night. I don't understand.'

'Mr. March, Evelyn is in love with you.'

'But she knows — she must know that I — I love her, too. Surely . . . '

'That is just it,' Gay broke in. 'You see, Evelyn is already married.'

'Already married! It's impossible!'

For a minute or two the line was silent, then Gay said:

'I'm afraid it's the truth, Mr. March. Perhaps you will believe it when I tell you that Margaret is Evie's daughter.'

'Margaret! Evelyn's daughter!' Nicky's voice was utterly incredulous. 'But she's ten and Evelyn's only . . . '

'Twenty-five! And Margaret is only eight. She was born when Evelyn was only seventeen. Her father — Evie's husband — was visiting our parents . . . It is rather a delicate subject, but I suppose an explanation is due . . . Evie was very young at the time and didn't realize what was happening. When they knew the baby was coming, Father made him marry her to give the child a name. But he returned to Italy before Margaret was born and has not returned.'

'But this is all incredible!' came Nicky's voice, strained, a little hoarse. 'If she wasn't in love with him, couldn't she get a divorce?'

'Margaret's father is an Italian,' Gay said, 'and therefore a Roman Catholic. His religion does not recognize divorce. Oh, I know this must come as a shock to you, Mr. March. Evelyn has wanted to tell you for a long time, but she did not have the courage. She asked me to tell you that it is because she cared that she can't go on seeing you. She said she hoped you would not try to write or see her, for her sake, and for Margaret's.'

'No! I see!'

'I'm most awfully sorry,' Gay said.

'It's all right! Goodbye, and thank you for ringing.'

Nicky felt the irony of his words even as he said them, but never for a moment did he doubt Gay's story. It all fitted so perfectly — Margaret's unusual likeness to Evelyn; their avoidance of social interests; Evelyn's intense love for the child; Gay's reluctance to mention them. Yes, the missing piece of the puzzle had been found and the mystery was a mystery no longer.

Bitterly, he realized that in finding the solution he had wanted so desperately he had also found the means of breaking his own heart.

He went back into the drawing-room in search of his mother.

'I'm going away,' he told her abruptly. 'Tomorrow! I think I'll go abroad.'

Seeing his white face and tragic, stricken eyes, Mrs. March forbore to ask the questions that burned into the front of her mind. Instead, she put an arm round the shoulders of her favourite son, and said lightly:

'Of course, if you want to, Nicholas dear. Where will you go?'

7

It was a beautiful morning — fresh and crystal-clear — and as Evelyn stood at the open window in her thin nightdress, she shivered a little in the cold. But she did not move.

It was nearly nine o'clock and time the postman usually went past their gate. In the three weeks that she and Margaret had been at Nanny's little cottage, Evelyn had never known him to be unpunctual.

At first she had run out to meet him, eagerly requesting the expected letter that would surely come from Nicky. But when a week had passed and still no letter had come, she could not bear that the postman should see her disappointment, guess at the anguish in her heart; and because of her pride, she had even gone to the trouble of deceiving him into thinking it was Gay's letter she wanted so desperately, forcing herself to smile and say, 'Ah, there it is at last!'

Now she waited in her room, her heart beating swiftly when the old man came bicycling down the lane, standing still as he paused by the gate to search through his mailbag, dropping with a sick little bump when he climbed back on to his bicycle and rode away. Only three times had he come up the little flagged path and pushed a white envelope through the letter-box into the tiny hall.

Then Evelyn had made herself walk slowly down the twisted oak staircase while her heart raced ahead and her mind worked furiously, thinking, 'He has written at last! It must be from Nicky! If it is from Gay again, I'll die. Oh, Nicky, Nicky! Dear God, let the letter be from him!'

Hardly daring to look, she had stooped to pick it up, knowing even as she did so that it was not the letter she wanted; staring blindly at Gay's handwriting and feeling more utterly wretched and disappointed than she had thought possible for any human being to be.

This morning brought yet another letter from Gay — this time to say she would be arriving that very afternoon because she had a lot of important things to talk over with Evelyn.

'And I, too, have several things to ask Gay,' thought Evelyn. 'Perhaps she has given Nicky the wrong address. Perhaps he wrote home and she is bringing a letter with her!'

She walked slowly along to Margaret's room, the waiting, the hoping starting all over again. Perhaps she would write a note to Nicky after all, she thought. She had fought so hard against the desire to do so, her intense pride only just preventing her taking such action as the days went slowly by, always without word of him, from him. She would write a short, newsy letter, not mentioning this burning desperate emotion that filled her heart at every thought of him — the undeniable love that she knew now could never be quenched, never be given to another man.

She would tell Gay everything. Gay would understand and advise her. It would be such a relief to pour out her heart to someone. Margaret was much too young to be worried by such things and Nanny, sweet old thing that she was, was yet too much a person of the last generation to be able to offer any practical advice.

When first they had arrived at Cherrytree Cottage, Evelyn had not expected Nanny to survive her illness. But the heart attack had been short even while it was severe, and the old woman pulled through, weaker, now an incurable invalid, but still alive and likely to be for several more years, the doctor had said, if she took care of herself. Immediately Evelyn had volunteered to take care of her, saying that if necessary Nanny could go home with them and Cherrytree Cottage be closed or sold.

The doctor, a young man of twenty-six, had only just qualified and had bought the small country practice in preference to working in one of the large London hospitals. He was amazingly keen and thorough, and Evelyn had liked him so much that she had introduced Margaret to him and asked him to give her a complete account of the little girl's health.

The young man, Dr. James Cathy, had shown great interest in Margaret's eyes, but although pronouncing her healthy in every other respect, could give Evelyn no hope as to restoring the little girl's sight.

'I hate to have to admit it, Miss Challis,' he had said.

'I did not really think anything could be done,' Evelyn had answered. 'I just wanted to be quite sure.'

'You don't look any too well yourself, Miss Challis,' James Cathy had remarked, noting her extreme pallor accentuated by the cloud of dark hair, the hollow cheeks and large circles under her eyes.

Evelyn had turned away, saying lightly:

'Oh, I'm quite all right, Dr. Cathy!'

But he was not convinced, and Evelyn realized she would have to hide her unhappiness more skilfully if she wished to escape this young man's keen observation.

'Oh, Nicky, Nicky! Why haven't you written? Did it all mean nothing to you, after all?' Evelyn asked herself for the hundredth time. But still there was no answer.

With a little sigh she lifted the wooden latch of Margaret's bedroom door and went over to her little sister.

The child lay sleeping deeply with her head turned towards the window, through which a shaft of golden sunlight was centring on her face. Her eyes were closed and the long dark lashes lay on her soft little cheeks.

As Evelyn stood there, lost in thought, Margaret stirred and turned over in bed, and although she could not see her sister, she was instantly aware of her presence. She reached out a hand and touched the folds of Evelyn's nightdress, felt for her hand.

'Why, Evie, you're freezing cold!' she said. 'Come and get in beside me. I'm ever so nice and warm.'

Evelyn turned her attention to Margaret.

'It's time to get up, darling,' she said.

'Oh, never mind!' Margaret said, pulling at her hand. 'Just come and cuddle up for five minutes. We can't be late for breakfast if we are getting it ourselves, can we?'

Evelyn smiled her quiet, thoughtful smile and climbed in beside the little girl. The touch of Margaret's warm young body comforted her in some way, and she felt a little happier, less lonely.

'Gay is coming down this afternoon, darling,' she said. 'She has lots of things to talk about.'

'Do you think it's anything very 'portant?' Margaret asked. 'Do you think she has decided to come and live here with us?'

'No, I don't think it would be that,' Evelyn replied gently. 'I should say it was something to do with getting married.'

'Married?' Margaret echoed. 'Who to, Evie?'

'Someone very rich and handsome,' Evelyn told her.

'Do you know him?' Margaret questioned curiously.

'Well, not exactly,' her sister answered. 'But I'm sure if Gay likes him, he will be very nice.'

'Oh, Evie!' Margaret cried in an excited squeak. 'Do you think Gay will have a little baby then? If it grew up quickly I could play with it, couldn't I?'

'Why, Margaret!' Evelyn said, studying the child's face carefully. 'You aren't lonely, are you?'

'Well, no, not 'zactly!' Margaret said. 'But it would be nice when you were busy. You often are, you know!'

'Yes, I suppose I am,' Evelyn answered slowly.

'Do you think Gay's baby would see

like everyone else or would it be blind like me?' Margaret prattled on. 'Evie, am I the *only* little girl who is blind, or can all the other children see?'

Evelyn felt her heart contract painfully. This consciousness of her blindness was new to Margaret — a thing she, Evelyn, had not been prepared for. She supposed it was natural now that Margaret was growing up.

'Of course you aren't the only one,' she said, keeping the pity from her voice. 'There are lots of little girls and boys who can't see.'

'Then where are they?' Margaret asked. 'Why haven't I met any of them, Evie?'

'Well, we don't meet very many people,' Evie said. 'I never thought you — you would specially like to meet them, darling. I suppose that is the reason. Most of the blind children are at St. Dunstan's.'

'Where's that?'

'It's a special school for boys and girls, and grown-ups, too, who can't see.'

'A school!' Margaret echoed. 'Oh, Evie, will I ever go there? What fun it would be!'

Evelyn gave the eager little face a puzzled look.

'Would you really like to go to school, darling?' she asked. 'You could learn to read and write on a Braille typewriter and sew and make baskets, and things like that.'

'Oh, Evie!' Margaret's voice was husky with excitement. 'Oh, I would love to go! Do you really think I could? Would you come with me?'

'No, I couldn't come with you,' Evelyn said. 'But of course you shall go if you want to, Margaret. We will talk to Gay about it when she comes this afternoon. I expect Dr. Cathy will be able to tell us more about it, too, when he visits Nanny this evening. We'll see!'

Suddenly she felt Margaret's strong young arms round her, the soft lips against her cheek.

'Evie, you're always so nice to me!' the little girl said, almost in a sigh. 'I love you ever so much!'

Evelyn hugged the child to her and said in a voice which was not quite steady:

'You won't be lonely by yourself, darling?'

'Not if there are other little boys and girls there,' Margaret said happily. Then with quick childish intuition she sensed Evelyn's emotion and added: 'Of course, I'd miss you terribly, Evie! Would you be lonely without me?'

'Oh, I expect I shall go and live with Gay,' Evelyn said lightly. But even as she said it, she knew she would not do this. And if Nicky did not write, did not answer her letter, she could not bear to return home where he had been so much part of her life. There would be too much there to serve as a constant reminder of him. No, she would go out into the world, away from all the bitter memories and start life again — free from the ties of a young child and household duties and all such trouble-some commitments.

But Evelyn did not convince herself by such thoughts. She knew she would be more than lonely. She would be the loneliest person in the whole world.

*　*　*

Gay had not said by which train she would be arriving, so her two sisters waited for her in the sunny little orchard. Just before tea-time she drove up to Cherrytree Cottage in a small sports car which she proudly exhibited as her own.

'Gordon has given it to me as an engagement present,' she announced airily. 'It's a good thing you let me learn to drive last year, Evie! Do you like it?'

'Why, Gay, it's lovely!' Evelyn said, and Margaret tugged hard at Gay's hand and cried excitedly:

'Oh, Gay, do tell me, what does it look like? What colour is it? Can I feel?'

When Gay had given her little sister a detailed description, Evelyn led them both over to the porch where tea was waiting. Nanny sat in one of the wicker chairs, looking very old and wrinkled, but no less observant of eye.

She gave Gay a quick look and then said shrewdly:

'Well, you have grown up like your mother!'

Gay's eyes narrowed and she said in a small, hard voice:

'That is not a compliment, Nanny. I would rather you did not make a remark like that again.'

'Nonsense!' said the old woman. 'She was a very lovely woman at one time — very lovely.'

Gay's expression softened a little and, as she sat down to the tea-table, she held out her left hand and showed Nanny and her sisters a beautiful emerald ring. It was a large stone, set in diamonds, and Evelyn gasped as she saw it.

'Gay, how perfectly lovely!'

'Must have cost your young man a pretty penny!' Nanny remarked point-edly.

'Three hundred!' Gay said airily, and pretended not to notice the look in Evelyn's eyes — not a jealous or envious look but one of utter amazement.

'You have just the right hands for rings,' she said presently. 'When are you going to be married, Gay?'

'Oh, in about a month or two, I think. Gordon's mother wants you to meet her in town, Evie, some time next week to discuss arrangements.'

'Why doesn't she come down here?' Nanny put in with a sidelong glance at Gay.

Gay did not meet her eyes, but said:

'I thought it would be better in town. Besides, I want some clothes for my trousseau, and Evie can come up and help me choose them on the same day.'

'Oh, Gay, I should love that! We must try and find some money from somewhere.'

'That won't be necessary. Gordon's given me a cheque,' Gay said. 'He knows we aren't well off and his mother says as I shall be Lady de Verriland one day, it's time I started to dress like someone.'

'Gay!'

'Well, she didn't meant to be rude,' Gay put in quickly. 'It's just her way of being generous. Besides, Evie, it's stupid to pretend I do look well dressed or smart enough to mix with Gordon's crowd. I don't! And you know perfectly well that we couldn't afford the sort of trousseau I shall need. Now could we?'

Evelyn shook her head, trying to convince herself that Gay was right — that it was senseless trying to scrape a few pounds together when their future-in-laws could so easily afford to throw a few hundred away.

Deep inside her, however, she still felt that Gay should have refused — that by accepting their generosity she had somehow lowered the family pride. But could Gay be expected to have any pride in a family such as theirs where the past was always coming up to threaten their happiness with its sordidness.

'I'm frightfully hungry! Let's start tea,' Gay said cheerfully. And to Margaret, 'Come on, Hilda! You're supposed to hand round sandwiches if you're a parlour maid, you know!'

Margaret gave a little squeak of happiness and Evelyn sat back in her chair, the frown disappearing from her forehead, and prepared to enjoy the all too rare pleasure of Gay's company.

Gay took Margaret for a ride in her new car when tea was over, while Evelyn cleared away and washed up. When they returned, she left Margaret with Nanny and took Gay up to her room.

Gay lit a cigarette and sat down on Evelyn's bed.

'Heard from Nicky?' she asked casually, although she had already divined Evelyn's reason for bringing her up to the privacy of her own room.

'No, no I haven't!' Evelyn said. 'Oh, Gay, what shall I do? You *are* sure you gave him the right address?'

'Yes,' Gay said. 'Of course I did, Evie! He distinctly said he would write.'

'Did he say anything else?'

Evelyn tried to keep her voice from rising on that note of anxiety she knew to be there.

'Well, he seemed a little surprised you had gone,' Gay answered. 'But when I told him the reason, he said he quite understood and that he would write.'

Evelyn walked up and down the room, no longer able to conceal her emotions.

'Gay, I can't bear it!' she said, rolling and unrolling the little white handkerchief in her hand. 'Don't you see I love him? He said he loved me, too! Oh, why hasn't he written? I can't understand!'

Gay did not look at the pitiful, strained face.

She said slowly:

'Evie, you don't suppose he — he is married?'

'Oh, no, I'm sure he isn't,' Evelyn

said. 'He would never have told me he loved me. No, Gay, no!'

Gay did not stress the point.

'Someone said he had gone away,' she went on.

Evelyn's voice was hoarse — full of fear.

'Gone away?'

'Yes! I think he has gone on a holiday,' Gay said. 'Perhaps that is why he hasn't written.'

'Oh, but he could still write,' Evelyn said desperately. 'Even if it was only a postcard. Gay, I must find out what has happened. I'm going to write to him.'

'Write to him?' Gay repeated sharply. 'You can't do that, Evie! Where's your pride?'

'I have none left, Gay!' Evelyn said quietly. 'You see, I love him.'

Gay was silent for a minute. Then she looked up suddenly and said:

'O.K., Evie! You sit down and write now. I'll post it for you on my way back through London.'

'Oh, Gay, you darling! I knew you

would understand. It can't matter, really, can it? If I make it a short, newsy letter that one might write to any friend?'

She hurried over to the little table and sat down, drawing the blotter towards her. Gay lit another cigarette and smoked in silence, listening to the hurried scratching of Evelyn's pen. It was only a short note and did not take Evelyn long to write it. On the envelope she put a note in the left hand corner requesting that it be forwarded if necessary. On the flap at the back, she put 'If undelivered, return to Miss Evelyn Challis, Cherrytree Cottage, Plumton, Sussex.'

She handed it to Gay with a great feeling of relief.

'Now at least I shall know one way or another,' she said. 'If I don't hear from him and don't get the letter back, I shall know he received it but doesn't want to answer. If I get the letter back, then I can write again when he returns from his holiday.'

'I ought to be going,' Gay said, stubbing out the cigarette end and putting the letter in her pocket. 'See you next Thursday week, Evie. I'll meet you at Peter Jones' at eleven-thirty. O.K.?'

'Yes, I'll be there, darling.'

Margaret joined them downstairs and the three sisters walked out to Gay's car together, discussing Margaret's proposed entry into St. Dunstan's. Gay thought it was an excellent idea and encouraged Evelyn to go ahead with arrangements. As soon as possible, she made her escape and was soon on her way to London.

Evelyn felt immeasurably comforted by the thought of her little note to Nicky. Deep in her heart she was sure his silence was due to some misunderstanding. He could not have pretended that last evening together, nor that kiss which she was certain had meant as much to him as it had to her.

'Now at least I shall know,' she thought. 'I'm glad I wrote!'

Meanwhile, Gay had stopped the car

by the edge of the road and found the envelope in her pocket. She tore it open and pulled out a single sheet of paper.

'Dear Nicky,' she read. '*This is just a short note to explain why I left so suddenly the other day. Nanny was taken seriously ill and I was needed to look after her. She is better now and I hope to be home in a month or two.*

'*Margaret has been asking after you and wants to know if you have been on any picnics since our last one.*

'*Do write some time and let me know how you are.*

                '*As ever,*

                      '*Evelyn.*'

A short, simple little note, but enough to make Nicky doubt Gay's story. She pulled out her cigarette lighter and held the paper over the flame. Then, with a little sigh of resignation, she restarted the engine and was soon speeding on her way to town.

8

Evelyn and James Cathy sat in the deck chairs on the front porch listening to Margaret's shrill little voice coming from the kitchen where Nanny was instructing Martha, a girl from the village, how to cook the supper. Usually, Evelyn did all the housework, but tonight Nanny had insisted in asking Martha to come up.

'Dr. Cathy is your guest, my dearie,' she had said. 'And you must do the entertaining. Margaret and Martha and I will manage together.'

'I believe you are trying to do a little match-making, Nanny!' Evelyn had said, smiling, and had not been convinced by Nanny's vigorous denials of any such intentions. She knew the old woman had quite lost her heart to her young, fair-haired, blue-eyed doctor and strongly suspected she was trying to make him fall in love with her, Evelyn.

Not that James Cathy needed much persuasion. Already he was looking forward more and more to his now less frequent visits to Nanny, and he knew the attraction that Cherrytree Cottage had for him was entirely due to Evelyn's presence there. He wanted a wife — a companion, and she fitted so perfectly into the picture that he had to warn himself against the danger of being blinded by the obvious unsuitability of such a match.

James wanted to marry for love, and although at times he thought he did love Evelyn, at other times there seemed to be so great a distance between them that he felt they could never be spiritually close to each other. He had tried to break down this invisible barrier on one or two occasions when he had paid calls at Cherrytree Cottage that were not professional, dropping in for a friendly chat.

But they had not brought him any closer to her, and he was beginning to despair of ever making her realize him as a person of flesh and blood instead of just a doctor. Then suddenly she had telephoned him, asking him to dinner. Now here he was, wondering at this unexpected move on her part; wondering if she could possibly be growing to care for him a little bit; wondering why she had arranged this little twosome on the porch with Margaret and Nanny so obviously out of the way.

'It was very kind of you to ask me in to a meal,' he said formally, turning to offer her a cigarette. 'Doctors are such unsatisfactory guests as a rule, arriving late and being called away in the middle of a bridge four or the most important course of a meal.'

Evelyn smiled her quiet, thoughtful smile, and said:

'I'm glad you could come, Dr. Cathy. I want to ask your advice.'

'Professionally?'

'Well, yes and no! I want your

opinion about Margaret.'

'Oh!'

Without a doubt he was disappointed, but he gave her his full attention nevertheless.

'She wants to go to St. Dunstan's,' Evelyn was saying. 'As you know, she has always been with me, and I dare say I have spoilt her a little. Do you think she would be happy there? That it would be the best thing for her?'

'If she wants to go, yes!' James Cathy said after a second's hesitation. 'You could always remove her if she were not happy.'

'That's another point to the argument,' Evelyn said. 'You see, my other sister is getting married shortly and I had thought of going abroad. I would have liked to take Margaret with me, but I'm afraid she is more anxious to go to school.'

He detected the hurt tone of her voice, but did not refer to it.

'Margaret is right,' he said. 'It would be a lot easier for her to be with her own kind where she can learn so much. I think it is very unselfish of you not to keep her with you when you are obviously so fond of her. There are many people in your position who would have clung to her against their better judgment.'

'I shall miss her,' Evelyn said.

'So you had really already made up your mind to let her go?' James said with a smile.

'I suppose I had, really. But it was your view — being so definite about it, I mean — that really decided me finally,' Evelyn answered with unconscious tact. 'But I am not yet certain whether I should go away myself.'

'Do you want to go?'

Evelyn looked at the glowing tip of her cigarette and said in a low passionate voice which surprised him:

'Yes! I must get away. I can't go back to that house alone!'

'Will you go for long?'

'I don't know. It depends how Margaret settles down. I should like to go out for some winter sports. I shouldn't choose a holiday resort — just somewhere away from everybody, up in the mountains. I have always loved the look of them from those photographs you see of pine trees, weighed down by snow, and white stretches broken by single ski-tracks. The solitude, the quiet, is what I need . . . '

She broke off, horrified to find her voice was trembling and her eyes smarting with tears.

'Oh, Nicky, Nicky,' she was thinking. 'Why didn't you answer my letter? Why did you make me fall in love with you just to leave me like this?'

A month had passed now since she had written, yet still there was no reply. She had asked Gay about the letter, but Gay had posted it, she said, and advised Evelyn to forget Nicky, who was so obviously unworthy of her affections.

Forget him! She had tried, was still trying, but without result. At night she could not sleep for thinking, worrying about him. Through the day, she dreaded the coming of another long, sleepless night.

'I am sorry to hear you are going away.'

James Cathy's gentle, soothing voice broke in on her thoughts, and something a little wistful in the tone broke down the last vestige of her control and she burst into tears. Evelyn, who had not cried since she was a little girl.

James was out of his chair in an instant, had his arms round her, and was saying all kinds of things he had been thinking but had not been certain of meaning until this moment.

'Please, please don't,' he begged. 'Don't cry, Evelyn. Darling, don't!'

'I'm so — so lonely!'

The childish pathos of those few simple words caught at his heart, appealing to the protective male instinct that was so strong in him.

'There's no need to be lonely,' he said. 'So many people love you.

Margaret does, Nanny does, I do, too! I want to marry you, Evelyn.'

She drew away from him then, blowing noisily into her handkerchief like a small girl, gazing up at him with wet, puzzled eyes.

'Marry me?' she repeated. 'But you don't even know me!'

'Enough to know I love you,' he said, smiling down at her from his kind, laughing blue eyes. 'I've met you every day for one month and every other day for a second month, you know.'

She looked away from him, leaning against the supporting post of the veranda, staring down the little lavender path to the white latched gate where the postman stopped.

'I never thought — I didn't know . . . '

'No,' he interrupted gently. 'Of course not. Up until now I have been here in a professional capacity only. But that has not stopped me thinking about you. I hope I may see you more often now — as a friend?'

'I'm going away.'

'Yes, I know. But not until Margaret is safely in St. Dunstan's, and your sister married, surely? May I see you sometimes before you go?'

'Yes, but Dr. Cathy . . . '

'It would be nice if you would call me James!'

She smiled at him suddenly, shyly.

'James, I must tell you. It is only fair to do so. I can never feel the same towards you. You see, I am in love with another man. I always shall be.'

He looked at her sharply.

'He is already married.'

'No! I don't think so! He — he just doesn't care for me now. Our affair is over — finished. There is no more to it — except that I love him still.'

'I see! You don't think perhaps you could one day grow to care for me — not the same way, of course, but sufficiently to become my wife?'

'I — I don't know! It wouldn't be really fair to you, would it? Besides, I don't really want to get married just yet. It's all too recent — too much on my mind to even contemplate such a thing.'

'Of course!'

'I'm so sorry!'

'There's nothing to be so sorry about, my dear. Look, Evelyn, we won't mention this again until you come back from your holiday. Then, if I may, I will ask you that last question again. I shall go on asking until you say 'Yes' just for the sake of peace.'

'I may be away some time,' Evelyn answered him seriously. 'It isn't fair to give you any hope when I don't know if — if there is even a chance of my growing to care for you as much as you deserve.'

'We are under no obligation to one another,' James said quietly. 'If you fell in love again with some other fellow, I should quite understand. And if I decided I wanted to marry someone else, I should consider myself free to do so. But that is not very likely. There is no tie between us — except that of friendship.'

'You are very kind,' Evelyn said thoughtfully.

'No. I am very selfish! May I write to you when you're abroad?'

'No, don't let's write!' Evelyn said firmly. No more waiting for letters, watching for the postman.

'All right,' he agreed. 'We won't even write. I shall just have to trust to my good fortune that you don't forget me.'

She smiled up at him, and putting a hand on his sleeve, said:

'No, I won't forget. You are the only friend I have, Dr. Cathy — James! And you have paid me a great compliment. I shall think of you often.'

She stood up and added shyly:

'Please forgive my childishness just now. I think I am over-tired.'

'As a doctor, I strongly recommend this holiday,' James answered. 'I think you need it, my dear. But as a man, I'm all against your going, Evelyn.'

Evelyn released the hand which he had taken in both of his own and excused herself, saying:

'Supper will be ready, I expect. I must go and tidy. I won't be long!'

Left alone, James leaned back in his chair and wondered heartily at himself and the trend the last half-hour's conversation had taken. He had not been certain he loved her until he heard himself saying he did. Then he had been quite sure, and now he knew it was going to be a long and lonely time for him while Evelyn was away.

But he comforted himself with the thought that she had not entirely rejected his proposal, and broken hearts, like broken bones, could be put together again and be made whole.

He smiled at his own simile and resolved to treat Evelyn very gently.

'She needs a long rest and a complete change of environment,' he told himself. 'Then we will see!'

He stood up as Evelyn came to the door to take him in to supper. He was sure he could cure anything and everything — even a broken heart, and Evelyn, he thought with a smile, made a very lovely patient.

'Tell me,' he said, following her into the hall. 'Have you any idea where you will go?'

* * *

A week before Gay's marriage to Gordon de Verriland, Margaret went to St. Dunstan's and Evelyn went home to help her sister with preparations for the wedding.

Not that there were any social preparations to be made. Lady de Verriland had arranged for one of the big London catering firms to organize the entire reception, and nothing remained for Gay to do but sort and pack her many new clothes.

Evelyn was amazed by the quantity and the sheer loveliness of Gay's trousseau — gossamer fine stockings, shimmering pure silk nighties, sets of fine delicate chiffon undies, and several long, glamorous housecoats and négligées.

'I wish we could have afforded to buy your trousseau ourselves,' she had remarked to Gay with a thoughtful little frown. But Gay had only laughed and said it was silly to mind other people spending lots of money if they had so much they did not know what else to do with it.

Evelyn had held fast to her opinion, but had to admit that Gay had the most wonderful outfit — one that all girls dreamed about but few ever possessed.

The night before the marriage, the two girls went to the de Verrilands' house as arranged by Lady de Verriland.

'Gordon can go to his club,' she had said. 'I don't want little Gay tired by a lot of travelling before the wedding. She must be looking her very best.'

'You have been to so much trouble for us,' Evelyn said, half-apologetically, half-gratefully. But Lady de Verriland swept aside the remark with a wave of her hand.

'Nonsense, child! We must not have it

thought that Gordon's wife is — well, not on the same social level.'

Evelyn had flushed a bright red, hating Lady de Verriland in that moment as much as she hated the words and the air of condescension that went with them. But for her sister's sake, she hid her feelings and tried to retrieve some measure of the gratitude that had been uppermost in her mind at the thought of all Gay's future mother-in-law had done for them.

Gay's wedding-dress and veil, for instance — it had been worn by the family brides for many years, and Lady de Verriland had not hesitated to offer it to Gay. Perhaps 'offer' was the wrong word. She had ordered Gay to wear it, and she had been only too willing to do so. The long creamy satin folds showed off her slight, rounded figure to its best advantage, and in it she looked very lovely — very virginal and sweet and as every bride should look — ethereal, young, innocent.

The last of these adjectives was not

really applicable to Gay any more than was the word 'sweet.' In the last few months, Gordon had taught her a thing or two and told her quite a lot more, and Gay had no false illusions as to what her marriage to Gordon would entail. She was not frightened by, nor afraid of, what lay in front of her, but a little excited and not a little curious. She wanted to do all there was to do — live life fully and every moment to its extreme. She hoped that her marriage would make this possible, and when she walked up the aisle the following day it was to be with a bright, hard confidence in herself and in her ability to get all the happiness out of life that it could offer.

Evelyn, however, was far from happy. She had tried to talk to Gay as she felt an elder sister, who was also a guardian, should do, but she knew so little herself of the 'facts of life' that her attempts to instruct Gay were useless, and Gay soon stopped this heart-to-heart talk by telling Evelyn she knew all she wanted to know 'from the girls at school,' and told her not to worry about anything, as she intended to be very, very happy.

'No doubts at all?' Evelyn asked as she kissed Gay goodnight.

'No, none at all!'

'I'm so glad, Gay. If you do love Gordon, that is all that matters. Nothing can stay wrong for ever if you mean enough to each other. Goodnight, darling. Sleep well!'

Left alone, Gay thought over her sister's words, and for one moment she felt a little nagging fear in her heart. Was love the only thing that really mattered? The only way to find happiness? Did she begin to love Gordon?

But almost immediately that other, harder self conjured up the picture of all Gordon's gifts — the flat they were to have in Berkeley Square, the expensive furs he had promised her, and the French woman who was arriving tomorrow to be her own personal maid.

How could she fail to be happy with

all this? And Evelyn? She thought with a sudden sinking sensation in the pit of her stomach. What of Evelyn and Nicky? Should she tell her tomorrow of the 'mistake'? She would be safely married to Gordon by then, and Nicky could do no harm even if he did meet Lady de Verriland and tell her about Margaret.

As suddenly came the memory of something Gordon had said only yesterday.

'We will have to go damn carefully at first, my sweet! Don't forget that dear Mamma still holds the purse-strings, and if we spend too much, she'll tighten them up. And if we do anything of which she doesn't approve, anything to damage the famous family name — there'll be hell to pay.'

'What sort of things?' Gay had asked, and Gordon had replied rather vaguely:

'Oh, getting caught in night clubs when they're raided or mixed up in some public scandal or something of that sort. Mother's got a bee in her bonnet about the family name. Otherwise she is really quite a nice old girl!'

To bring Evelyn and Nicky together now *would* be a risk. It was not very likely, but it might lead to the discovery of the taint that had been in their mother's blood and eventually to Lady de Verriland's disapproval of Gay in the family and the suspension of Gordon's allowance.

This last week Evelyn had not even spoken of Nicky — had, in fact, talked about some new young man — a doctor who had asked her to marry him. Surely there was no need even to mention what had happened, Gay told herself.

When she decided on a policy of silence, she saw no wrong in her action and really genuinely believed her elder sister had got over her affair and was interested in someone else. She did not know how bitterly, how vividly the memory of Nicky March lay in Evelyn's heart, how deep and lasting had been the love she had for him, nor how impossible she was finding it to forget him in spite of James Cathy's constant attentions. Gay did not realize the extent of Evelyn's suffering, because even on the day of her wedding, she had no idea at all of what it meant to be in love — to give your heart to one man, into his keeping for better or for worse.

But Evelyn, standing in the church pew with Gay's bridal bouquet in her hands, heard the words of the marriage service and knew that she would love Nicky March until and after the day of her death, and now, alone in the world without him, without Gay, without even little Margaret, she wanted to die. She had reached the end of her tether and had come to a crossroads in her life where she must choose her way but did not feel she had the strength to do so.

As she knelt with the congregation, Evelyn prayed for help and guidance, and almost immediately came the thought of her journey abroad. When James had asked her of her destination, she had not known where she wanted to go, but now she did know. She would go to Munich and find comfort in the music and the surrounding mountains of Bavaria. She would travel and travel until at last she found release from Nicky's memory. She would search for peace.

Lifting her bowed head, she heard Gay's sharp clear tones as she said:

'I will!'

9

'Madam is alone?'

'Yes, quite alone!'

'And Madam wishes to go somewhere quiet?'

Evelyn looked at the Munich agent for Cook's travelling bureau and nodded her head.

'Madam would not prefer the company of some nice English people? I can recommend . . . '

'No!' Evelyn interrupted firmly. 'I would prefer to be by myself.'

The young man looked over the top of his spectacles and cleared his throat.

'That makes it a little difficult,' he said. 'Unless, of course, you are prepared to be without some of the usual comforts . . . '

He stared at her a little doubtfully.

'I don't mind,' Evelyn said. 'What had you in mind?'

The young man pointed on a map to a range of hills round the well-known ski resort of Garmisch and placed his pencil point on the top of one of the mountains.

'There is a little ski-hut here,' he said. 'It is run by a Bavarian peasant and his wife and son. Not many English people go there because there is no bath, only rough straw palliasses on hard, wooden beds. The food is excellent, I believe, and the ski-ing perfect. The son earns his living as a teacher to the few visitors who do go there. But I don't think it is really up to Madam's standards. It is very rough and ready.'

'It sounds ideal!' Evelyn said. 'Would I have to book in there?'

'Oh, no, Madam! I don't think so. I only happen to know of the place as I have been there myself. It is not on our lists. At weekends some of the skiers come up from Garmisch for the run down, which is a good one, and the snow up there is, of course, less beaten down and icy than where there are more people. But during the week there is nobody there at all but old Hans and his family. They would be delighted to have you, I know.'

'How do I get there?'

'You can get a train from the Bahnof direct to Garmisch-Partinkirchen. From there, there is a funicular up to a resort three-quarters way up to the mountain. Hochalm — that is the name of the hut — is about an hour's climb beyond that.'

'Climb? Then it is rocky?'

The clerk shook his head.

'Oh, no, Madam. I meant an ascent. You can go on foot and carry your skis, or else climb on skis if you are practised.'

'No, I can't ski at all. I am hoping to learn.'

'You will take lessons from Hans' son, Peter?'

'Yes, I should like to do that.'

'Perhaps Madam would be good enough to remember me to them when you go. They are great friends of mine.'

'Of course!' Evelyn said, smiling. 'Thank you so much for your help. It has been very kind of you.'

'I hope, Madam, you will enjoy your stay there. It is a very happy little place.'

Evelyn picked up her handbag and walked out into Marienplatz and back towards the Fierjahrzeiten Hotel where she had stayed since her arrival. For the first time since the day of Gay's marriage, she felt some satisfaction in being alive. The farewell to England and Nanny and James' goodbye kiss had all seemed quite unreal, and even the excitement of her first sea voyage, the long train journeys across France and Belgium and into Germany had failed to rouse her from the peculiar state of apathy into which she had fallen.

Since arriving in Munich, she had seen the famous churches, the Englischergarten, the parks and streets, museums and well-known beer kellers; she had slept and eaten and walked and talked and listened to all her favourite operas at the large opera house — but all the time she had not really felt alive — as if her body were dissociated from the big lonely well of pain that was herself.

Now at last she felt better, happier. The thought of the mysterious grandeur of the mountains brought a spark of interest which was growing brighter and brighter as she made her plans. The energy that she had lost came seeping back into her blood and she felt a great urge to go out and tackle some climb that would require all her resources to accomplish the ascent — something too difficult that she would need all her strength if she were to be the vanquisher and not the vanquished.

When she caught a train to Garmisch-Partinkirchen the following afternoon, she did not notice the several curious glances that were thrown in her direction, nor understand their whispered questions as to who the attractive young *Englische mádchen* could be; what was she doing by herself with a pair of new skis over her shoulder and a packed rucksack strapped on to her back.

Most of the inhabitants of the student town of Munchen only went ski-ing during the weekends. They would catch the dawn ski-train on Saturday morning to their favourite resort in the Bavarian Alps, and return on the late Sunday night train. Later, Evelyn was to travel with them, listening to the accordions and the choir of young, eager voices singing as happily and unselfconsciously as children. She was to see the laughing, happy, sunburnt faces, smell the appetizing odour of hot sausages as they were passed round the crowded carriages by attendants, to be eaten with much noise and gusto and a good deal of mustard. She was to see the tired, exhausted bodies stretched out on seats, curled up on luggage racks, propped up against rucksacks, and skis in the corridors, and to wonder how they could sleep so deeply in all the noise of hundreds of chattering voices of every nationality raised against the singing ones with their accordion and mouth-organ accompanists.

Above all, she was to envy the brown-faced, fair-haired girls, sleeping against the broad shoulders of their *liebchens*, exhausted, contented, cared for, loved.

But as yet, she knew none of this and as the train pursued its journey towards the mountains, she gazed eagerly out of the window, waiting to catch the first sight of the snow-clad peaks, rosy in the setting sun.

It was quite late when the train pulled in at the station, and, with difficulty, Evelyn asked her way to the funicular that would take her up to Hochalm.

'The last one goes in a half hour,' she was told. 'But it is not many minutes' walk from here.'

She shouldered her skis and took the direction of the man's pointed finger. The little station from where the

funicular climbed up a sheer perpen-
dicular slope, was quite deserted.
Evelyn searched round for several
minutes before finding someone who
gave her a ticket and told her that there
was still another quarter hour before it
would be time to go, and directed her
to a little hotel nearby where she could
get a cup of chocolate and a cake for
tea.

Evelyn was welcomed into the tiny
tea-room by a red-faced, beaming old
woman who stood beside her while she
drank the hot rich chocolate, and
answered Evelyn's questions in surpris-
ingly good English.

'Tomorrow it will be fine weather for
the *gnadiges fräulein*. The mist — he
come down have now, but the sun he
shine tomorrow. You will see very pretty
view.'

'And Hochalm?' Evelyn asked. 'Is it
pretty there, *Shoenes*?'

'*Ach, ja!* Yes, indeed. Fräulein is not
at the hotel staying? English visitors
stay there!'

'No! I am staying at Hochalm. I wish to be alone.'

'*Ach, ja. Ich Verstehe!* I understand, Fräulein will find it solitary up there. And the *Ski-laufen* — they are *sehr gut* — very goot, yes?'

Evelyn complimented the old woman on her excellent English, and after paying her bill, went out again to find the funicular ready to depart.

A young peasant, in ski-costume, helped her into the single compartment, and with a shout to the old man who operated the electrical turning gear, they swung up away from the ground.

As the peasant woman had said, a thick wet mist had come down, entirely obscuring the top of the mountain. Visibility was only a few yards and, looking out of the window, Evelyn could see nothing but the tips of the pine-trees showing through the cloud below them and the two dark heavy wires that held the funicular, disappearing into the mist above. Then suddenly another little funicular swung into view on its downward journey — passed them and was soon lost to sight.

Evelyn felt her ears deaden as they gained height, and saw the young peasant smile as she covered them with her hands. He said something in German, but she could not understand the dialect and shook her head. He smiled again and did not seem to expect an answer.

Presently the funicular jolted and almost before she saw it, they were drawing up to the tiny station, and she was climbing out on to the wooden platform, her skis over her shoulder.

'Hochalm? Where is it?' she asked. '*Wo ist es?*'

The young man pointed to a little beaten track winding up away from the funicular, but a light, steady fall of snow made it impossible for Evelyn to see further than twenty yards or so ahead.

'How far?' she asked in English, but as he did not understand, she tried again in German. '*Wie viel kilometres?*'

This time he understood.

'*Nur ein*,' he said, grinning, and held up one finger.

Evelyn wondered for a moment if she would be able to find her way. The falling snow was fast covering the little track that had been beaten by previous climbers, and she had no map, no possible way of knowing which direction she should take.

'I'll ask the young peasant to show me,' she thought, but as she turned she saw he was already climbing into the funicular for its downward trip, and she did not like to call him back. Obviously Hochalm could not be hard to find or on a treacherous track, or they would have given her some warning. They would not have allowed her to set off on her own — an English traveller who did not know her way. The young man would think her very silly if she called him back now.

So she turned up the path and, shifting her rucksack more comfortably on her shoulders and carrying her skis, she started to walk.

The new snow was thick and soft and made stiff going. Unaccustomed as she was to her heavy studded ski-boots and the weight of her pack and her skis, Evelyn was tired out before she had been moving ten minutes. She put her skis down beside her and paused for a rest, the exhilarated, excited feeling dying a little in her fatigue.

All around her was the white wall of falling snow. It covered the scarf over her hair, her gloves, her ski jacket, and clogged the soles of her boots between the studs. It was very cold.

For a minute or two the sound of her own irregular breathing was all she could hear, so she held her breath only to find that there was no other sound at all — not even the faint sigh of a breeze. It was so still that for one fleeting second she felt afraid. Then she let out her breath and held it again, so that she could listen once more to the silence. It was unlike anything she had ever experienced before and, trying to sort out her emotions, she wondered if this complete calm, this nothingness was the true meaning of the word peace. Movement without sound, without effort; space without limit, yet confined within six walls of whiteness. There was no sky, no view, nothing tangible except herself and the large falling flakes, and even they dissolved at the touch of her warm hand.

How long she stood there she did not know, but when at last she regained full consciousness of herself and remembered that she was on her way to Hochalm and that it was rapidly growing dark, she was surprised by the emotion that still assailed her — a feeling that nothing really mattered very much after all — that here was peace — a numbness that was vastly comforting to her tired mind, her aching heart.

With a little shock, she realized she could easily lie down in the snow beside her skis and go to sleep, knowing full well that she would probably freeze to death if she did so.

She was too practical, too common-sensical to allow such a state of apathy to take a real hold of her. Nevertheless, as she took up her skis, she felt frightened again by the strange power that had momentarily had the better of her, realizing the danger of such a state of mind. She could understand now how easy it must be for people marooned alone in the extreme cold or stranded on some solitary peak, to succumb to the inertia that she had just experienced in a minor degree.

She pressed forward, now eager to be out of the cold; anxious to reach the little ski-hut with its welcoming warmth and light. Once the track disappeared completely and she felt a moment's panic before a half-buried signpost pointed upwards in the direction of 'Hochalm.'

Gradually as the day lengthened, it grew darker and darker and looking at her watch, Evelyn saw the time was after four-thirty and realized she had been walking nearly an hour. It should not have taken her so long to cover one kilometre, she was certain, and the panic rose inside her, adding to her weariness, to the extreme cold of her face and hands.

The little path seemed interminable. She trudged forward a further five minutes, then the track curved and broadened and suddenly there was the ski-hut about a hundred yards further on. It had stopped snowing and the twinkling orange lights flickered out towards her through the twilight. Thick snow lay piled up high on the window ledges and the sloping roof was completely covered with a deep white layer. The whole building lay snugly on a flat plateau, guarded on three sides by tall mountains.

It looked to Evelyn like a little mouse crouching in the corner of a room, so small and hunched was its appearance. But on drawing closer, the hut appeared larger and more solid and with a little sigh of relief, she put down her skis and knocked on the wooden door.

'*Wer ist da?* Who is it? *Ach, guten abend, Fräulein. Sind sie sehr kelt? Kommen sie herein.*'

Evelyn had not understood his warm welcome, but nevertheless allowed herself to be led inside by the old man. The heat of the room met them like a wave and Evelyn gratefully sank into a wooden rocker chair by the big stove and watched her host disappear outside. Presently he returned with a broad grin and a lot more to say which she could not make head or tail of. She realized that he had been seeing to her skis and allowed him to lift the rucksack from her shoulders and start unlacing her heavy boots.

As he was pulling them off, a rosy-cheeked Bavarian peasant woman came hurrying into the room and chattered away at her husband and Evelyn without waiting for a reply, and was almost immediately gone again, leaving Evelyn alone again with her attentive host.

She watched him stuff thick wads of

newspaper down her boots and place them with her wet scarf and gloves and ski-jacket by the large, tiled stove. This erection filled half the room, emanating the waves of warmth that she had first felt on her arrival.

'*Wie geht es jetzt?*' the old man asked suddenly, and this time he waited for Evelyn to reply.

'*Ich kann nicht Deutsch sprechen!*' she attempted with an apologetic smile. 'English!'

The old fellow's face deepened into a huge smile and he held out his hand, shaking hers enthusiastically.

'We haf plenty English people here! I speak ver goot English. We ver pleast haf English visitors. From London you come, yes?'

'No, I come from the country,' Evelyn said, smiling at the excitement on the old man's face.

'You stay hier ver long?'

'I don't know! A little while,' Evelyn answered vaguely. 'If I may.'

'Oh *ja, ja!* We ver pleast to haf you. I

tell Ingeborg you are English Fräulein. She cook you ver goot meal.'

'Oh, no, please,' Evelyn protested, but he had already disappeared. Left to herself, she leaned back in her chair, unbelievably tired after her long journey, and enjoyed the relaxation that the warmth afforded her limbs. In some strange way, she felt she had come home, that her journey ever since leaving England had just been for this and much as she had appreciated the beauty of Munich with its gaiety, its festivity, its music, yet it was this quiet isolated spot that she had been seeking in her heart.

She thought she ought to have enquired where she was sleeping, to have unpacked her rucksack and changed into some dry clothes, but she was too tired and decided to let her host do all the organizing.

He returned in ten minutes with his wife, who was carrying a snow-white tablecloth. Between them, they laid the table ready for the evening meal.

'Peter is not yet in!' the old man said. 'He is my son. He ski very late with the junger Herr. But they come in soon. It is not goot to ski in the half-light. *Fräulein machen Ski-laufen?*'

'No, I don't know how,' Evelyn answered smiling. 'But I hope to have lessons from Peter.'

'*Ach, ja!* Peter very pleast to gif lessons to such a pretty *mädchen*,' old Hans said, laughing. 'He like the pretty girls, yes?'

Evelyn laughed with him, and the old woman shook her head at them and disappeared back into her kitchen, from whence came the appetizing smell of sausages and coffee and sauerkraut — a vegetable Evelyn was trying to like since there was so much of it in this country.

Just for one moment, Evelyn allowed her thoughts to drift back home. How much little Margaret would have enjoyed this, she thought! But the letter she had had from her before leaving Munich was one full of contentment at her school. She had made several friends of her own age and the nurses and doctors and teachers were all very kind. She missed Evie, she wrote, but she was quite happy otherwise. James Cathy had taken her out to tea and had promised to take her to a concert in London next week.

Evelyn smiled to herself, and mentally resolved to write to James and thank him for looking after Margaret. He really was a dear and she was extremely fond of him. Yes, in spite of the fact that she had asked him not to write, she thought she would drop him a line — perhaps a postcard.

'Have you any picture postcards?' she asked old Hans on the spur of the moment.

He produced a large variety of pictures of the ski-hut, and Evelyn enjoyed looking at them and felt a rising impatience to see Hochalm for herself with the sun on it and all the skiers on the slopes.

She chose one of the hut itself and scribbled a line to James — a non-committal line that was just to let him know she was thinking of him. She put it in her pocket and forgot about it for the time being.

And Gay, she wondered. How was she enjoying married life with Gordon? One letter from her written on her honeymoon was full of details of Gordon's latest gifts to her and what fun they were having. Gordon had decided to take her to the south of France for a week, so Evie mustn't expect to hear from her for a bit.

Yes, there was no doubt about it that Gay was quite happy.

She looked up as the front door opened and saw a young man whom she took immediately to be Hans' son, Peter, brushing the snow off his ski-suit and boots, and stamping on the wooden floor to warm his feet.

But her gaze went past him to the other man who was following him in — whose back was turned to her but who yet seemed horribly, fascinatingly familiar.

'It can't be,' she thought. 'It would be too much of a coincidence . . . It can't be . . .'

But as he turned round and caught sight of her, her heart leapt with a sickening lurch and she knew that she had not been mistaken. With a great effort she steadied her voice and said quietly:

'Hullo — Nicky!'

10

Hans was watching Evelyn and Nicky with his frank peasant's stare, but neither of them noticed him. They were staring at each other, hungry for every little detail in the other's face after a separation that seemed to each of them to be of many years' duration. 'I — you're looking well, Nicky!'

'Yes! I've been on holiday — plenty of ski-ing and mountain air. Evelyn — how in God's name did you find this place? It's fantastic — unbelievable . . .'

His voice trailed away and Evelyn lowered her eyes from his burning, searching glance.

'A man at Cook's in Munich recommended it to me,' she said, speaking hurriedly. 'I've only just arrived; I never dreamed — I never thought I would see *you* here.'

'Evelyn — Evie!'

The involuntary cry went straight to her heart and she turned towards him and was instantly caught in his arms.

Neither of them noticed Hans as he went through to the kitchen, leaving them alone. They were already in a separate world where nothing mattered, where no earthly troubles could reach them. Their love carried them to such exalted realms that each forgot the long months of loneliness, of hurt pride and distrust. They were together again.

'I love you, Evie. I love you!'

'And I love you, Nicky!'

As she raised her face for his kiss, Evelyn remembered the evening Nicky had driven her home through the starry night and told her for the first time that he loved her. It seemed so long ago and yet only yesterday.

Then his lips met hers and she forgot everything but the dear, remembered thrill of his proximity.

They broke apart as the door opened and old Hans came towards them with outstretched hand.

'Then my *junge Englische* friends each other know, *ja*? Ve celebrate, *ja*?'

And he went to the cupboard to bring out a cherished bottle of schnapps and poured out five little glasses. Ingeborg and Peter were called from the kitchen and there was much noise and laughter.

Evelyn's cheeks were flushed and her eyes bright as Nicky's glass clinked against her own.

'There will be time enough to sort things out later,' she thought. 'Nothing matters now — only that he loves me.'

'To you, Evelyn!'

'To you, Nicky!'

With a feeling of complete joy that was touched with recklessness, Evelyn tipped the stinging liquid down her throat; felt its fiery warmth inside her rush to meet the burning throbbing centre of her heart.

Watching her, Nicky knew that if he lived to be a hundred, he would still love this girl; that there could and would never be any other woman in his life but her, and that life without her would be a mere existence, devoid of the very essence of happiness, of understanding, of comfort. He loved her, and that was a simple fact which he now accepted, knowing it to be for always and even after death.

'Ve vill eat now, *ja*?' old Hans was saying happily. 'Ingeborg has a vere gut supper prepared. Come now, Fräulein, Herr Nickolaus. *Essen, ja*?'

Later, thinking back on that meal, Evelyn could remember very little about it. Nicky joked and talked a lot with their host and hostess, using their native dialect with great fluency and skill. Occasionally Hans addressed her in broken English, and Evelyn made suitable answers, but her eyes never left Nicky's face. Unconsciously, she was learning now while she could yet do so, every line, every feature, every little gesture of the man she loved. Some inner instinct warned her of another parting, another separation, encouraging her to take this mental photograph of him so that this much at least she could have with her always.

Fortunately, no one noticed Evelyn's preoccupation, or if they did, they attributed it to her scanty knowledge of the language. Occasionally Nicky would look across at her and she would smile back at him, feeling her heartbeats quicken and the colour rush to her cheeks. As if reassured, he would turn back to Hans or Ingeborg or Peter and continue his discussion, keeping them amused with his quick wit and endless supply of amusing incidents that had occurred during his journalistic career.

With simple tact, the family left them alone soon after supper, and as the door closed behind them, Evelyn realized that the moment had come for questions and explanations.

Nicky came across to her chair by the big stove and would have put his arms round her, but she evaded him, rising quickly and walking over to the window where a big bright moon was showing its cold face over the ridge of the surrounding mountains.

Nicky stood silently, watching her.

'Why didn't you write, Nicky?'

He answered her simple question with a straightforward reply.

'I wanted to, Evie, but Gay told me the truth. After that, I thought it better not. I wanted to get away.'

He could not see the quick hurt in her eyes.

So Nicky had not been able to face the truth. His love had not been great enough to surmount the story of her mother's past.

'The sins of their fathers shall be visited upon the children . . . ' she quoted to herself bitterly. Oh, no wonder Gay had been afraid to tell Gordon the truth! No wonder she had not allowed him to meet Margaret!

Gay had realized in time what she would lose — everything that she, Evelyn, had lost.

'Then it made so much difference?'

She could not help the question although her pride forbade it. Nicky looked at her quickly.

'It had to make a difference,' he said, thinking of her disastrous marriage. 'There was our future to be considered. I — I wanted to marry you, Evie.'

'Yes!' thought Evelyn. 'Children. The risk of passing the taint on to another generation. Nicky was right. He could not be blamed.'

'I'm so sorry!' she said in a small, pitiful whisper.

In an instant he was behind her, his arms encircling her waist, his head against her soft hair.

'Oh, my darling,' he said hoarsely. 'You are not to blame. Oh, if only it hadn't happened this way. But I can't be sorry I met you, Evie. I have no right to say it, but I love you — with my whole heart, my whole soul. Just to be with you, to hold you for this moment is worth all the pain, all the unhappiness that is in store for me. I shall always love you, my very very dearest.'

'But not enough,' Evelyn cried involuntarily. 'You don't love me enough!'

Nicky turned her towards him with a rough gesture and bruised her lips with a long hard kiss.

'Too much!' he said then. 'Look, Evie, if you want it, we will live together as man and wife. We'll take a chance on the world finding out the truth. We'll go away together — miles away where nobody knows us, and make our life together — just you and I . . . '

Evelyn released herself from his arms, her face white and strained.

'No, Nicky,' she said. 'That can never be. I — I wouldn't — even if there were not Margaret's future to be considered. But she must come first.'

'Margaret!'

Of course, Evelyn's child. Nicky had forgotten her.

'She can come with us,' he said quickly. But even as he suggested it, he knew Evelyn would never consent. Even if she were to agree to an illicit relationship between themselves, she would never allow herself to set such an example to Margaret. No, it was a dead end. Evelyn was married and there was no alternative but for them to say goodbye. Friendship? No! That would never be possible on a platonic basis — not between two people who loved each other as he and Evelyn cared — body and soul, heart and mind.

'Then it must be goodbye again!' The words were wrung from him.

'Oh, Nicky!'

She was in his arms again, and he was covering her face, her eyes, her hair with kisses, robbing her of speech or even thought.

'I can't leave you,' Nicky whispered brokenly. 'Oh Evie, my darling darling heart. I can't leave you.'

For a moment Evelyn's heart leapt to his words. Perhaps even now he would change his mind; decide to take the risk. Then her natural common sense prevailed and cold realization replaced her hope. Nicky might marry her, but if anything were to go wrong with their children's lives, she would be to blame and she would never, never forgive herself. She loved him too much to ask him to take that risk.

'Nicky, we must be strong,' she said, trying to convince herself as well as him. 'We will have to say goodbye!'

She smoothed his hair very gently from his hot forehead and her eyes were soft with tenderness. In the great unselfishness of her love, she felt no malice for his seeming lack of courage. She did not question whether she would have felt the same in his place; because she loved him, she accepted his decision and felt only a heart-breaking sorrow for them both. It was not his fault. It was not her own. But the fault of circumstances.

'I'll leave tomorrow!' she said gently, and in spite of her resolutions, she gloried a little in his tightening grasp.

'No, Evie! I'll go. You need the holiday.'

'I couldn't stay here without you,

Nicky. I'll go in the morning.'

'So soon!'

'No!'

Evelyn suddenly felt quite reckless, crazily so. Perhaps it was the schnapps, she thought with an attempted smile. 'No, I'll stay out my week. We will have one week together, Nicky — one glorious week.'

'Evie, do you really mean that?'

She nodded her head, her eyes feverishly bright, her breath coming quickly.

'Yes, Nicky! I do mean it.'

'Then we will never go to sleep,' Nicky said, his heart leaping with happiness at this unexpected reprieve. 'I couldn't waste those hours sleeping when I might be with you. We will stay up twenty-four hours out of twenty-four.'

Evelyn shook her head, laughing a little through the tears which had filled her eyes.

'No, we will have to get some sleep,' she said. 'I want to learn to ski, Nicky. I'd never be able to stand up if I didn't have at least six hours a night!'

'I'll teach you to ski!' Nicky said eagerly. 'You'll soon learn, darling. We'll take our lunch with us and go out all day tomorrow. I'll ask Ingeborg to pack up my rucksack and we'll start early — immediately after breakfast.'

'Then I'll have to go to bed now,' Evelyn said, sinking into the chair by the stove. 'I'm very tired.'

'No, not yet,' Nicky said. 'Stay a little while longer, darling. It's such a long, long time since I last saw you.'

He sat down on the floor at her feet and leant his head against her knees, and for a while they sat in silence, listening to the occasional soft thuds of the lumps of snow dropping off the roof outside.

Once Evelyn reached out a hand to touch his cheek and then Nicky pressed her fingers to his lips, kissing each of them and then the palm of her hand.

'Can Fate have been so unkind as to bring us together only to part us again?' he murmured.

'Don't talk about parting!' Evelyn said softly. 'Let's live this week in the present, Nicky. The past and the future don't matter — must not matter. Only now!'

'You're beautiful!' Nicky said inconsequently. 'Not just to look at, Evie, but through and through. Small wonder that I love you!'

'And small wonder that I love you, Nicky. There's never been anyone but you — never will be.'

'Oh, Evie, my very dearest. When you say such things to me, I don't know how I can bear to leave you. If it were not for Margaret, I think I . . . '

'No, Nicky, please! Don't let's talk about it. I don't want to discuss it any further; the subject is such a painful one for us both. Please promise me not to mention it again.'

'Oh! Evelyn, I'm only human,' Nicky burst out passionately, thinking with jealousy and hatred of the Italian who had taken such a mean advantage of a young, inexperienced and lonely child.

He could cheerfully murder the man who had brought all this unhappiness to his darling, and succeeded in parting them so irrevocably.

'And I, also, am only human,' Evelyn said quietly. 'I do understand how you feel about things, Nicky, otherwise — well, I couldn't go on loving you as I do.'

Nicky never realized the depth of those words, nor the unselfishness that prompted them. Evelyn had put her understanding before her pride. For his sake, she was renouncing his love for ever. Inexperienced as she was, she realized the influence she had — could have over the man she loved; realized that she could probably persuade him to marry her if she used her feminine wiles cleverly.

But she was too honourable, too selfless to even contemplate such a thing, even knowing that to give him up would mean a long and lonely life without love, without comfort, for there would never be another man in her life.

Marriage, now, would not be for her. She must devote her life to Margaret, centre all love and devotion on the little blind girl who was her sister, and try to forget the overwhelming love she had for this man.

'Not yet, though, not yet!' she thought silently, and impulsively she bent and kissed the top of his head.

Immediately responsive to her mood, he turned and caught her in his arms, and kissed her again and again until she begged him to let her go.

'It's hot in here,' she said breathlessly. 'Let's go outside, Nicky. I'd like a short walk — it is safe to walk at this time of night? I'd hate to get lost in these mountains, darling, even with you!'

Nicky smiled at her lovingly.

'Oh, it's safe all right,' he replied, helping her to her feet. 'That is if it has stopped snowing. Occasionally people get lost in heavy snowstorms; they're apt to be very misleading however well you know your way. If you climb up these particular mountains round here, you will find some nasty precipices the other side, and believe me, it's no joke having to climb down and fish somebody up from the bottom of one.'

'How horrid!' Evelyn said, shuddering. 'Have you ever had to do that, Nicky?'

He nodded his head.

'Yes! Two weeks ago. A lot of city people come up here for the weekends and two young girls went out after lunch and did not return.'

'What happened?' Evelyn asked.

'Old Hans sent word to the barracks in Garmisch. There is a regiment of ski-troops there and they organized every available man who was an experienced skier to go out on a search. It was snowing hard by then and nearly dark. I shall never forget seeing them leaving the hut here one by one, in silence, carrying storm lanterns and ropes and medical supplies. I was one of the last to leave and by the time I had started to climb, the first men were quite high up and I could see the little orange glow of their lanterns, winding up into the darkness . . . '

'And the two girls?' Evelyn asked. 'Did you find them?'

'Yes! We were out searching four hours before any trace of them was found. Then we heard a feeble shout for help. One of the two girls was still conscious and had seen the light of the lanterns above her. It took us some considerable time to get down to them and when we did so, they were both more dead than alive. Neither was wearing warm clothes as it had been a beautifully warm, sunny day when they started out, and they suffered severely from exposure.'

'Were they all right?' Evelyn asked.

'Yes!' Nicky said with a tender smile for Evelyn's solicitude for two girls she did not and never would know. 'Yes, they recovered in due course. Ingeborg put them to bed with hot drinks and hot bottles and the rest of us celebrated downstairs. You should have been here, Evie. It was a wonderful experience. We all sat round that long wooden table and pooled a small amount of money each and ordered large mugs of beer — mugs like those long thin ones on the shelf over there which hold six pints! Someone brought out an accordion and we started singing. Some of these Bavarians have the most lovely voices, you know, and it was a pleasure to listen to them. The mug was passed round from person to person, each one taking a good long draught before handing it on. When it was empty, more money was put into the kitty and another six pints bought.'

'It does sound fun,' Evelyn said enviously.

'It *was* fun,' Nicky cried reminiscently. 'I can picture now in my mind the hot, steamy heat; the music and the deep harmony of men's voices raised in song. Most of all, I think, I was struck by the grand companionship and 'cameraderie' that prevailed. Everyone had been united in saving two lives. Now they were united in celebration of the fact. They were good men, those fellows — born and bred in the mountains; interested only in them and the fresh air and the exhilarating sport of ski-ing. Not that it is really a sport to them. It is as much a part of and a necessity to their daily lives as food and drink. Even Army life had not contaminated their minds. Politics meant nothing to them. They had just accepted the Nazi regime as a lot of small children accept a new teacher. They were told it was a good thing and they believe it. In a way one wishes there were more people in this country like them, and yet it is their ignorance that will be their downfall. Believe you me, Evelyn, I heartily look forward to the day when the Nazis go well down the drain, and all those better educated Germans who have allowed themselves to be led down the wrong road. But I have it in me to be sorry for these few simple folk who, nine out of ten, are good, God-fearing people.'

'God-fearing?' Evelyn repeated. 'But

I thought there was practically no religion recognized here?'

'Very little!' Nicky answered bitterly. 'But you will find these mountain peasants different. Many of them are Roman Catholics and attend church service regularly. You will find little tiny stone churches wherever there is a small gathering of huts. Up here, it seems impossible to conceive another war. But I'm absolutely certain it will come. Otherwise why all this tremendous mobilization? Why all the swastikas and tanks and aeroplanes. What is it all leading to if not war?'

'Oh, Nicky, no! Surely not!' Evelyn cried. 'Even in Munich I was made welcome and treated like a queen as soon as it became known I was English. One isn't polite to one's future enemies.'

'I don't know so much!' Nicky answered quietly. 'It may be all part of the scheme. Just supposing they are intending to declare war on us. They aren't ready yet themselves so the obvious thing to do is to keep us ignorant of their intentions. At the moment, England is totally unprepared for war. From all appearances Germany is preparing for total war! But very few people realize it. I meant to give up journalism, as you know, but I can't help probing into these things. I can smell a rat, Evelyn, and I don't like the smell. When I get back to England, I'm going to do my best to open the eyes of the powers that be . . . '

He broke off suddenly, his brown, boyish face lit with his quick smile.

'Fancy wasting time talking politics!' he said softly. 'I'm sorry, darling!'

'Oh, but I'm interested, Nicky!' Evelyn answered quickly.

'Right now I am only interested in you!' was Nicky's retort. 'And we were going for a moonlight walk, darling!'

Evelyn smiled up at him as he took her arm and pressed it against his side.

'Yes,' she said. 'Let's go out for a short while.'

They walked out through the little

door, and for a moment their eyes were dazzled by the sparkling whiteness of the moon's reflection on the new-fallen snow. The whole brilliant carpet twinkled with a myriad little lights, and Evelyn felt her heart contract by the beauty of it all.

High around them on three sides the mountains towered, shadowing each other with dark black patches. On the fourth side there was a sheer drop into a deep, pine-grown valley several thousand feet below. The trees were so small that the whole appearance was that of a toy model.

It was soundlessly quiet. Occasionally a soft fall of snow would break the stillness, and once Nicky struck a match to light his pipe, and even such a tiny noise seemed to fill the air around them.

How long they stood there Evelyn did not know. Glancing at Nicky's face, she saw a look of such sadness, such hopelessness, that her whole heart melted towards him. Once again the thought crossed her mind — if his grief was at the thought of leaving her, why would he not take the risk and ask her to marry him?

But she shied away from the question, pride and shyness that were so much a part of her forbidding her to speak outright.

'Why won't you marry me, Nicky?' she could ask him silently. But never aloud.

Neither of them realized as they stood there, hand in hand, that one simple little question, so easily asked, yet so impossible to do so, would have cleared the whole dreadful misunderstanding that Gay's selfish wilfulness had put between them. Yet so incalculable a thing is Fate, that when the question reached her lips, Evelyn turned away from the man she loved so desperately, and the moment was gone, lasting no longer than the foam on the edge of a wave.

'I'm going in, Nicky,' she said abruptly. 'I'm very tired. Goodnight, darling!'

She did not raise her face for his kiss, nor did he try to stop her. He just stood there, watching her slim dark figure as it moved quietly away from him, disappearing into the orange light of the little hut.

It was some time before he followed that shadow's footsteps, and even then, tired as he was, he did not go to bed but sat in the room by the stove, his head buried in his hands, until the first pink light of the rising sun tipped the mountain tops with rosy splendour.

Then only did he go quietly and silently to bed.

11

Evelyn was woken early the next morning by a soft thud against her window pane. She sat up in bed, rubbing her eyes sleepily, and as full consciousness returned a smile spread over her face and she touched her lips gently with her fingertips, remembering Nicky's kisses, so strangely stirring and exciting; recalling the whole of the last wonderful evening together.

'If I choose,' she thought, 'I can get up now and have only to call out and I should see Nicky in a matter of minutes!'

But she preferred to remain there for a few moments longer, savouring the sweet realization that the man she loved was somewhere near to her and knowing utter content in the thought that she had one whole week in which to see him, hear his voice, feel his kisses, his arms about her; knowing that he loved her in his way.

But Evelyn was not to be permitted this luxury for long. Another soft thud against the window pane and this time she saw a snowball burst into a thousand little pieces before it fell to the ground.

She jumped out of bed and ran to the window to find a bright-eyed, laughing Nicky only a few feet below her.

'*Guten morgen, Fräulein!*' he said, blowing her a kiss. 'Did I wake you, darling?'

'You certainly did!' said Evelyn, smiling. 'You're up early, Nicky. What time is it?'

'Time to be kissed!' Nicky returned. But he glanced at his watch and added: 'Nearly seven-thirty. Come on down and have a breath of fresh mountain air before breakfast!'

'Give me ten minutes!' Evelyn called back.

But she stood at the window a moment longer, taking in the picture of

Nicky looking ridiculously young and boyish in his ski clothes. He had on a white, cable-stitch jumper which accentuated the brown of his skin and the bright blue of his eyes.

'Do you love me?' he asked suddenly and with an impish grin.

'No!' Evelyn lied, her eyes and smile telling another story.

For answer, Nicky stooped and gathered a handful of soft snow, and aimed it directly at her. But Evelyn closed the window swiftly and laughed to hear his pretended annoyance when it hit the window pane.

She dressed hurriedly and went downstairs to find somewhere to wash. Last night the family had already retired to bed when she and Nicky had come in from their walk and she had not liked to disturb them. If she had expected to find a bathroom now, she was to be disappointed. Peter met her at the bottom of the stairs and explained in halting English that the wash place was in the shed by the side of the hut.

On entering, Evelyn found a row of tin bowls and old Hans calmly shaving in front of a cracked mirror hanging from one of the rough wooden beams. She drew back hurriedly, but Hans called her back, explaining that everyone washed together as one big family and that she would find plenty of hot water on the stove in the kitchen.

Evelyn privately resolved to take one of the bowls of water up to her room where she could strip down to bath herself that night, but meantime she did as Hans had told her and carried her washtub through to Ingeborg. The rosy-cheeked old woman soon filled it for her from a steaming cauldron, and she rejoined Hans in the shed.

'This wouldn't appeal to Gay,' she thought with an inward smile. Gay was not happy unless she had a hot bath and at least half an hour in which to dress and make up her face in the mornings.

Within five minutes Evelyn had completed her own toilet and went to find Nicky outside.

Everything looked very different in the rosy sunlight from the impression she had received the night before. The snow was dazzlingly white and the mountains seemed to slope more gradually and no longer looked treacherous or dangerous, but most inviting.

'You're looking very lovely — as always!' Nicky said as he came up to greet her. 'You're not tired, are you, darling?'

Evelyn shook her head, allowing him to take one of her hands tightly in his own.

'It's beautiful, isn't it?' she said, with a glance around her. 'Oh, Nicky, I'm so glad I came!'

'So am I, darling!' Nicky said, looking down at her tenderly. 'Let's walk a little, Evelyn. Your hands are cold.'

They walked slowly round the little plateau on which the ski-hut had been built, and Evelyn listened with delight to the soft crunch of their nailed boots in the new snow.

'It'll be nice for you to fall in!' Nicky told her, laughing. 'It's really easier when you are learning turns to have a nice flat, hardened surface. But if you're on skis for the first time, this couldn't be better.'

'I think I'll put a cushion in the seat of my pants all the same,' Evelyn answered him with her quiet smile. 'I'm sure I'll never be any good at it, Nicky. You would do better to leave me to Peter's care. I'll be such a nuisance and you'll get tired of watching me sit down and get up again the whole day.'

'Nothing you could do would ever bore me,' Nicky said, with a loving glance at her. He loved to see the quick colour rise to her cheeks whenever he paid her a compliment. 'Besides, darling, I should be jealous of Peter. Why should he have the pleasure of your company?'

'Oh, Nicky, what nonsense!'

'Nonsense or not, you're going to spend every second of the day with me!'

Nicky said authoritatively. And he pressed her arm close against him, feeling his heartbeats quicken with his love and his eyes losing their laughter and deepening with a wistful longing as he remembered how brief this short holiday was to be.

But he pushed the thought quickly to the back of his mind and turned back in the direction of the hut.

'I'm hungry!' he said. 'Let's go and sample Ingeborg's breakfast. It's bound to be good!'

And Evelyn followed him obediently, happy to do anything he should suggest.

They were out again soon after their meal and spent a hilarious morning in the snow. Evelyn at first found her skis incredibly cumbersome, and sat down almost as soon as she stood up. Nicky persevered with advice and encouragement, and by lunchtime he made her climb with him to the top of one of the more gradual slopes, and with his arm round her waist he guided her down to the bottom, showing her a little of the speed and exhilaration that the sport could provide.

They reached the ski-hut without mishap, but as soon as he released his hold of her, Evelyn sat down with a bump and lay in the snow, her hair windswept and snow-flaked, her cheeks rosy and her eyes sparkling with laughter.

'Oh, Nicky!' she cried, 'I'll never be able to do that on my own and it was so wonderful!'

'I think you'll manage far steeper slopes than that in a few days,' Nicky said encouragingly.

'Let's do it again!' Evelyn said eagerly.

Nicky laughed as he helped her to her feet.

'Teacher says that's enough for one morning,' he told her, knowing how tiring such exercise could be to one who is not used to it. 'We'll come out again after lunch.'

By tea-time Evelyn had progressed so

rapidly that she was attempting the easiest slope on her own. Nicky was sincere in his congratulations.

'You're going to be a damn good skier, darling!' he praised her. 'I should really start you on turns tomorrow, but, being a Saturday, there will be dozens of people up from the towns like a lot of honey bees, and I want you all to myself. We'll ask Ingeborg to pack us up a picnic lunch and we'll go to the Weissepitze for the day.'

'Oh, Nicky!' Evelyn cried breathlessly. 'Do you really think I could manage it? Perhaps you ought to go off on your own, darling, and leave me here to practise. It must be so dull for you . . .'

'Don't be such a silly little goose!' Nicky chided her tenderly. 'For one thing I am never bored with you, and for a second I'd no more think of leaving you here by yourself than I'd jump into the valley, and for a third I'm quite sure you can manage it.'

He dropped a kiss on her cheek and

stooped to unfasten her skis for her. In a minute he had strapped them together and slung them crosswise with his own across his shoulders, and they walked together towards the hut.

They made a good-looking pair, thought Ingeborg, watching them from the kitchen window. She had known Herr Nikolaus some years now, for he had come up regularly every weekend during his days at the Universität in Munich, and she had grown very fond of him in her motherly way.

Fräulein Evelyn, too, she had liked from their first meeting. She had been attracted instinctively to the goodness and sweetness that shone from her eyes, and Ingeborg's simple soul delighted to see the two young English people together. She knew also that they were deeply in love with one another. One had to be a fool not to see it, and she hoped it would not be long before Herr Nikolaus asked the *junge* Fräulein to marry him. She had such a wistful longing in her eyes when she looked at him.

Ingeborg turned from the window and concentrated her thoughts on a more practical channel — namely that of preparing the evening meal.

But the days passed slowly by and Ingeborg waited in vain to hear the two young people announce their engagement. Each morning, they left the ski-hut with a packed rucksack and their ski batons slung over their shoulders. Every evening they would return as the light was fading, and join the family round the big marble stove. More often than not, Hans and Peter and Ingeborg would retire early, tactfully and sympathetically leaving their two guests alone.

Sometimes they would all sit silently, listening to old Hans playing his zither and joining in the folk songs which he sang so well. Then Nicky and Evelyn would unashamedly hold hands and delight Ingeborg's sentimental heart. Other times they would play cards — simple games like 'Snap' and 'Donkey,' and Ingeborg would always laughingly be the last to call 'Snap' — the first to be dubbed. 'Donkey.'

Lying restless and sleepless in her little wooden bunk at night, Evelyn would relive every minute of those all too precious days — counting at first the number of days and as time grew shorter, the number of hours. The night preceding their last day, she knew that she could not continue the light banter which had dominated her conversations with Nicky. Among all their interesting discussions and the dear moments of light-hearted flirtation, they had studiously avoided any mention of the future — of what was to happen to them both and their love for one another. Evelyn had longed to ask Nicky if they would meet again sometimes — as friends; whether they would correspond or if their goodbye was to be final and irrevocable.

Even before Nicky said he thought it better to make the break complete, Evelyn knew in her heart that this was their only chance of finding some measure of happiness.

It was their last day together and they were having a picnic lunch on a flat piece of rock several hundred feet above the little ski-hut. Nicky lay outstretched, stripped to the waist to allow the hot rays of the sun to burn his already sun-burnt body an even darker brown. Evelyn sat with her knees hunched and her arms encircling them. She wore dark sunglasses to protect her eyes from the glare, but the three-cornered scarf she sometimes had over her curls lay beside her and her hair was blowing softly against her cheeks, stirred by the cool mountain breeze that was nearly always to be felt at this height.

Their skis were stuck into the snow a little way below them and looked like dark sentinels guarding the entrance to their hideout.

'When will you go, Nicky?' Evelyn asked hesitantly, trying to keep the fear from her voice and the trembling from her lips.

'Sometime tomorrow, I suppose,' Nicky answered, his voice almost inaudible. 'I — I wish this didn't have to happen, Evie. Of course, I realized this week would be bound to make the parting even harder. There are so many more chains to bind us now — so many precious memories holding us together . . . It hurts . . . I hadn't thought it possible to love anyone as I love you, Evie. It consumes my whole heart and torments my mind. There is never a moment when I am not thinking of you — never a touch from your hands, your lips that I do not thrill to. At night I cannot sleep for longing for you. I am happy only when I hear you say you love me or when you are so close to me that I know this to be so. How can I live without you, my very dearest?'

Evelyn did not reply because she could no longer trust her voice. She felt the hot tears stinging her eyes and bit her lips hard, determined not to make things harder for him although it might have afforded some small measure of relief to her own heart. She longed with an almost irresistible force to throw herself into his arms and sob out her wretchedness against his strong shoulder and beg him again and again not to leave her.

'Give my love to little Margaret,' Nicky said, forcing himself back to a more casual tone of voice. 'She's a sweet kid and you must be very proud of her, Evie.'

He did not mention Gay, remembering too vividly the blow she had dealt him over the telephone. Not that she could have done it more gently or with more understanding, but always he would associate not only her, but anyone with her name, with the most painful moment of his life. Her words had meant the end of all his hopes and dreams — the finish of his love. But not really the finish. He would love Evelyn always, every minute of his life, every second of every day.

'Let's go, darling,' he said, unable to bear the strained silence between them.

Evelyn rose obediently, allowing him to fasten her skis for her; permitting herself to gaze with all the love and longing in her heart at his curly head, bent at handtouch nearness as he knelt in the snow at her feet.

Before he fastened his own skis, Nicky put his arms around her and kissed her — once — fiercely on the mouth.

'Always remember I love you,' he said, and turned quickly away from those quivering lips, leaving her puzzled and afraid.

That kiss was the last she was to receive from Nicky before he left. After their evening meal, at which Nicky had been strangely silent and preoccupied, he excused himself and disappeared up the wooden staircase, saying he was in need of some fresh air. He did not look at Evelyn, nor ask her to go with him as was his custom, and presently she heard the back door slam and knew that he had gone out. Even then she did not think he had gone for good. Was this not their last evening together and had he not said he would go 'tomorrow sometime'?

She tried to talk to Peter and Hans and Ingeborg and answer their questions as best she could, but her ears were straining for the sound of Nicky's returning footsteps, and she soon excused herself, pleading a slight headache, and went upstairs to her room.

She did not put on the light but stood for a while at the open window, feeling the cold air on her face and a weird, unaccountable anxiety in her heart.

How long she stood there, she did not know, but eventually the intense cold penetrated her awareness and she closed the window and drew the curtains.

There was still no sound of Nicky returning. The fear in her heart grew until she felt she must occupy her mind or go mad.

'I'll go to bed and read,' she thought.

Then realizing that she would not be able to go down to greet Nicky, she decided to lie down on her bed, fully clothed, and she went to the door and switched on the light.

Immediately, she saw the folded sheet of paper propped up on her dressing-table. She knew instinctively that it was from Nicky — guessed at its contents with a sick lurch at her heart. He could not be returning after all.

The shock of this realization took all the strength from her legs and she sat down on her bed, the paper clasped in her long, slender hands. Two banknotes floated to the ground and she automatically bent to pick them up.

Presently, she opened Nicky's letter and read it through.

'*My dearest darling,*' he wrote.

'*I must go now. I can't bear the thought of another sleepless night knowing that there will be no comfort in tomorrow since we must then say goodbye.*

'*Forgive me if this way hurts you but I am hoping to spare us both the pain of those goodbyes.*

'*Please give Hans the money for me.*

'*I shall never never forget you, my darling. I love you more than life itself.*

'*Always heart and soul,*
'*Your*
'*NICKY.*'

Evelyn did not cry. Yesterday tears had seemed so easy but she had not allowed them to relieve the ache in her heart. Now she wanted desperately to cry and no tears would come. She stared around the little room with large, vacant eyes, and absently remembered her first morning when Nicky had awakened her by throwing a snowball at her little window. How long ago it seemed now!

The silence and the bright glare of the lamp became intolerable to her ragged nerves. She switched off the light and opened the window again. It had started snowing very gently and several tiny flakes blew in from the darkness and settled a moment on her white, cold hands, then melted into nothingness — nothingness.

Somewhere out in this snow, Nicky was speeding downwards with all his skill and aptitude for the sport towards Garmisch. She followed him in her mind's eye, seeing his dark outline twisting and turning through the trees. She had no fear for him even though it was a dark night. He was as much at home on his skis as was Peter, who had been able to tackle the nursery slope even before he could walk.

'I'll go out for a little while,' Evelyn said aloud. 'I must get out of this room — away from the hut.'

She tied a scarf over her hair and pulled on her ski-boots and jacket. She did not use the back door but went through the living room and said in a queer, strained voice:

'Herr Nikolaus has left. He asked me

to give you this money, Hans. I am going for a short walk.'

'No, it snows now . . . ' began old Hans, but she had already closed the door behind her. He rose quickly to follow her, but Ingeborg laid a restraining hand on his arm.

'Leave her, Hans!' she said softly. 'Perhaps she wishes to be alone!'

'But it is snowing!' said the old man anxiously. 'It is easy to lose your way if you do not know it well.'

'She knows these parts as well as you or I now,' said Ingeborg quietly. 'She will not go far, I think. Poor little Fräulein. She truly loves Herr Nikolaus!'

'I wait here until she comes back,' said Peter, his large brown eyes reflecting his father's anxiety. 'If she does not come soon, I go to look for her.'

The little family sat in silence round the warm stove and the old clock on the wooden shelf ticked by the minutes with determined regularity. Ten, twenty, thirty . . . and still Evelyn had not returned.

Ingeborg looked white and unhappy.

'If anything has happened to her, it is my fault!' she said, breaking the silence. 'Peter, you had better go look.'

'I, too!' said old Hans, and he reached for the hurricane lamp and brandy flask that were always ready by the clock for such emergencies.

Within a few minutes the two men stood heavily muffled with set white faces, awaiting Ingeborg's farewell. Peter bent to kiss his mother, saying gently:

'If we do not return in one hour, telephone for the ski regiment. *Auf wiedersehen, Mutti!*'

Ingeborg stood by the open door until they were lost behind a curtain of snow. Then she closed the door and went back to her rocking-chair by the stove. Her eyes were on the clock as she rocked to and fro, and her lips moved in prayer to the Shepherd of the Mountains. Slowly and certainly, the minutes ticked by.

12

Peter lowered the slight weight of Evelyn's body on to the carpet by the stove as easily as if he had been carrying a rucksack. Old Hans stamped the snow from his boots and needed no second glance into his wife's anxious face to follow her unspoken question.

'No! She is not dead!' he said, his voice harshened by his recent fear for this girl. But his eyes softened as he saw the unaccustomed tears rolling down Ingeborg's cheeks.

'Come now, *Mutti*!' he said gently. 'Put her to bed quickly with hot bottles and she will soon be well again.'

Ingeborg hurried to do his bidding, Peter carrying Evelyn's still unconscious body upstairs to her little wooden bed with a look of adoration in his eyes. He worshipped this beautiful English girl with the same passionless adoration that he felt for the picture of St. Agnes that hung above his bed. He would have laid down his life for her without even considering the thought twice.

But that had not been necessary. After half an hour's search, he and his father had found Evelyn's partly covered footprints and had followed them to the ledge where she and Nicky had picnicked the previous day. It was on this rocky space that they had found her, unconscious, numbed with cold. Old Hans had correctly surmised that she meant to sit only a little while with her sorrow and unhappiness but that the cold had sent her into a stupor and she had given way to the inevitable impulse to sleep, soon drifting into a state of apathy. It had not then taken long for the cold, driving snow to gain the upper hand.

'Should we send for Herr Nikolaus?' Ingeborg asked when she rejoined her two menfolk in the living room.

'No, I think not!' said old Hans

thoughtfully. 'If he wished to go, it is for some very good reason. Now the Fräulein must get well quickly and forget him.'

But Evelyn did neither of these things. By the morning, she was flushed and feverish and her words jumbled and incoherent.

'If she is not better by afternoon, we telephone the Herr Doktor in Garmisch,' said Hans with a worried frown. 'It may be the pneumonie. Then the little Fräulein will have to go to hospital.'

Peter refused to leave the house, wandering round as a dog will do when its master is ill. He asked no questions but he listened to his parent's words, and when the hospital was mentioned, he felt physically sick with anxiety. To go to hospital meant inevitable death in Peter's simple mind. Then only did he leave the house, and trekked high into the mountains where he could pray in the soft solitude to the Shepherd, asking him to save his little Fräulein's life.

So sincere was his faith that when he returned to the ski-hut, he was quite confident of Evelyn's recovery and it did not worry him unduly to hear Ingeborg and Hans discussing the possibilities of finding Herr Nikolaus.

'But we have no address to write to,' said Ingeborg tearfully. 'He did not tell us where he was going.'

'Perhaps we could write to the Universität!' suggested Hans, but he knew there was not much chance of reaching Herr Nikolaus in this way. It was many years now since the *junger Herr* had been studying.

'I think we should tell her family,' suggested Ingeborg. 'I will look in her room, Hans, and see if I can find some English address.'

So it was that she came across the postcard Evelyn had written to James Cathy and, since meeting Nicky, had completely forgotten to post. Ingeborg's spirits rose when she saw the prefix to James Cathy's name. Undoubtedly the English doctor would be the very person for them to send word to.

Old Hans approved the idea at once. 'Peter shall go into Garmisch this afternoon,' he said. 'He can fetch the Herr Doktor and at the same time send a telegram to this Dr. Cathy.'

With the aid of his dictionary, he composed the contents of the telegram and as Evelyn's condition was in no way improved after midday, Peter fastened on his skis and sped off in the direction of the town.

It was past tea-time when he returned with a doctor from Garmisch. The little bespectacled physician gave one look at Evelyn and pronounced that she was seriously ill with pneumonia and that on no account was she to be moved.

'We cannot possibly carry her down through the cold mountain air,' he told Hans with a frown. 'Has she relatives here? She should have a nurse, too.'

'Ingeborg shall nurse,' said old Hans promptly. 'She was a nurse in the last war and will look after the Fräulein as her own child.'

'*Gut!*' said the doctor. 'And her family?'

'We have sent for an English doctor friend of the Fräulein,' answered Hans. 'We do not know of any relative or friend already in Germany.'

'We must inform the British consulate in Munich!' said the doctor, 'if she is not better very soon. We do not want to be held responsible for her death.'

'Death!' echoed Hans, his brown, weather-beaten face looking grey and drawn.

'Ach! Perhaps it will not be so serious,' said the old doctor comfortingly. 'It may not be so bad but we cannot be sure until after the climax is reached. However, if Peter will return with me I will give him medicines and supplies and I would like to see Ingeborg before I go, to give her some instructions.'

'Of course,' Hans assented and showed the doctor into the kitchen.

Two days went by and Evelyn's temperature rose steadily. Sometimes she was delirious and then she would call ceaselessly for Nicky. The tears would fall down the vigilant Ingeborg's cheeks as she sponged the girl's thin hot body and forehead. At other times, she would speak of someone called 'Gay' and again of 'little Margaret,' and Ingeborg would wipe her eyes with the corner of her apron, feeling frustrated by her powerlessness to help her little Fräulein.

Every day, Peter went down to the post office to see if there were a reply to his telegram, but nothing came and then suddenly, James Cathy appeared in person. With a sigh of relief, old Hans welcomed him to his humble little home, saying with charming simplicity:

'We are all so glad you come, Herr Doktor. We love the Fräulein Evelyn as our own daughter, but she need her own countrymen. You will surely make her well.'

'I hope so!' said James, holding Hans' roughened hand in his own white, strong fingers. 'You see,' he said softly,

'I hope one day to make the Fräulein my wife.'

Hans gave him a quick look. He wondered if he should speak of Herr Nikolaus in spite of the fact that he did not like to interfere in such personal matters.

'You do not by chance know a young fellow-countryman by the name of Herr Nikolaus March?' he enquired carefully.

James looked momentarily puzzled.

'Nicholas March?' he repeated, and suddenly he remembered Evelyn's story of the man she had loved who had so mysteriously disappeared from her life.

'Yes! I know the name!' he answered, choosing his words carefully. 'Why do you ask?'

Hans looked embarrassed.

'I — we have had a visitor of that name, staying here. I think the Fräulein knew him in England. She — she sometimes calls for him. I thought, perhaps, we should send for him, but now you are here . . . '

'I think perhaps I should hear the

whole story!' James broke in quietly. 'You see, if I am to make the Fräulein well, it is necessary that I should help her mind as well as her body. You need not fear that I will repeat what you say — even to the Fräulein.'

Hans hesitated for a moment. He instinctively liked the fair-haired young doctor — judged him as sincere and honest and finally decided to trust him. After all, he thought, if it were to help the Fräulein, it was best Doktor Cathy should know all he, Hans, could tell him.

'Will you be seated?' he asked the young man politely, indicating a chair by the stove.

James breathed an inward sigh of relief, and taking off his coat and muffler, he gratefully accepted the offer of a seat. It had been a tiring journey and one charged with anxiety and fear. As soon as he had received Hans' telegram, he had telephoned for a seat in the next British Airways 'plane to Munich. From then onwards, he had

259

tirelessly arranged another G.P. to take over his practice, dashed up to London to see about his passport and money, and back to the village to pack. Some delay had occurred over his passport photograph, forcing him to stay another day, which meant cancelling his 'plane bookings and re-booking for the following morning.

During those twenty-four hours, he put a call through to Gay, telling her of Evelyn's illness and suggesting she should follow him out if she wished. Hans had said 'probably pneumonia' in his telegram and although he did not wish to alarm the girl unduly, he knew that when the crisis was reached, Evelyn's life would be in the balance.

But Gay seemed satisfied to leave Evelyn's welfare in James' hands.

'I'm frightfully busy just at the moment, Dr. Cathy,' she said. 'But if you think Evie really needs me . . . '

'I don't think your presence is essential to her recovery!' James answered caustically, taking a thorough dislike to this girl. She was Evelyn's sister, Margaret's sister, and yet she sounded so very different, so incredibly selfish and unfeeling. 'If she asks for you,' he added quietly, 'I will send for you immediately.'

'Oh, that's *sweet* of you,' came back Gay's voice, softened and pleasant with her relief. She and Gordon had arranged to spend a fortnight with Lady de Verriland and Gordon was going to ask for a larger allowance. So much lay in the balance and she did not want to be absent (tearing round the Continent after Evelyn who had been silly enough to get ill in some remote spot in Germany), so leaving Gordon to go by himself. He had been against asking his mother for more money — an attitude which had surprised as much as it had annoyed her and she was afraid that he might not stress their need of a bigger allowance. He would probably just say *she* wanted it, or something stupid . . . No, she would rather be with him.

'Give Evie lots of love for me, Dr.

Cathy,' she said sweetly.

'I will give her your message!' James had replied in a stilted voice. And as soon as he could, he had rung off.

He had then written a quick note to the Matron of the Sunshine Home, asking her to tell Margaret that her elder sister was ill but that she was not to worry as he was going out to look after her himself. He knew that little Margaret would be concerned and upset and even want to go with him, and he resolved to write as often as possible, and hoped he would soon have some good news for her.

'The Herr Doktor from Garmisch who has been caring for the Fräulein will be here shortly,' old Hans said, breaking in on James' thought. 'Would you like to visit the Fräulein now?'

'No! I will wait for the doctor, thank you,' James answered. Professional etiquette forced him to this decision. Much as he would like to see Evelyn, he did not want to antagonize this German fellow. He had every intention of taking

262

over the case, but he knew he must do so tactfully.

'Then I will tell you all I know of Herr Nikolaus while we are waiting,' said Hans, and the two men lit their pipes.

Hans had finished his account of the past week when the German doctor arrived. It was with a worried frown that James greeted him and followed him up the little wooden stairs.

'It is more than pneumonia!' he thought when he heard the other doctor's diagnosis. 'It is also a severe nervous breakdown.'

The German doctor was only too willing to hand his patient over to the Englishman's care. He did not enjoy the daily trip up to the ski-hut and in spite of the cleanliness of the place, he preferred to work in better conditions. Besides which, he knew the Fräulein's condition to be serious and he did not want her death on his hands. With the political situation as tense as it was, he knew the consequences of allowing an

English patient to die were severe. It was the Führer's wish that the best of everything — food, hospitals, courtesy, attention, should be extended to all British and American visitors.

No, he did not enjoy his task and was sincere in his last remark to James Cathy.

'I hope the Fräulein will soon be well!' he said. 'Anything you need, you may send Peter for. I shall be delighted to supply everything you require.'

'Thanks very much,' said James with equal courtesy. 'I may have to avail myself of your kind offer.'

'Then *auf wiedersehen*,' said the little physician. He clicked his heels smartly and raised his arm. 'Heil Hitler!'

He wondered once he was outside why this greeting, so familiar in all the towns, should sound so out of place in this little mountain retreat. But he did not worry himself too much about it and with a sense of relief, he fastened his skis and departed hurriedly down the frozen track towards the town.

James made his way back up the stairs and found Ingeborg still by Evelyn's bedside.

'You must be tired!' he said gently, noting the old woman's red-rimmed eyes. 'How much sleep have you been having lately?'

'Not so much!' Ingeborg answered truthfully. 'I have not liked to leave the Fräulein alone.'

'I will stay with her now,' James answered with a kindly smile. 'You go and get some rest. Would it be possible for me to have something cold up here for my supper?'

'*Ach, ja, Herr Doktor!*' Ingeborg answered, rising wearily to her feet. 'I will leave a tray and Peter shall bring it up to you.'

'Thank you!' said James simply. '*Schlafen Sie gut!*'

Ingeborg gave him a deep, trusting look and closed the door behind her. She had complete confidence in the *junger Doktor*. In spite of his youth, she was certain of his skill in his profession.

Her four years of nursing in a hospital in the last war had not slipped her memory so much that she could not recall the way all the nurses knew instinctively the good and the bad. He would make the Fräulein well if it were humanly possible to do so. Of that she was sure.

As soon as she had prepared a cold meal for the men, she retired to her bed and fell into a deep exhausted sleep.

How many hours James sat watchful and attentive by Evelyn's bedside, he did not know. Days merged into nights and nights into days. Sometimes Ingeborg would relieve him while he snatched a few hours' rest or while he stretched his cramped limbs in the fresh, open air.

Afterwards, when it was all over, he could remember only certain incidents of that vigil. One night, for instance, when Evelyn had partly regained consciousness and had thought he was Nicky. She had caught hold of his hands and gripped them with all her strength, begging him not to leave her again.

The pain in his heart had been transcended only by his immense pity for her and by his anxiety to help her. She was so thin and drawn that she seemed to have shrunk away to nothing. The high, delicate cheekbones stood out through the angry, fever-heated skin, and the tears had dripped from her brilliant, vacant eyes as he sat there, anxiously watching her. Then in a sudden rush of compassion and love for her, he put his arms round the frail hot body and said again and again:

'I love you, darling. Get well, Evelyn. I love you so much!'

In some strange way this had comforted her. She probably thought it was in Nicky's arms she lay. But he could feel no torment of jealousy — only a bitter hatred towards the man who had caused her this suffering, who had virtually been responsible for her illness.

Another incident he recalled was

when she regained complete consciousness, and recognized him.

'Hullo, James!' she had said, her
voice weak and hardly recognizable as
her own. 'Where am I?'

'You've been ill, Evelyn,' he had
answered her, keeping his voice calm.
'But you will get well soon. Now try
and drink some of this.'

But she had lapsed back into
unconsciousness before he had been
able to get her to drink the hot tea.

Eventually Evelyn started to recover.
The improvement was so slight at first
that James did not mention it to the
family in case he should raise their
hopes in vain. But her temperature had
dropped. still more the following day, so
that he was able to say:

'The Fräulein is better. I think she
will recover!'

There had been tears in Hans' as well
as Ingeborg's eyes. Peter alone did not
show any sign of emotion, but the look
in his eyes as he followed James' figure
up the stairs, was one of complete

devotion. James had now only to hint at his wishes before Peter had disappeared to fulfil them. Sometimes he was incredibly clumsy, slopping the boiling water as he brought it up from the kitchen, but it was not in James' heart to reprove him. Once the boy burnt his hand in this way and suffered in silence for a whole day before James noticed the burn.

'Why didn't you tell me?' he asked.

'Because you very busy with the Fräulein,' Peter had answered simply, and once again James had been unable to chide him. It was rare to find such complete selflessness among human beings. After all, what did the boy hope to receive in return for his adoration of the English girl? He knew very well that Peter expected nothing. It was only the civilized peoples of the world, the so-called educated people, he thought bitterly, who expected something in return for everything they did.

As the days passed, Evelyn's condition improved steadily. She was very,

very weak and James did not try to force her to speak, although he sometimes worried at her strange, prolonged silence. Her large, bright eyes followed him around the room, and if he questioned her she would shake or nod her head. But she never spoke to him, and Ingeborg said that she, also, was unable to persuade the Fräulein to say a single word.

James realized Evelyn was suffering — not physically, but mentally, and that she had for some unaccountable reason of her own, decided to keep it to herself. He felt sure that if he once mentioned Nicky's name, he could break down this unnatural reserve. But he had promised old Hans not to say a word of his story of that strange week Evelyn had spent with Nicky, and there was no other way in which he could have learned of Nicky's presence.

But Evelyn's silence could not last for ever. One evening, James gave Peter permission to enter the sickroom, and busied himself downstairs in the kitchen while the boy was there.

Peter had been to the town earlier and bought some flowers. He laid them shyly on the bed and sat down beside her.

'Fräulein is better, *ja*?'

Evelyn nodded her head.

'Fräulein does not look very happy. Are you not pleased to be well again, Fräulein?'

Evelyn shook her head and closed her eyes, afraid of the tears that had forced their way into them.

'But Fräulein, what would the Herr Nikolaus think to see you ill? Herr Nikolaus, he be very worried.'

It was more than Evelyn could bear. She buried her head in the pillow and for the first time since she had regained consciousness and realized where she was and all that had happened to her, she allowed herself to give way to the utter despair and hopelessness in her heart.

Seeing her crying, Peter went quietly out of the room, his big brown face creased with worry. James hurried into the room and sat down on Evelyn's bed.

'There, darling,' he said gently, gathering her into his arms. 'Don't cry, Evelyn. Everything will be all right. Don't cry, darling.'

Evelyn threw her arms round his neck and the tears flowed faster and faster.

'Oh, James!' she sobbed. 'I want Nicky! I want Nicky! Oh, James, James!'

He held her tightly to him, and very tenderly, he stroked her hair.

13

James sat quietly listening to the deep gasping sobs that seemed to come from the very depth of Evelyn's body. He knew that the mental relief this outburst would eventually afford her would far outweigh the harm to her physical status, and even while the man in him felt protective and helpless, the doctor in him was glad that the repressed emotion should at last have found expression.

Presently she lay back on the pillow, her face paler than usual and her breath coming in short, painful gasps. But she was no longer crying.

'I'll give you a sedative, Evelyn,' James said. 'You should try and rest now.'

She turned her large, unhappy eyes towards him and he read in them both fear and hurt.

'Don't leave me, James!' she said urgently. 'Please don't leave me alone.'

'Of course I'll stay if you want me,' James answered soothingly. 'Now take this like a good girl. It'll help you to sleep.'

Evelyn obediently swallowed the sleeping draught and lay back exhausted. James took hold of her hand and was surprised at the strength in her grip as she clung to him.

'James — I'd like to tell you — about Nicky!' she said, her voice calmer, her eyes already growing less brilliant as the drug started to take effect.

She gave him a truthful account of the week preceding her illness, confirming Hans' story and completing the picture in James' mind.

Then her eyes closed and presently her breathing came more regularly and the grip of her fingers relaxed. James covered her gently with the bedclothes, confident that she would sleep now for at least eight hours.

He left the room and finding his

ski-boots and jacket, he went outside into the cold, bracing air. He wanted to be alone — to try and think this whole thing out. There was still one point of the story which was not clear to him. It simply did not make sense. Why, he asked himself, if this fellow Nicholas March was really in love with Evelyn, was he not prepared to marry her? Surely he could not be letting his fear of the slight taint in Mrs. Challis' blood get the better of him. After all, any doctor he might have consulted would tell him that unless hereditary for some generations, the fact that Mrs. Challis virtually killed herself by over-drinking by no means proved that her children or her children's children would do the same.

From all accounts, it appeared that none of Evelyn's relations or ancestors had had alcoholic tendencies. It looked to James as if this case were just one in which the woman herself had acquired a bad habit and had been insufficiently strong-minded to overcome it. He had studied the case fairly thoroughly because little Margaret Challis had been his patient and there was no doubt about the fact that her blindness had been caused by lack of attention to her mother before the child was born. But he had never considered there would be a danger of the children following their mother's footsteps, and would not have called it a blood taint.

Perhaps, James thought, the fellow March had not consulted a doctor. In any case, James told himself scornfully, he sounded completely lacking in courage and Evelyn was well out of it.

When he returned to the ski-hut, James was filled with a desire to protect Evelyn from any further hurt or disillusionment. He loved her and when she recovered from this attack, he was going to ask her to marry him. She needed a man's help and understanding and he had every hope that she would eventually turn to him. Beside her own need of him, he could stress the need Margaret had for a man's care and guidance, and he was certain that Evelyn would let her consideration for Margaret influence her decision. In time she would learn to love him and he would teach her what kindness and tenderness meant.

James did not realize as he planned that love is not a thing which can be taught. It is either there or it is not. In Evelyn's case, it would either grow from the already existing friendship between them, or it would never exist at all in the way James wished. Nor did he fully realize at that moment quite how deeply she had loved Nicky; how tremendously she had suffered by his desertion of her, nor how finally and irrevocably she had given him her heart.

It was two weeks later before James learned the true state of Evelyn's mind. For some nights now she had not been able to sleep and he had given her a small morphine tablet to take before she settled down for the night. He knew the danger of the drug becoming a habit, but the one night he had refused it she had lain awake until dawn and he had found her in such a pitiful state of nerves the following morning that he decided he would wait until she was stronger physically before stopping the tablets.

The following week he tried again, but she again worked herself into a panic of nervous despair, begging and pleading with him, saying again and again:

'Oh, James, please! Please let me have it. I can't sleep without it. I just lie here and lie here and the hours are like years. James, please! Just this once. Please, James!'

He felt completely nonplussed. He knew how dangerous the habit of drug-taking could be and yet he did not like to refuse her when it was so obvious that she could not sleep without them.

'You shouldn't keep taking these things, Evelyn,' he said at last. 'They are bad for you, and if you take too many of them you might poison yourself.'

She had looked momentarily scared and he pressed his point home.

'Too many of such things can even prove fatal,' he said. 'Now, Evelyn, will you try without one tonight to please me?'

'Oh, James, please! I'll be better soon,' Evelyn answered weakly.

So it continued for another few days. Then James said it must come to a stop.

'You're better now,' he told her firmly. 'This time I mean it, Evelyn!'

She cajoled him, reasoned with him, even tried vamping him but to no avail.

'Look, James, just let me finish the box. There are only a few left,' she said at last. 'Then I'll stop. That's a promise!'

James looked triumphant.

'Very well, Evelyn!' he said. 'I'll leave the box with you. When they are finished, it will be no use asking me for more. You understand that?'

She nodded her head, and he left her, satisfied that the whole business of the drugs would soon be over.

Evelyn lay still in her bed, the little box containing the pills clutched tightly in her hand. She opened the lid and counted them. There were ten — ten more nights of forgetfulness, of ease for her aching heart, and then she would be without comfort, without the merciful relief from her memories. They were such bitter-sweet and painful memories. Agonizing, wonderful memories of her days with Nicky.

The years of lonely, sleepless nights stretching beyond those ten little pills, grew and grew in proportion until she felt weak and utterly desperate. She could not face them. She could not face any of it any more. She did not want to go on living without Nicky.

The hot tears stung her eyes and flowed down her cheeks in thin, salt streams. Her illness had left her so weak that she felt she had no will-power to stop those tears. Sleep would not come. She tried hard to sink into that merciful state of unconsciousness but she knew even as she tried that she would not be able to sleep — without the drug.

She sat up in bed and switched on the light.

'They are bad for you,' James had said, but she did not care. She didn't care if they did poison her, if they did prove fatal.

'Was he trying to scare me?' she asked herself. 'Supposing he wasn't! Supposing I did take too many, would it — kill me?'

She opened the box and counted them again.

Yes, there were ten! Would ten be fatal? Would she go to sleep and never wake up again if she took all of them — all ten of them — now?

It seemed suddenly to Evelyn as if she had reached the end of her endurance. She could not go on. There was nothing left for her to live for. Nothing, nothing . . .

She reached for the glass of water by her bedside and with a little sob, she emptied the pills into the palm of her hand, and hardly conscious of her action, she took them, one by one.

'Now it is done!' she said aloud, her eyes wide open and staring as those of a sleep-walker. 'I have taken an overdose. I am going to die. I'll never see Nicky again — never. Tomorrow I will be dead . . . James will be sorry. I hope he isn't blamed. I ought to have written a note to someone . . . Gay! I ought to have written to Gay. She must look after Margaret for me.'

She sat up suddenly, her eyes frightened out of their dullness into a bright, feverish brilliance. Her heart was beating rapidly and she felt very weak and sick.

'Gay wouldn't want Margaret,' she whispered. 'She never has done. And Margaret will be alone — completely alone. James will do his best for her but it isn't the same. He can't give her the love and the care that I could.'

And now it was too late. She was going to die!

Sheer panic gripped her. She wanted

desperately to undo this dreadful, ghastly thing which she had done. She wanted to live . . .

'James!' she cried. 'James! James!'

She could hear her heart thumping, and in her imagination she thought she felt the effects of the drug, and fought against her drowsiness.

'James!' she shouted. 'James!'

But there was no answering call from him.

She staggered weakly from her bed, feeling her legs give way under her, and lay in a heap on the floor. She knew she must get to James, ask him for an antidote quickly, but after weeks in bed she had no strength left.

With a superhuman effort, she dragged herself across the floor and raised herself by clinging to the door knob.

At this moment James opened the door and as Evelyn fell backwards, he caught her in his arms.

'James!' she cried, her eyes wild with fever and panic. 'James, I've taken an overdose. I'm going to die. Save me! Save me . . . '

Suddenly she went limp and her lids closed over the brilliant, blazing eyes.

James felt the slight weight of her body as it fell against him, and as he gathered her into his arms, his face was grey and drawn and he looked an old man.

'This is my fault!' he thought. 'Poor Evelyn! Poor, poor little girl.'.

It was some minutes before Evelyn came out of that faint. During this time James sat silent and thoughtful, wondering what he should say to her — how he could explain.

Over a week ago he had resolved on the idea of substituting the morphine drug with some harmless white powder. He knew that in most cases of insomnia the effect of taking tablets was chiefly psychological, and this had proved one of those cases. Evelyn had told him she slept perfectly with the aid of the substitute, little realizing that it was not the usual drug.

As he sat there, watching for the first sign of returning consciousness, James thanked God for enabling him to have been treating Evelyn at this moment. If it had been the German doctor, he might never have thought of changing the components of the tablets, and even he, James, had little realized the full extent of Evelyn's nervous illness although he was able to talk to her in her own language. He blamed himself bitterly for not taking more notice of the state of her mind. So far he had only succeeded in healing her body from the pneumonia.

As a doctor he knew that the M. & B. treatment necessary for such illnesses had an extremely depressing effect on the patient, and he should have realized that coupled with a nervous collapse such as Evelyn had experienced following Nicky's departure, the effect might be serious enough to make even suicide probable.

Evelyn stirred and opened her eyes. James took her hand and held it tightly between his own.

'You're going to be all right, my dear!' he said, forcing his voice to calmness. 'There is no need for you to worry at all.'

She stared at him as if trying to remember what had happened. Her lips moved and he strained his ears to catch her voice. Her eyes never left his face.

'Margaret . . . '

'Margaret is fine!' James said quickly. 'Would you like her out here with you, Evelyn? I can send for her, find someone to bring her out.'

Evelyn shook her head.

'No, don't upset her . . . how is she, James?'

'She's getting along splendidly!' James answered. 'I knew she would be happy when we left her there. And well looked after, too.'

Evelyn looked less tense. He waited for her to speak again.

'I'm sorry, James!'

James hesitated only for a moment. Then he made up his mind.

'I want to marry you, Evelyn,' he said. 'We won't discuss it now because you must try and sleep. But I want you to know that I love you and that although I realize how you feel, I know you need my love and someone to look after you — and Margaret.'

'But James . . . ' she began.

'No!' he silenced her. 'We won't discuss it now. First you are going to get well. That is all you must think about, Evelyn. Margaret needs you, and I need you. You must make us your reason for wanting to — to go on. Life holds so much for you, and you must get better, my dear, if not for your own sake, then for Margaret's and for mine.'

He could not have made a better appeal to her, and his words had an instantaneous effect. He saw the expression in her eyes soften and become calmer.

'Now you must sleep,' he said gently. 'I shall stay with you so you won't be alone.'

'I'll be all right, James,' Evelyn murmured.

But he remained with her until her eyes closed and he was really certain that she slept. Then only did he go to his own room, leaving both their doors open so that he could hear if she stirred.

The sun was high over the snow-covered mountains and it was nearly noon the following day before Evelyn awoke. She seemed very much better and ate a fair bit of Ingeborg's carefully prepared lunch. After her meal, she asked for some writing paper and a pencil and James left her writing a long letter to Margaret. When he went in again she was eating a large tea and even managed a smile for him — the first he had seen since her illness. He felt greatly cheered.

'If you feel strong enough, you may go downstairs for a little while tomorrow,' he told her, anxious to make the best of this obvious improvement. 'Peter shall carry you down and you can sit in Ingeborg's rocking-chair.'

Evelyn looked pleased.

'Oh, James, I'd love that!' she said eagerly. 'I'm so tired of this room!'

'I'm going to take you away altogether in a week or two,' James went on. 'We're going to have a holiday — both of us. I thought we might go to Brittany. I know a little fishing village there called Audierne. It's near Quimper. I used to go there when I was a boy. It will be quiet and the sea air will do you good.'

'But, James, what about your practice?' she asked. 'You've been here so long . . . '

'I need not return for another month at least,' James answered, pouring her a second cup of tea. 'The fellow who substituted for me is a friend of mine and he had just sold his practice. He doesn't mind stepping in for me as he wants to get to know what a country practice is like. He has always been in town previously. Now, what do you think of the idea, Evelyn?

Do you like Brittany?'

'I've never been there!' Evelyn answered. 'But if you like it, James, I don't mind a bit.'

'Then that settles it,' James said quickly.

'James!'

He looked at her quickly, surprised at the note of urgency in her voice.

'Yes, Evelyn?'

'I want to know . . . about the other night. I . . . you . . . James, what did you do to — to counteract the . . . '

She seemed unable to go on.

'My dear, if you want the truth,' James said, making his voice as casual as possible, 'you did not take an overdose at all. There was nothing in the pills — in the last box, that could possibly harm you. Not even if you had taken fifty.'

'But you said . . . '

'Yes, I know,' he broke in. 'The first lot would have been fatal. But I had to stop you taking so much morphine, Evelyn, and knowing that the reason you did not sleep had become purely psychological, I also knew that as long as you thought you were taking something you would be able to sleep.'

'Then I didn't . . . take anything poisonous? I didn't . . . '

'No! Now forget about it, Evelyn. There's nothing whatever to worry about. The M. & B. you'd been having for the pneumonia was entirely responsible for that attack of acute depression and you have nothing whatever to worry about.'

Evelyn seemed immeasurably relieved.

'I've been so ashamed of myself,' she said quietly. 'It was so uncourageous of me — so very weak!'

'Nonsense!' said James briskly. 'Your health was entirely responsible. Now you must get well, Evelyn. I don't want a sick fiancée on my holiday.'

'Fiancée?' Evelyn echoed. 'But, James, I can't — I can't get engaged. I don't love you. I . . . '

'I know!' James broke in gently. 'But there's plenty of time ahead of us,

Evelyn. We will have a long engagement — really get to know one another. You need not feel as my fiancée that you have committed yourself in any way. We will both be entirely free to break the engagement at any time. But you need someone to care for you, to love you, and I would like to be that person.'

Evelyn reached out and took his hand in her own.

'You are terribly kind to me, James!' she said. 'I appreciate the compliment more than I can say. But I can't agree to it. I'm no good to you — no good to anyone. I have nothing whatever to give you.'

'My dear,' James replied simply. 'I don't ask anything of you. It is enough to know that you regard me as a very good friend.'

'It wouldn't be fair to you!' Evelyn burst out impulsively.

James looked satisfied.

'If I don't like the situation I am free to break the engagement in the same way as you are,' he said. 'Now we won't argue about it further. It is decided, yes?'

'All right, James,' she said slowly. 'But only on the condition that you promise me faithfully that you will break our engagement if you should want to — the moment you should want to. You are so kind, so generous and thoughtful that you might be afraid of hurting me. Will you promise me, James?'

'Of course, Evelyn!' James answered quickly. 'Of course, if you wish it.'

He was to remember that promise later — one that he made so easily and with such confidence that it would not be necessary, but one he was going to find almost impossible to fulfil.

14

Evelyn was sorry to say goodbye to Ingeborg and Peter and Hans, but she was glad to leave the little ski-hut with all its memories of Nicky and her long illness there.

She had been greatly touched by the tears Ingeborg had shed at their parting; by the look of dumb misery in Peter's eyes, and by Hans' parting gift — a little miniature beer mug which he had carved for her himself. She had promised to write to them all and now, as she sat in her little room in the Auberge St. Michael, she was going to do so.

It was a week since she and James had arrived here. At first sight of the little fishing village she knew she was going to love it. She had been immediately fascinated by the cobbled streets; the multi-coloured sun blinds covering the market stalls along the quayside; the little stone houses and the beautiful blues, greens and reds of the sails. She soon put on plenty of weight eating the freshly caught *langoustine* and Madame de Marqué's famous mayonnaise.

Madame de Marqué was the owner of the *auberge*, and an incurable romantic. At first she had been disappointed to learn that James and Evelyn were not a young honeymoon couple, but later she decided that the fiancés were not even in love with one another and that it was her duty to see that this unhappy state of affairs should be improved upon. Rather to Evelyn's disappointment, her first move was to give them a very secluded table in the *salle-à-manger*, and she saw that there was always a vase of spring flowers on the little checked table cloth.

To Madame de Marqué's simple mind, flowers were the inspiration for love and romance, and although the whole place was kept spotlessly clean and fresh, the privilege of flowers on the table was not afforded her other guests.

Evelyn would have preferred to observe her neighbours more closely and to join in the conversation. She liked to see the funny little Frenchmen tuck their white table napkins into their lapels and to hear them suck up their soup with such obvious enjoyment.

James, a true Englishman, said the noise was disgusting and he was glad they had moved to their own table. Evelyn had looked at him a moment, unable to prevent a mental comparison of this man and Nicky who had mixed with Ingeborg and Peter and Hans as one of them, loving their individuality and their simplicity.

But Evelyn knew she must not make such comparisons. Nor must she even think of Nicky for that only led to unhappiness . . . She dipped her pen into the ink and started her letter.

'*Dear Ingeborg . . .*'

Her eyes wandered out through the open window, and the beauty of the scene before them destroyed all hope of concentration.

The brightly coloured fishing boats were just entering the harbour. The blue sea was dotted with their gay red and blue sails and the fishermen, in brick-red trousers and jackets, were plainly visible standing up in their boats, singing in deep musical voices.

'The catch must have been a good one,' she thought with a smile. She was glad because James had told her that the winter had been severe and the men were entirely dependent on their fishing for their livelihood.

This year the spring had come early, bringing with it fresh warm winds and sunshine and the little village had an air of happy anticipation which reflected itself in Evelyn's mind, for how could one feel that life had nothing left to offer one when all around was such happiness, such colour and so much to hold one's interest.

On market day the canvas coverings to the stalls flapped gaily in the breeze and she would awake to the loud chatter of the women as they decorated their counters. The children ran wild, their little clogs clicking cheerfully on the cobbles and their shrill, high-pitched voices mingling with the deeper tones of their parents.

Evelyn and James would always have a large following of these children when they went walking. Sometimes she would stop and talk with them.

"*Jour, M'dame, M'sieur!*" they would call politely, but their Breton dialect made further conversation difficult to understand. James, always a generous person as she was already learning, gave them a handful of five centime pieces, and they would grin happily all over their grimy little faces and run away towards the shops, calling over their shoulders,

'*Merci, M'sieur! Merci!*'

She loved to see the little boys, exact miniatures of their fathers in sail-red trousers and jerkins, hanging over the quayside with improvised fishing rods; managing with great skill to catch a fair-sized fish with a bent pin and a length of string. It was in their blood and as soon as they were old enough, they would join the men who set sail in the morning and return as the sun went down, singing and laughing if the catch were good.

Most of all, Evelyn liked to see the fishermen hanging out their nets to dry. These nets were the most beautiful things she had ever seen — fine as lace and blue or blue-grey in colour. No two nets appeared to be the exact same shade and yet the general effect, as they decorated the harbour, was that of a delicate, aquamarine spider's web stretching from mast to mast. She had never seen such colour before and, always sensitive to beauty, Evelyn could sit at her window and stare at the little harbour for hours on end.

James had found a fellow Englishman and spent a good deal of his time playing table billiards in the little salon. Sometimes Evelyn joined them, but more often she would plead tiredness and retire to the solitude of her room, where she could sit like this and drink in the beauty around her. She would not admit, even to herself, that she wanted to be alone so that she could think about Nicky. In all honesty, she always brought her thoughts sharply back to the present when she found them wandering, but nevertheless, memories of him would crowd her room and her mind and she cherished these quiet moments when it was no longer necessary to force a smile to her lips for James' sake. He had been so good to her, so undemanding, so understanding, and it was for his sake that she was doing her best to get well, to put all thought of the past from her.

With an effort, she returned to her letter and forced herself to finish it. As she sealed and addressed the envelope, there was a knock on the door.

'*Qui est là?*'

'It's James! Can I come in?'

'Of course!'

He came into the room, looking very young and rather like an undergraduate in his grey flannels and white shirt.

Evelyn felt a sudden rush of affection for him. He seemed suddenly so much younger than herself. How could one help being fond of him!

'Hullo, Evelyn! What've you been up to?'

'I was writing to Ingeborg!' she answered with a smile. 'I sent them all your love, James.'

'Fine! I expect they are missing you.'

He sat down by the window and lit a cigarette.

'You don't mind me smoking here?'

She shook her head.

'I'd like one, too!'

'No!' said James firmly. 'You've got to take care of those lungs, Evelyn. Besides, it's a bad habit to get into.'

'All right, doctor!'

She did not argue with him because there was something else she wanted to discuss — the letter she had received that morning from Gay.

'I'm worried about Gay,' she told James with a frown. 'She — she isn't very happy.'

'Not happy?' James repeated. 'But she must be. She has only been married about six months!'

'I know! But I think Gordon's mother has been making trouble. I never did like her, James, although, of course, I only met her once that week before the wedding. Gay doesn't actually say she's to blame. She's much too loyal a person ever to say such a thing — even to me.'

'Then what makes you think her mother-in-law is responsible?'

'You'd better read Gay's letter!' Evelyn said. 'I'm sure she wouldn't mind.'

James felt a moment's swift repulsion. That telephone call he had had with the girl . . . he hadn't taken to her, but of course it was hardly fair to judge a person on one short conversation on the 'phone. After all, she was Evelyn's sister and Evelyn obviously loved her. But, then, was Evelyn's judgment to be relied upon? Look at this fellow Nicholas! Obviously a bounder, a complete cad. Evelyn was too good herself, that was the trouble. Never could see any bad in anyone. Still, he might have misjudged this sister of hers. He took the letter and read it slowly.

'*Darling Evie,*' she had written.
'*I'm so glad to hear you are up and about again and feeling more cheerful. Congratulations on the engagement. Of course, I rather expected it.*'

Why? wondered James. What reason had she to expect such an engagement? Of course, he had been in a bit of a flap that day he had 'phoned her. Worried about Evelyn and all that, still . . .

'*No doubt you will be surprised to hear I am now living in London. I have got a little flat in Chelsea and am really enjoying myself very much. Gordon is staying with his mother. I think she's horribly selfish to keep him from me but if Gordon chooses to stay that's his fault.*'

Not much loyalty there, thought James. Either to Gordon or his mother!

'He says we can't afford to run our house in the country as well as spending odd days in town and wants me to go and live in that horrible vault with his mother. But I'm not going to. I honestly don't see why I should shut myself away in that hole. It's all very well for Gordon. He's got his golf and his friends and everything and he doesn't consider me at all. He's changed terribly since we were married. You know how fond he used to be of having a good time.'

Is that why she married him? James asked himself wryly, or because of the de Verriland money?

'Besides, it's nonsense about us not being able to afford it. I know we have rather overdrawn this quarter's allowance, but Gordon could easily get some more from his mother if he

304

liked to ask. But he's got some new silly idea about taking money from the old girl . . . '

Can this girl be Evelyn's sister? James thought. Can Evelyn really believe that Gay is sweet and good and — what was the word she had used — *loyal?*

'Anyway, I'm not going to bury myself down there and if Gordon wants to see me he can jolly well come up here. He's making me a small allowance of my own and I'm running the flat on that. Don't worry about me as I'm having a very gay time and have met some most amusing people. I'd ask you to come and stay here when you get back to England but I don't honestly think you'd like it much, Evie darling, so I won't be selfish.'

'Selfish!' James thought. 'What you mean is that you wouldn't like anyone to see what's going on.'

'Give my love to James. I'm sure you will be happy and of course you will make such a good doctor's wife.
'Lots of love for now,
'GAY.'

'That's about the only true sentence in the whole letter,' James thought as he folded it and handed it back to Evelyn.

'Well?' she prompted, watching his face.

'If you want my honest opinion,' James answered carefully, 'I think that Gay is the one at fault. If this husband of hers is any kind of a chap, he won't dream of asking his mother for money — even if she is rich. And if the question of financial difficulties arises, as it obviously has done, Gay should let her husband decide what is best.'

'But I don't see that Gordon is being fair to her,' Evelyn cried. 'She's young and lovely and enjoys town life. Gordon should live up there with her. Gay is young and . . . well, sometimes a little impetuous. She needs someone to look after her.'

'Perhaps she doesn't like being disciplined,' James remarked shrewdly.

Evelyn was instantly on the defensive.

'Oh, no, James! Gay has always been very easy to manage,' she said. 'She always did anything I asked her.'

How much did you ask her to do that she didn't like doing? James said to himself, knowing Evelyn's selflessness where those she loved were concerned. But he did not voice his thoughts aloud. To Evelyn he said:

'She seems to be quite happy. If you like, Evelyn, we'll pay her a visit as soon as we get back to England. I don't want you to worry unnecessarily.'

'I do worry about her,' Evelyn admitted. 'She's so vital, so impulsive, and of course she doesn't know very much about life yet. I'm afraid for her.'

'Afraid of what?'

Evelyn stared out across the harbour.

'I don't know, James,' she answered truthfully. 'I'm silly, I expect, but I just have a feeling all isn't well.'

'Evelyn, would you like to cut this holiday short? We could return immediately.'

She turned to face him and he saw her eyes were filled with a grateful tenderness for him which made his heart beat at an unaccustomed rate.

'It is typical of you to suggest such a thing,' she said softly. 'You always think of me and never of yourself. All the same, James, I'm not as worried as all that. Besides, as far as we know, there isn't anything to be worried about. No, we'll enjoy the remaining week of our holiday.'

James leant forward and caught her two hands, holding them tightly in his own.

'Evelyn, you are happy here — with me?'

'I love it here!' Evelyn said quickly. 'It's — very beautiful.'

It did not answer his question but James seemed satisfied with her reply.

'You're a very beautiful woman, my

308

dear,' he said, dropping her hands. He did not try to kiss her and Evelyn was grateful to him for this. It would be a long while, she thought, before she could bear to let another man kiss her as Nicky had done.

Nicky also had told her she was beautiful and she had gloried in his praise of her, happy that he found her to his liking. James had said, 'You are a very beautiful woman,' in the same dispassionate way in which he would have admired the view. But Nicky . . .

She forced her thoughts back to the present.

'James, let's go for a walk before dinner.'

He rose immediately, and helped her into her coat. As they left the *auberge*, James took Evelyn's arm and Madame de Marqué, watching them from the doorway, smiled happily to herself. Already the young fiancés were feeling the call of Spring, she told herself. Soon there would be a little kiss — another, and *hoop-là*, a grand wedding!

But Evelyn's thoughts were very far from weddings, even though they encircled the man at her side.

'What was to become of them?' she asked herself hopelessly. How long would James be satisfied with the present platonic basis to their engagement? How long would it be before she could erase the memory of Nicky and allow another man to make love to her?

She looked at the pale sapphire ring on her wedding finger and recalled James' words to her when he had placed it there.

'I hope you will always wear it, my dear!'

What had he meant? That he hoped she would not want to return the ring to him — to break their engagement? James was so incredibly reserved always, that it was impossible to discover his real emotions. Perhaps his reserve was out of consideration to her. But sometimes she wondered if this were the right way to treat the situation; wondered how she would react if he pulled her to him and

310

crushed her lips with his mouth, blotting out the desire for those other lips.

'James!'

He looked at her quickly, hearing the unusual note in her voice.

'Yes, Evelyn?'

They had reached a secluded little cove on the beach and there was no one about — no one to see or hear Evelyn's desperate little voice saying,

'Please kiss me, James!'

He needed no second bidding for she looked very beautiful as he gathered her into his arms. The white woolly jacket she wore over a blue cotton frock showed her creamy, sun-tanned skin to perfection. Her eyes, always beautiful, in their depth and colour, were wide open and regarded him with a steady, child-like stare that reminded him incongruously of little Margaret.

Then he forgot everything but her quaint little demand, 'Please kiss me, James!'

He bent his head and as he thrilled to that long, passionate kiss, his eyes closed and he never saw the swift pain dart into those lovely eyes; was too carried away to feel the sudden stiffening of her body or hear the soft moan which came from the depth of her heart.

'You're the most beautiful woman in the world,' he whispered huskily. 'Such a sweet person! I love you, Evelyn.'

He drew her even closer, stroking her hair with a sudden rush of protective feeling, forgetting everything but the fact that this lovely girl in his arms was his fiancée, would one day be his wife, and that he wanted far more than the friendship that had up till now existed between them.

He did not know that she was already regretting the sudden impulse that had been responsible for his kiss. She knew now that it had been born of her desire for another man's arms, another man's kisses.

'Nicky, Nicky,' she thought silently. 'If only this were you. Oh, my dearest love, where are you now?'

But there was no answer to her

unspoken cry, no sound but the soft lapping of the waves against the rocks and the mournful cry of the seagulls as they dipped low over the beach in search of food.

'Evelyn, my dear, my darling, say something to me!'

'Nicky, I . . . '

James released her so suddenly that she had to step backwards to retain her balance. Then as she saw his white stricken face, the sudden hardening of his mouth, she realized too late what she had said.

She stared at him, numb with misery, angry with herself for hurting the one person who had done so much to help her.

'James, I'm so sorry,' she whispered. 'I wasn't thinking . . . it just came out before . . . '

'It's quite all right,' James said stiffly, turning back towards the hotel. 'You needn't explain.'

She fell in beside him, walking fast to keep up with him.

'James, I couldn't help it!' she said pitifully.

He softened at the sound of her helpless little voice.

'My dear, I quite understand,' he said more gently. 'Let's forget it, shall we?'

She nodded her head, feeling the tears stinging her eyelids.

'I won't cry, I won't,' she thought fiercely.

But as they walked back in silence, the tears dripped slowly down her cheeks and she knew that as long as she lived she could never love this man whose ring she wore, never love any other man but Nicholas March.

'Let's forget it,' James had said. But, although she might forget this incident, she knew she would never forget Nicky, and though she might one day marry James and bear his children, her heart would remain for ever within the keeping of her first and only love.

15

Gay pushed open the front door of her little flat and flung her forage cap on to the hall table. Then she slammed the door and stooped to pick up the letter lying on the mat. She glanced at it casually as she went through into the bedroom and flung herself on to the divan.

The thin line of her eyebrows shot up in a half-surprised, half-amused glance. A letter from Gordon.

'Now what the devil does he want!' she said aloud.

But she did not bother to open the letter and rose restlessly from the bed, going across to the dressing table. She sat down in front of the mirror and ran a comb through her short, fair curls.

'I look tired!' she thought. 'And small wonder!' Life in the A.T.A hadn't been as easy as she had anticipated. In fact it had been plain hard work all during her training. Now she had her wings but the powers that be kept her slogging away with only an occasional day off.

She reached across for the telephone and dialled a number. It rang insistently for a minute or two but there was no reply. She slammed down the receiver and the thin pretty face creased into a discontented scowl.

'Oh, blast!' she said irritably. 'Why does Jack have to be out the one evening I want to go dancing.'

She dialled another number and this time a man's deep tones answered.

'Bob? Oh, it's Gay here!'

'Why, hullo, poppet! Still as beautiful as ever?'

Gay's expression softened and her eyes strayed back to the mirror, surveying the tall slim figure in its neat blue uniform.

'I'm in town!' she proffered casually. 'Thought I'd put on some glad rags and forget I ever joined this racket.'

He was quick to take the hint. It

wasn't every day that a girl of Gay's popularity wanted his company.

'You mean you're free?' he asked eagerly.

'That's what I said!' Gay answered with a low laugh.

'Listen, sweet! I'll be around in ten minutes!' came Bob's voice. 'We'll do a show and dine and dance afterwards. O.K.?'

'Sounds nice,' was Gay's reply. 'I'll be seeing you!'

She rang off and the expression on her face changed as she saw Gordon's letter, still unopened, lying on the pillow where she had tossed it.

She picked it up idly and glanced at the postmark. Twenty-first of April, forty-four. Nearly a week old. She opened it and read it, then re-read it more carefully.

'*My dear Gay,*' he had written.

'*I am going on embarkation leave next week. No need to tell you what this means. It is two years now and in*

317

spite of everything that caused our separation, I would like to see you again before I go. You see, Gay, I have not forgotten you! After all, you are still my wife and although I'm not fond of this angle, I may never see you again.

'I will be at the Club if you care to ring me from the twenty-eighth to the seventh May.

'Yours, GORDON.'

Gay sat down on the bed and somewhere around her heart, the hardness cracked and a little softness crept in.

Gordon still loved her. She could tell that from his letter. Two years of separation hadn't altered his feelings towards her. And now he was going overseas. Probably on this invasion racket all the papers were so full of.

Gay forgot Bob and the fact that she should be dressing, and allowed her mind to wander back over these last five years of war. Gordon had joined up right away. He was a captain now, but he had joined as a private. She had been furious about it, of course, and they had had a ghastly row. It had ended with Gordon telling her he was refusing any further allowance from his mother and that he was going to make his own life, whether she liked it or not.

She had threatened to divorce him, but as Gordon said, she had no grounds for divorce, and even if she had, she would get practically no alimony from a private in the army.

'Far better stick to me, my dear!' he had said with a short, sarcastic laugh. 'No doubt I will get a commission in time and then you will get a fairly decent wife's allowance.'

She had stormed and raged at him, but of course, she had seen the reason in his advice. Evelyn had agreed to her having her share of their father's money and she hadn't been too badly off. Now, with her own flying pay and Gordon's army allowance, she was sitting pretty.

But she had never forgiven Gordon, and although at first she had seen him occasionally, always hoping that she could talk him into accepting Lady de Verriland's offer of a steady income, Gordon had remained adamant and she, Gay, refused to see him at all. She knew he could have divorced her, if he chose, but she was shrewd enough to realize that for some reason or other, Gordon still loved her and in his way, remained faithful to her.

Army life had undoubtedly changed Gordon. At those occasional reunions he had always tried to preach to her, telling her she was going to the dogs and running her own life as well as his. He wanted her to join one of the women's services, but she certainly wasn't doing that!

Oh, yes! Gordon had changed all right. He was not recognizable as the same man who had asked her to marry him, saying:

'There's nothing more reliable than an income with five figures to it!'

Gay had to admit that the Army had made a man of him. He was no longer a playboy, and earning his own living seemed to have given him a self-respect which she wasn't sure she liked. Not that he hadn't been self-confident enough in the good old days, and Gay preferred that other side of him — the sophisticated, debonair young man about town.

He had changed himself out of all recognition but pride forbade Gay allowing him to change her. God alone knew how he had tried! But she was obstinate. She wanted a good time, and war or no war she was going to have it. No cooking meals and washing babies' clothes for her!

If Gay had been less pretty, less attractive to men, she might have given in. But there had always been a crowd of young officers on leave only too ready to take her out to dances and amuse her, and at last Gordon had given up trying to alter her, and they had agreed on a separation.

But he hadn't forgotten her. His letter proved that.

'Ring me at the club!' he had written.

Well, for old times' sake, she would do so. But not yet. She wasn't going to let him think she really wanted to see him. He could wait another twenty-four hours, wondering if she were going to ring; if she was going to be kind-hearted and see him before he went abroad. She could not leave it longer than a day because she only had a forty-eight-hour break.

The expression on Gay's usually discontented little face was, since she was alone, completely revealing. A curious half-smile played about the petulant mouth and her eyes were soft-ened almost to gentleness even while the brightness betrayed her excited antici-pation. To see her one might have said she was in love, but Gay herself would have denied this strongly.

'In love with Gordon? Rubbish!'

But all the dissatisfaction of the past year crowded her mind, digging its way into her heart. She was sick of parties, sick of the eternal round of drinks followed by the inevitable petting and the effort of refusing just that particular thing the men always wanted.

'I'm faithful to Gordon in *that* way,' she had said fiercely in answer to Evelyn's worried questioning. 'But you needn't think it is because I love him. I'm sick of love. The whole thing revolts me!'

'But Gay, darling, you shouldn't feel like that. It's all wrong. It should be the most wonderful, beautiful union of two people who really care . . . '

'Well, I must say you're a fine one to talk,' Gay had retorted bitterly. 'You and James have been engaged five years — five whole years, and you're still not married. When is the beautiful, wonderful union of two people who *really* care coming off?'

Evelyn had turned away, miserable and sickened by this hardness that seemed to have taken complete possession of Gay's soul. She blamed the war,

Service life, and in fact anything but Gay herself. For as long as she lived, Evelyn would never be able to see Gay as she really was.

'James and I are the best of friends,' she had said gently. 'I couldn't get along without him.'

'Well, you seem to do very well without this love racket you keep preaching about,' Gay retorted. 'What's stopping the wedding bells?'

Evelyn had not replied. How could she tell this strange, hard young woman who was nevertheless her sister, that she could not bring herself to marry James because she was still in love with Nicky. Even after five years, she had not forgotten him. She knew she would never forget him as long as she lived. And James had not seemed so desperately anxious to get married lately.

At first, during the two years following the announcement of their engagement, he had been most persistent. But she had put him off with vague promises of 'next year.' Then little Margaret had come home, a young woman now, and Evelyn had been so busy with her W.V.S. work and all the local committee work she did, that she had been able to say truthfully to James:

'I simply haven't time to get my trousseau,' and he had answered, understandably caustic:

'Will the time ever come, darling?'

Evelyn had loved having Margaret home. Her schooling at the Cedars had been thorough and she had continued studying at the Eicholz Clinic, from where she emerged a fully trained masseuse. She had wanted to put her training into practice and James had readily agreed to let her work with him, answering the telephone, receiving his patients and generally acting as his secretary when she was not actually doing massage work.

The three of them, thought Evelyn, had settled into a happy, contented little rut of hard work and companionship. Gradually James had ceased to press her with questions of when they would be married, and Evelyn had been only too glad to let him take Margaret out in the evenings. She herself was usually dog-tired after her days at the canteen and would want nothing more than an early night and bed. But Margaret, with all the energy of a girl in her teens, seemed tireless and Evelyn knew she needed company and was happy that James could take her for an occasional evening's dancing or a day at the seaside.

It never occurred to her that her little sister was grown-up — old enough to fall in love and need attention and admiration and the company of more than a friend. Margaret was completely happy with James; of that Evelyn was certain, and she never paid any attention to the young officers whom she sometimes met at the canteen.

Margaret had grown unbelievably pretty. She had Evelyn's hair, Evelyn's figure and was, in fact, so like her that they might have been mistaken for twins but for the obvious difference in their ages.

Five years of war had undoubtedly left their mark on Evelyn. At twenty-seven she was no longer a pretty girl but a slim, beautiful woman. Too thin, perhaps, but there was a quiet resigned look in her pale face that gave her an air of composure, and in a world of uncertainty, of death and all the horror of warfare, men turned to Evelyn for reassurance. There was something so essentially feminine about her, and although none of her admirers ever succeeded in winning more than a smile from her, they all loved her and many carried her photograph as the incarnation of all they were fighting for — goodness, truth, charm and freedom of spirit.

But how little they realized, thought Evelyn, the ties which held her spirit captive. She could never be free again because her memories of Nicky bound her to him and to the past, and freedom of heart would never be hers again.

She did not think of him so often now. There was, after all, so much else to think about, to worry over. Apart from her work in the village which took up all her time, she had Gay on her mind, an ever-present responsibility that she felt she was not doing justice to. Gay was not happy. Evelyn knew it for a certainty. She went to parties and had plenty of friends, but Evelyn could see beneath the hard, bright exterior and although she could not understand Gay or reach through the barrier that her hardness put between them, she never ceased trying to find a way of gaining her sister's confidence.

Once Evelyn had been to see Gordon. It was, strangely enough, their first meeting since the wedding, but in that short afternoon spent with him, Evelyn revised her opinion of her brother-in-law. He had told her frankly that he still loved Gay and would have liked a reunion, but that Gay was not of the same opinion. He said he hoped Evelyn would have a good influence on her and that perhaps they might one day come together again, and she, Evelyn, had promised to do all she could to help him.

But what had she done? What had she been able to do? Gay resented criticism and refused even to discuss Gordon with her sister. She had made one attempt to change Gay's outlook, persuading her to spend a weekend in the country. But it had not been a success. Margaret had been very excited at the thought of having Gay to stay and had made every attempt to win her sister's love and affection. But Gay had been aloof, hard as ever, and Margaret, always oversensitive to rebuffs, had closed into a shell of silence.

Nor had Gay seemed to get on with James. Evelyn had been very annoyed with him for being so critical, so mocking and blamed him entirely for the furious arguments that had ensued. She had defended Gay with unusual force and surprised James by her anger. Evelyn was so seldom stirred from her gentle, quiet demeanour.

The little house had had a complete shaking during those two days, and Gay had not come again.

'My dear old thing,' she had said when Evelyn offered a second invitation, 'I know when I'm not wanted, and although I much appreciate your generous and forgiving nature, I am *not* coming.'

'But you *are* wanted, Gay darling,' Evelyn cried. 'You know I always love having you.'

'But our dear doctor does not enjoy the stimulating effect of my delightful company,' Gay had returned with an amused glance at her sister's anxious face.

'James was rude and impossible,' Evelyn had said with unusual disloyalty. 'Anyway, Gay, you know he doesn't count. You come first and if he doesn't like it, he can lump it.'

Gay had raised her eyebrows and given her sister a half-amused, half-grateful look.

'Really, Evelyn,' she said, her voice toned to an unaccustomed tenderness, 'I can't think why you stick to me like a limpet to a rock. Heaven knows I'm not very pleasant company nowadays, and you have no cause whatever to — to care for me.'

'Gay!' Evelyn had cried. 'You're my sister!'

Gay had shrugged her beautiful shoulders, and the old mocking light returned to her eyes as she said:

'Does that really make so much difference?'

'Of course!' Evelyn said. 'Gay, please come again.'

'Perhaps I will, one day,' Gay said.

But she had not gone.

There was something about Evelyn, something about the quietness and simplicity of her life which had touched Gay on the raw. Although it was not the life she liked, she was jealous because they seemed so happy, so at peace. Jealous, also, of the bond that held her two sisters so close together. Not that they excluded her, but she felt an outsider and resented it, even while she was honest enough to admit that she was different through her own making. She hadn't wanted to be a home-girl. She had wanted sophistication, gaiety, life, fun, money. And what had she got? Certainly not happiness.

But was Evelyn happy? she asked herself as she climbed into her bath hurriedly before Bob should call for her. Was she really in love with James?

For one sickening moment, Gay remembered Nicky, remembered the light, the beauty in Evelyn's face when she had talked about him that same evening that she, Gay, had met Gordon. She knew, in that second, that Evelyn was not in love with James, and that she, Gay, had undoubtedly parted her from the one man she really loved.

Then the doorbell rang and she forgot everything else in her hurry to dress. As she finished her toilet, she remembered again, but she thrust the thought quickly from her. This was her evening out, and she was going to enjoy herself. No one, least of all Nicholas March, was going to spoil it for her.

'Sorry to keep you waiting, Bob,' she said, and allowed him to take her arm as they went through the door.

But by some trick of Fate, Gay was not to be allowed to forget Evelyn, or Nicholas March. After the show, Bob took her to one of the most fashionable restaurants where he had booked a table, and as he seated himself opposite her, she looked across the room and her eyes met the curious, puzzled gaze of an Army major.

She knew at once who it was, and although it was a matter of minutes before Nicholas March recognized her, she felt the colour leave her cheeks and mount again in a dark, angry flush.

'Someone you know?' Bob asked, following her gaze jealously.

'Someone I used to know,' Gay answered, leaving her companion to draw his own conclusions.

'Someone you know?' asked Nicholas' companion.

'Yes!' Nicky said quietly. 'She's the sister of a girl I — I wanted to marry.'

The young captain looked at his senior officer with some surprise. Major March was unofficially known in the mess as The Woman Hater. Yet now he confessed to a past affair and with such a look of — what could one call it? — poignant sorrow, in his face, that it was easy enough to tell he had been in love.

'The sister's pretty enough,' he volunteered.

Nicky tossed his drink down in one gulp and drew out his cigarette-case.

'Not as beautiful as — as the other one.'

He could not bring himself to say her name.

'Shall I speak to Gay?' he asked himself. It would be easy enough. Junior officer at her table. How d'you do, Miss Challis. How are you? How is your sister? No, he couldn't do it. But he wanted to. He wanted desperately to find out where Evelyn was, what she was doing. He wanted to know what had become of Evelyn's little girl. What was her name? Margaret! Little blind kid. He'd taken a great fancy to her. Looked so like Evelyn. God, how many years was it since he had last seen her? How many years since he had dragged himself away from that wretched little ski-hut and all that life could ever hold for him in love and happiness?

Gay had changed. Grown up. Wonder why she blushed like that when she recognized me. Evelyn used to blush . . . Couldn't he ever forget her? Hadn't five years of slogging hard work in the Army done anything to change his feelings? Soften the pain? Dulled it perhaps, but not destroyed it. Seeing that sister of hers brought it all back, as cruelly as ever. He could hear Gay's voice, faintly distorted by the telephone saying:

'You see, she's married!'

Married! To a wretched Italian. An enemy, well not any more, but an Eytey all the same. Perhaps . . .

Nicky dragged his thoughts away from the trend they were taking, but when he had ordered another drink, they reverted again to the same subject. Perhaps the man was dead, killed fighting, and Evelyn was free. Rotten thing to wish, but still, he'd been a rotten fellow, seducing a girl and leaving her with a baby. Gay would know.

'I'll ask her,' Nicky told himself, but almost immediately, he told himself he couldn't do it. Supposing the chap were not dead. The disappointment . . . She might have married again. Surely, if she still cared for him and had found herself free, she would have communicated with him. No, he couldn't even expect her to care. Not after five years. And she had been such a kid when he met her. Such a lovely, unspoiled, beautiful girl . . .

He stubbed out his cigarette and turned to his companion.

'Shall we go?' he asked abruptly.

The young captain rose obediently,

wondering if the Major was going to give away more of his murky past. But Nicky remained silent and thoughtful and as soon as he could politely do so, he said goodnight, and spent the last few hours of his leave sleeplessly tossing and turning in the hard hotel bed.

Gay watched his departure with some anxiety. When she was sure he had gone, she breathed a sigh of relief and made Bob guide her across the room to the dance floor. She was gay, mocking, even mildly flirtatious, but although she deceived Bob, she did not deceive herself. She could have spoken to Nicholas March, told him the truth; told him that Evelyn was not married and that it had all been a stupid story invented by herself. She could have told him, but she had not.

Evelyn, lying awake in spite of the severity of the day's work, never realized that a word from Nicky, a word from Gay, and her whole life would have been altered. Only a word or two. But they had not been spoken.

16

'Coffee?'

'Please, Gordon!'

He gave the necessary order and turned back to his wife. Gay was looking exceptionally lovely, he thought. A little thin and drawn but nevertheless very attractive.

Realizing the importance and delicacy of the moment, he did not hurriedly broach the subject on his mind. He wanted her back — as his wife. He was more in love with her now than he had ever been and even though he realized their reunion, if he could bring such a thing to pass, would only be very temporary, he wanted to leave the country knowing Gay was his. He wanted her to love him; to know when he was in the thick of battle that she was at home, thinking of him, writing to him. Perhaps even bearing his child.

So far, he had allowed this lunch to proceed with no more than the light banter of two acquaintances to pass between them. He wasn't going to hurry his move.

'Like a game of chess,' he thought with a humourless smile. 'Got to go carefully, think it out first. Sound her, lead her into thinking it was her idea.'

She was smoking now, blowing a little blue cloud into the air through soft red lips.

'How long since I kissed those lips?' he asked himself wryly. Two years since he had held the lovely slim young body through the silent hours of the night. Now she was almost a stranger — an exciting stranger. He felt as if he were about to suggest some illicit affair to her, so different was the poised, sophisticated young woman at his side from the angry, spoilt little girl he remembered from their last meeting.

He could recall vividly her shrill voice, shouting all sorts of unrepeatable things at him; see the now cool amused eyes flashing with childish temper and the carefully set fair curls in a riotous disarray.

'You know, you have grown into a very beautiful young woman!' he said aloud.

Gay smiled at him lazily.

'You've grown quite attractive yourself!' she retorted.

And it was true, she thought. He had put on weight and was every inch a man, a soldier. The lines of dissipation had left his face and clean, strenuous work had hardened his muscles, given a more determined line to his jaw.

'Where did you get the Monte Carlo tan?' she asked with an amused, yet admiring, glance at his sunburnt face and hands.

'Battle course I was on last month!' he returned easily.

'Preparing for invasion?'

'Aren't we all?' was Gordon's evasive reply. 'How do you like your work, Gay?'

A small discontented frown creased

her forehead, making her seem more real to the man beside her, more like the old Gay.

'It's not too bad really, I suppose! But they work us damned hard!'

'I'd like to see you in your uniform,' he said. 'Should think it suits you.'

'I'm sick to death of uniform,' said Gay petulantly. 'The first thing I'm going to do when this coupon-racket is over is buy myself a complete new trousseau.'

He looked at her quickly, trying to judge her words, see if there had been a second meaning behind them. She met his look, and her eyes dropped. He felt he had missed a good opening but it was too late now.

'I've got a few odd coupons to spare,' he said, breaking the awkward silence that had fallen. 'Anything you particularly want?'

Gay shot him an amused smile.

'That's very generous of you, Gordon,' she said, her tone slightly bantering. 'I wouldn't mind some silk stockings.'

'I'll send you some from abroad!'
Gordon promised.

Gay raised her eyebrows.

'When do you go?'

'I don't know. But I don't suppose it will be long . . . What else do you want? I mean that I could get you now?'

'He's absolutely serious,' she thought. 'He really does want to get me something. Well, and why not?'

A sudden imp of mischief prompted her to say:

'Well, I could do with some undies and a new nightie!'

Gordon looked down at his plate.

'Good Lord!' he thought. 'I'm embarrassed. Because my wife says she wants some undies! But she doesn't seem like my wife . . . only a stranger.'

'Why, Gordon!' Gay said, looking at him from under her lashes. 'I believe you're blushing!'

'Don't be a fool!' he said more rudely than he had intended. But he did not deceive her.

'Well, how about it, then?' she prompted.

He met her glance squarely and this time it was Gay who looked away.

'We will go and choose them — together!' he said, watching her face. 'I'd like a little feminine diversion. One gets sick of masculine company at times.'

Gay recovered her poise quickly.

'I suppose you do!' she said, and her voice was very young and demure.

Gordon beckoned the waiter and asked for his bill. She watched him, noticing his self-assurance, wondering about him. Had he been faithful to her?

'Shall we go?' he asked.

She rose immediately and he followed her out into the hall, waiting while she disappeared to powder her nose. When she returned, he managed to get a taxi with some difficulty, and told the driver to go to Fortnum's.

'I believe there is a ladies' department there, isn't there?' he asked Gay as he climbed in beside her.

Gay laughed, a sudden spontaneous laugh which crinkled her eyes at the

343

corners and caught at his heart because of its very naturalness. He loved her. Even though she was hard and spoilt and sometimes bad.

'If only she will allow herself to be natural,' he told himself. 'She isn't really bad at heart. If I could make her love me . . . '

He tried unsuccessfully to quieten the quickened beating of his heart, but the faint, intoxicating scent of her perfume seemed to be enveloping his mind, drugging his thoughts.

Gay appeared unaware of his emotion. Her hands were playing idly with her suede gloves and he noticed that she was wearing her wedding ring. The ring he had placed there, promising to love and cherish her 'until death us do part.'

The thought sobered him.

'Mightn't be so long before death does part us,' he told himself grimly. 'Bound to be a lot of casualties before it's over. Then she will be free — and without the fuss and bother and publicity of divorce. Free to marry another fellow.'

Sudden anger swelled up within him, anger and jealousy, too. Gay belonged to him. He was going to see that she did — in every way.

She was leaning towards him, smiling provocatively, maddeningly. He felt the desire to crush her in his arms, kiss the life out of her, coursing through his veins.

'Flirt with me, would she?' he thought violently. 'I'll teach her!'

But reason sobered him like a dash of cold water. No, let her wait, reason said. Don't kiss her now. Play her at her own game.

Nevertheless he was glad when the taxi came to a standstill and it was no longer necessary for him to undergo the strain of her proximity.

She *was* flirting with him, Gay admitted to herself. But why not? He was very attractive — and it was fun teasing him, playing with him. She was sure of her ground, knowing he loved her. Besides, he *was* her husband! She smiled to herself, seeing suddenly the humour of the situation.

Watching her, Gordon wondered what was amusing her now. Hatching some plot, if he knew her, and he thought he understood her pretty well now.

Gay was her most charming self throughout the afternoon. Even though she had most of one of the shop's goods on the counter and ended by buying only one nightdress, the saleswoman was left smiling and in good temper. Gordon, watching her, had to admit that she could be very sweet when she chose.

She was charming to him, too, asking his opinion, accepting his advice, following his taste. Once or twice she said to her assistant in a shy, demure little voice.

'My husband is on embarkation leave, you know. I want something *really* special.'

And she looked across her shoulder

at him, for all the world like a young bride buying her trousseau.

He knew she was play-acting; knew that Gay knew she was not deceiving him, but he could not help being pleased by this suggestion of their intimacy — by the thought that there might be something behind her play-acting, and that she intended the evening to end with more than a good-night kiss.

In actual fact, Gay had not even thought so far ahead. She was enjoying herself tremendously and Gordon was being extremely generous, both with his coupons and in accepting the bills without questioning her extravagance. She had bought a lovely nightie — palest blue chiffon with long bishop sleeves, and two sets of rose-pink undies which were hardly suitable for flying, but definitely to be snapped up while the going was good.

They had tea at Fuller's and when Gordon suggested a show before dinner, she readily agreed. They went to see *Pink String and Sealing Wax*, an original murder story which held Gay enthralled. But Gordon afterwards could remember little about it. He had been observing Gay's profile, seeing the changes of expression in her face, seeing her without the artificial make-up she used when she knew she was being watched. Once she turned and gripped his arm in her excitement and he had taken hold of her hand, feeling for the first time in his life, protective and tender towards her. Beneath that sophistication and poise, she was still such a child — young enough to be completely carried away by a mere story.

He felt immeasurably cheered by those few hours in the theatre — confident now that there was good in Gay — a fine character if only it could be developed before this other person she had become took possession of her.

'Whatever the cost to myself,' he thought, 'I am going to do my utmost to change her.'

But not to go about it the way he had once tried. No preaching or arguing. He must find a more subtle way.

'Where shall we dine?' he asked her as they went out into the fresh air. 'It will probably be difficult getting a table anywhere. I should have booked earlier.'

Gay shrugged her shoulders.

'I'd ask you back to the flat,' she said. 'But there's no food there. Besides, I'm a rotten cook!'

He laughed and linked his arm through hers.

'Then we had better go to my club,' he said. 'We can get a meal there any time. Will you mind not dancing?'

'There doesn't seem to be any alternative,' Gay answered without rancour. 'But I'm sorry about the dancing. You used to be pretty good.'

'So she remembers,' thought Gordon.

But he did not further the conversation and instead guided her through the crowded street towards his club.

Dinner over, they had coffee and cigarettes in the comfortable lounge.

Gordon asked after Evelyn and was surprised by the look of nervousness — or was it apprehension? — on Gay's face. He did not know he had reminded her of something she would rather forget — last night's encounter with Nicholas March.

'Oh, she's all right,' she said vaguely.

'Isn't she married yet?' Gordon persisted.

'No! Don't blame her really. I never did like James Cathy.'

'Why?'

The question caught her unprepared.

'Oh, I don't know! We never got on. I don't think he likes me much, either.'

'About the only man in the country!' Gordon said quickly. She was pleased with his flattery.

'How many boyfriends *have* you got?' he enquired with enforced lightness.

'Oh, not so many,' Gay answered with a laugh.

'No one in particular?'

The smile left her face and she studied his expression, trying to guess at the feeling behind his words.

'No! No one in particular,' she said.

'Surely I cannot hope that my wife is faithful to me?'

Gordon's tone was light, bantering, but it roused her to sudden anger.

'Since you're really so interested in my private affairs, I have been faithful to you!' she said curtly. 'Merely because men bore me in that respect.'

The rebuff did not hurt him as it was intended to do. It sufficed him to know that no other man had taken his place; had known the delight of Gay in those rare but infinitely sweet, surrendering moods.

'Not that she has surrendered sweetly to me for the hell of a long time,' he thought bitterly, but this feeling did not last long. The past was over, done with, finished. It was the present and the future that mattered.

He changed the conversation.

'How's the other sister?'

'Margaret? Oh, she's all right. Grown up now!'

'You never talked much about her,' Gordon observed casually. 'Why not? Don't you get on with her?'

Gay lit a cigarette, playing for time.

'I'll tell him now,' she thought. 'After all, what difference does it make now? It's funny that he should never have found out about Margaret. I suppose she was shut away in that school most of the time.'

'We get on all right!' she said, watching him. 'Did I ever tell you she was blind?'

He was shocked into silence for a moment. The incredible, casual way in which she announced the fact that her sister was blind!

'Blind?' he echoed. 'But how awful! How did it happen? Not one of these air raids?'

'I could say yes,' Gay thought. 'He would never know the truth.'

But something prompted her to be honest. After all, there was no point in lying now they no longer received an allowance from Lady de Verriland. Her

352

disapproval of the marriage could make no difference — now.

'She has always been blind,' she said aloud. 'Born like it. Mother used to get drunk and injured Margaret before she was born.'

'Good God!'

She watched the effect of her bombshell. It was quite a little while before Gordon spoke. Then he said:

'Why didn't you tell me before, Gay? I might have been able to do something to help. Financially . . . '

He broke off, remembering the quarrels they had had over money. Perhaps Gay had wanted it for her sister.

'Gay!' he said, his face working as a variety of emotions crowded his mind. 'Gay, was Evelyn hard up? I mean, could you . . . did you help them, financially?'

'Oh, a bit — after we were first married,' Gay answered. And then added with a laugh, 'But I never was particularly generous, Gordon, so don't think you have done my poor sisters out of much.'

'Heavens above!' she thought. 'Aren't I being truthful tonight! Must be that liqueur on top of all that gin!'

'Gay, if there is anything I can do now, please tell me. I know it's rather late, but before I go, I would like to get this settled. Do your sisters need money?'

'It's funny,' thought Gay. 'He doesn't seem to mind a bit about Mother. And I was always so afraid of him finding out. All he cares about is Evie and Margaret!'

'No, I don't think they need help,' Gay said. 'They live fairly economically in the country, Evie tells me. And we've all got the money our dear Papa left us.'

'If anything happens to me, Gay, I have left you everything,' Gordon said abruptly. 'I wanted you to know.'

Gay looked at him, her eyes curious, not fully understanding this man she had married. All those fights, those scenes over a small allowance and now he was telling her she was going to get the whole lot if he should get bumped off in the war. She certainly had not expected it. She felt suddenly very sentimental towards him and, always afraid of sentiment, she covered it with a hard little laugh.

'All rather dramatic, isn't it?' she said. 'Hero goes to war and makes will in favour of wicked wife!'

Gordon looked as if she had hit him. She was immediately contrite and wished the words unspoken. But she was too proud to apologize. She changed the subject.

'What's the time, Gordon?'

He looked at his watch.

'Nine-thirty!'

'I ought to be getting back shortly,' she said vaguely. 'I'll never get a taxi if I leave it too late.'

'We'll go right away,' Gordon answered.

She felt suddenly afraid. The game was over and somehow or other she had lost the lead. She felt the situation was more than she could cope with.

'Gordon must not come back with me to the flat,' she thought swiftly. 'I couldn't trust him in this mood.'

And could she trust herself?

'I've had too much to drink,' she told herself. 'I feel light-headed and — and rather miserable!'

Aloud she said:

'Oh, you don't need to come back with me, Gordon. The taximan won't murder me en route!'

He took no notice of her flippant remark.

'I'll take you home,' he said firmly.

'Well, why not?' Gay thought. 'That is sure to mean a kiss or two in the taxi, but I can cope with that. Only he mustn't come into the flat . . . '

She had not reckoned for Gordon's wishes and his determination when he really wanted something.

To her surprise, he made no attempt to kiss her in the taxi. She wondered if he intended to part without more than a handshake, and felt even a little sorry about it. He looked very mysterious and attractive in the half-light of the cab.

But when it drew up outside the flat, he said:

'It's early yet, Gay. I'm coming in for a minute or two.'

He paid off the taxi and followed her into the little hall, closing the door behind him. As the door shut, Gay felt again that sudden apprehension in her heart. It was so still, so quiet, and she was alone — with Gordon.

'I haven't done the blackout,' she said, forcing her voice to calmness. 'Don't put on the light yet.'

It was very dark, but he could see her silhouetted against the window as she reached up to draw the curtains.

He strode forward quickly, silently, and put his arms round her.

'Gordon, don't. I . . . '

But he silenced her with a kiss that seemed to knock all the strength out of her body, dulling her resistance and forcing her reluctantly at first, and then with a growing passion, to return his kisses. When at last he released her, he

357

was smiling. Gay was white, shaking, trembling with anger — anger at him for daring, anger at herself for letting him.

'Damn you!' she said in a low, hard voice.

He laughed, certain of himself now, knowing her well enough to understand the reason for her temper. She had given herself away, shown him that he was still attractive to her, whether she liked it or not.

He did not try to kiss her again but waited while she darkened the window and switched on the light. Then he seated himself comfortably on the sofa in the little sitting-room and surveyed his wife's beautiful, flushed face.

'You're even more lovely when you are angry,' he said calmly.

She turned her head sharply, giving him a quick, half-angry glance. Then she turned on her heel and ran up to her room.

'He is not staying for long,' she told herself fiercely as she repaired her make-up. 'Just because he is going abroad he need not think I am going to be the dutiful little wife!'

But she was still afraid of the swift beating of her heart and the unaccustomed trembling of her hands as she combed her hair. She lit a cigarette to give her confidence as she walked downstairs, but Gordon's direct gaze nevertheless succeeded in disconcerting her when she re-entered the room.

'Will you have a drink?' she asked, busying herself with glasses, soda water, bottles. 'I have some whiskey or gin.'

'Whiskey, please, darling!'

She poured it out, spilling a little of it as she handed him the glass. He did not remark upon her unsteady hands, but she knew he had noticed them. She poured a whiskey for herself.

'Shouldn't you stick to gin?' Gordon asked, and was instantly aware that he had said the wrong thing.

'What I drink is my business,' Gay retorted. 'Are you by any chance suggesting I'm tight?'

He ignored her sarcasm.

'Don't be silly, Gay,' he said. 'Drink whatever you like. Why should it matter to me?'

'It apparently does!' Gay answered bitingly.

Gordon rose to his feet and put his glass down on the table. She turned quickly at the sound and stood defiantly facing him. He caught her by the arms and held her so tightly that it hurt her, but she was too afraid of the strange light in his eyes to cry out.

'Since you seem to know so much,' Gordon said in a hard, controlled voice, 'it does matter to me what you drink and how much you drink. You see, my dear Gay, you are my wife.'

She opened her mouth to speak but Gordon cut in with a laugh:

'Oh, I know that doesn't mean anything to you, my dear. But it so happens that it does mean something to me. I love you. Do you hear? You're spoilt and selfish and hard as nails, but I still love you. Funny, isn't it?'

Gay struggled to release herself from his grip, but he held her firmly.

'I won't stand here and be insulted by you,' she cried fiercely. 'Let me go, you . . . you devil.'

'I haven't finished what I'm going to say yet,' said Gordon calmly. 'It is high time someone told you a few home-truths, and that someone is going to be me.'

'I won't listen to you,' Gay shouted wildly but he still held her in that merciless grip.

'Oh, yes you will, my dear. You can't very well do otherwise. Now let this sink into that pretty little head of yours. You're going to the dogs, do you hear me? You're letting the bad get the better of the good. And there is good in you, Gay. That's the part of you I love. Somebody's got to shake you out of the rut you're in — start you afresh. And that someone is me.'

He pulled her struggling against him and forced her head back until he could kiss her mouth.

'Let me go,' Gay gasped, but his grip only tightened and his lips came down on hers, bruising them with the hard passion of his kisses. One arm still held her against him; the other caressed her body, weakening her resistance, forcing the strength from her mind, her body, her knees.

'When he lets me go, I'll lock myself in my room,' she thought, fighting him with the little power that remained to her.

But Gordon had no intention of letting her go. When he had done with kissing her, he lifted her in his arms and laughed into her wide, frightened eyes.

'You shall remember this night, Gay,' he said. 'When I'm far away and you're letting some other fellow kiss you, you will remember me.'

'Don't, Gordon, don't!' she whispered. 'Please, Gordon. If you love me, leave me alone.'

But he paid no attention to her appeal.

'It is because I love you that I will not

leave you,' he said. 'But don't be afraid, Gay. I have no intention of assaulting you.'

He carried her upstairs and laid her on her bed. Then he kissed the soft, trembling mouth again and this time with such gentleness and such tenderness that Gay no longer fought against him.

Gradually her muscles relaxed and against her will, she felt herself responding to his kisses, answering them with equal passion, with growing desire.

'Gay, my darling. My darling wife,' he was whispering softly. 'I love you so much . . . Love me! . . . Gay!'

With no further will or effort to withstand him, Gay switched off the light and pulled his head down to her breast.

* * *

When she awoke, it was barely dawn. She stared at the soft grey light creeping through the chink in the curtains and as full consciousness returned, she remembered what had happened. She turned swiftly and her heart leapt to her mouth and sank deep, deep down inside her as she saw that Gordon had gone. Her eyes searched the room, looking for his cap, his tunic, his baton, but they had all gone. She was quite alone.

'Perhaps he left a note,' she thought, and switched on the light. She ran downstairs to the sitting-room, but there was no envelope, no folded paper waiting for her.

'He'll ring me later,' she thought as she climbed back into bed.

But when she awoke again, the sun was streaming into her room and her watch told her it was eleven-thirty. And Gordon had not rung.

'Well, what do I care?' Gay said with a touch of the old defiance.

But she cared enough to wait in all morning in case he should ring. She cared enough to decide to catch the latest train she could instead of the faster, better one which went soon after lunch.

And Gay, who was so proud, so disdainful, cared enough to sink her pride and put a call through to the club where she knew Gordon had his luggage.

'I'm afraid Captain de Verriland left early this morning,' came the answer.

'I don't care. I don't give a damn!' Gay told herself fiercely.

But even if the hot tears which she brushed angrily from her eyes were not enough proof, the sinking miserable apprehension that was twisting her heart in cold, cruel hands told her that she did care, desperately, and more than anything in the world, she wanted to see Gordon again.

17

Evelyn stood with her arms elbow-deep in the warm, soapy water. Margaret stood behind her with a dishcloth and felt for the shiny wet plates where Evelyn had stacked them on the draining board. They worked in silence until the washing up was completed, then Evelyn sighed and dropped wearily into a chair.

'That's that!' she said. 'Now I'm for my bed!'

Margaret stood with her back to her sister, her long, thin hands fingering the edge of the last plate.

'Evie, do you mind if I go out?' she asked quietly. 'James said he would take me for a run in the car if I liked. Would you mind?'

'Of course not!' Evelyn said without hesitation. 'You know I'm only too happy that you two should enjoy each other's company. He's a dear, isn't he?'

'You love him — a lot, don't you?' Margaret asked, and listened acutely for her sister's reply.

'I don't know what I'd do without him,' Evelyn said with a little sigh. 'It's funny how dependent I am now on poor James!'

'Dependent?'

'Well, you know what I mean, darling,' Evelyn said vaguely. 'He's such a barrier against life, isn't he? So solid and dependable.'

Margaret heard the slight stress Evelyn gave to her last words, and she remained silent.

'Oh, God,' she prayed. 'Don't let me be weak. Help me to help James. He mustn't let her down.'

But Evelyn knew nothing of the turmoil going on in her little sister's heart. She was too utterly exhausted to notice anything these days. Work, eat, work, sleep — so it went on day after day, and she felt it could never stop. Ration cards, committee meetings, the canteen, billeting, queuing, catering, cooking, washing up. Days and days and days, all running through her hands in the same pattern.

'This is my war work!' she thought. 'And I wanted so much to join one of the services.'

But Fate had decreed otherwise. At the outbreak of war, Margaret had come home and attended school daily. Evelyn had not wanted her to remain in the town where bombs might be dropped no one knew when. Margaret had insisted on this course of training to be a masseuse and Evelyn had given in to her, but insisted on her travelling to and from work by train.

Nanny, old and nearly stone deaf, but otherwise the same dear old Nanny of Evelyn's childhood, promised to look after Margaret, leaving Evelyn free to volunteer for the W.R.E.N.S. But the day before her calling up, dear faithful old Nanny had had another, her last, heart attack, and Evelyn knew that she couldn't leave Margaret alone.

She was bitterly disappointed, but as James said, there was any amount of war work to be done in the village and they needed someone young like her to help on the local committees. In an effort to forget the thwarted plans, Evelyn threw herself into the job and was soon the main prop and stay for any war work that was undertaken.

The billeting authorities were sending down twenty London evacuees. All right, Miss Challis would see to it. The older women wanted to knit comforts for the troops but had no wool. Miss Challis would get them some. The local gun-site crews wanted to put on a Christmas show for the kids. Miss Challis would help them. The airmen billeted in the village wanted a dance. Miss Challis would organize it.

'It's because you are so terribly competent, Evie,' Margaret once said. 'You always do everything in half the time it takes anyone else and you're so thorough and so clever. Whatever you do is a success!'

Yes, most of the things she had undertaken to do had been successful, Evelyn thought as she lit another cigarette and rested her aching back. If she had been less efficient, people would not have continued asking her to do all these things.

Her mind covered each item of the following day's work and she did not hear Margaret leave the room or return carrying her overcoat.

'James should be here in a minute,' she said.

Evelyn started, and was conscious of the taut state of her nerves.

'War strain,' she thought, and to Margaret she said absently:

'Are you off, darling? Have a good time!'

'I won't be late,' Margaret promised. And silently she told herself, 'I mustn't be late. I daren't stay out too long with him . . . alone . . . in his car. Oh, James! James! What are we going to do.'

The sound of the car horn jolted her heart. She felt suffocated by its sudden angry beating and afraid lest Evelyn should hear it.

'That'll be James!' she said unnecessarily. 'Shall I ask him to come in, Evie?'

'What? Oh, no, darling. Not just now. I'm so tired. I'll just pop off to bed. You make some excuse for me, will you?'

'Does she really not want to see him?' Margaret wondered. 'Can she suspect? Does she realize how often she is throwing us together? No, she's tired. That's all. Dog tired!'

A sudden rush of pity engulfed her and she felt her way round to Evelyn's chair and kissed the top of her head.

'Sleep well, Evie!' she said.

'Goodnight, darling. Be good!'

(Be good! No, don't be silly. It's just a phrase. You've got a guilty conscience.)

Margaret moved certainly across the room — round the kitchen table, sink on the left, door knob on the right. Yes, there it was. Two steps down. Flagged path. Twenty paces. The little gate, latch low down. Another step, and then James' arms were round her, holding her against his rough tweed coat.

She knew it was the tweed. He always wore that ever since she had said it smelt so nicely of rain and heather.

'Margaret, darling. Kiss me!'

But she drew away from him, the sound of Evelyn's tired voice strengthening her resolve.

'Please, Jamie,' she said. 'Not — not now!'

His arms dropped to his side and his face looked unhappy, his eyes hurt.

She sensed it, and as she climbed into the car beside him, she felt for his hand and said with a naïve honesty that touched him profoundly:

'It isn't that I don't love you just as much, Jamie. But I can't. Evelyn's my sister.'

'Yes, darling, I know. I'm a brute to even ask you. She's my fiancée, too.'

He drove in baffled silence along the darkened village street and out across the moor. Somewhere along the rough track they were following, he pulled in to the side and switched off the engine and the lights.

'Shouldn't really be using petrol for this!' he said. 'Still, we've hardly done a mile.'

He pulled out a cigarette case and lit two cigarettes, placing one between Margaret's softly parted lips.

'God, you're lovely!' he said. 'Perhaps it's a good thing you can't see yourself, darling. You'd be so conceited!'

She attempted a laugh but it ended in a sob and immediately she was in his arms and he was whispering all sorts of loving, dangerous things to her.

'Don't Margaret! Darling, please don't! I can't bear to see you cry. I feel so guilty. It's all my confounded fault.'

'No!' she said, sitting upright and blowing into the handkerchief he had pushed into her hands. 'No, Jamie, it's nobody's fault.'

'I should never have told you I loved you,' he said bitterly.

'I knew — before you told me!'

'I should never have asked *her* to marry me,' James reproached himself for the hundredth time.

'You couldn't help it!' Margaret. 'Besides, she needed you.'

'Yes, Evelyn did need me. But she doesn't now. Oh, Margie, darling, why won't you let me tell her. I know she would release me. It was part of the agreement that if either of us should want to be free, we would break it off immediately. I promised her I would, and she would understand. Margaret, why not?'

The girl sat clasping and unclasping her hands. (Lovely, healing hands, James had once called them.)

'Because Evie does still need you,' she said quietly. 'She only told me tonight how much she relied on you. How dependent she was on you — how dependable you are.'

'Oh, God!' James whispered brokenly. 'Dependable! Me! I can't even trust myself any longer.'

'Yes, you can!' Margaret said firmly. 'That's one of the reasons I love you. I know I can always rely on you — to do what is right.'

Was it fair to appeal to his chivalry? She was being the stronger of the two. She *must* be. And it was easier for her than for James because she loved Evie so much. She owed everything to her and her sister's happiness was far more important than her own.

'More important even than Jamie's?' she asked herself.

But then that question did not arise. She knew James could never be happy with her, Margaret, knowing they had ruined Evelyn's life; that she was alone, disillusioned; that he had let her down in the same way as that other man whom he had called a cad, a rotter.

'If only you had been older,' James was saying. 'You were such a kid then. Very like Evelyn. I think that's why I thought I was in love with her.'

'Jamie, don't!'

'I must say it!' James answered with a bitter laugh. 'I'm not inhuman, Margaret, and I love you. So much. I just can't bear this much longer — seeing you every day, wanting you, loving you, always having to pretend that there is nothing between us.'

Margaret sat perfectly still. Only her lips trembled.

'Perhaps I'd better go away,' she said. 'You could forget me then . . . '

'Oh, you little fool, do you really think I could forget you?' James broke in harshly. 'Do you think that I could love you less just because you were living so many miles away from me? Distance makes no difference. Margie, would *you* forget *me*?'

She shook her head, knowing that no distance, no time, no single thing on earth could stop her love for this man. He was her reason for living, her entire happiness. There could never and would never be anyone else.

'Well then,' said James triumphantly. 'So what's the good, Margie, if I can never love Evelyn? I can't hope to make her happy.'

'She's happy now!' Margaret persisted.

'Is she?' James asked. 'Sometimes I wonder. Sometimes I think she still misses that other fellow. Heavens, if she felt for him as I am now feeling about you, I am sorry for her! When she was so ill — that time in Germany — I never realized what she must have been going through. No wonder she . . . '

He broke off, knowing that he was about to say something that must never be said — to anyone, and least of all Margaret.

'No wonder she what?'

'Was so ill,' James finished, and fortunately this seemed to satisfy her. 'No, she wouldn't be happy, Margaret.'

'It isn't love she wants from you,' Margaret replied with a curious instinctive perception of the truth. 'It's your companionship, James. You'd be there to take care of her. To make decisions for her. She needs you as a friend.'

'What hope has any marriage without love?' James asked bitterly.

Margaret turned to him and caught his hands.

'You've got to try and make it a success, James,' she said urgently. 'You must try! If not for Evie's sake, then for mine.'

He laughed — a hard bitter laugh without humour.

'You, who profess to love me, are begging me to marry someone else.'

'James!'

Her very tone was a reproach, and he knew he was being unfair. He caught her in his arms and kissed her with rough tenderness on those beautiful, unseeing eyes.

'Oh, my dearest darling!' he whispered against her hair. 'I'm so sorry to be like this. It's beastly of me . . . makes it harder for you. But I love you so much. I can't let you go.'

She did not draw away from him now, but leant her head against the rough, scratchy lapels of his coat.

'I won't leave you, Jamie!' she said softly. 'We will have our work together. We will still see each other every day, knowing that nothing can destroy our friendship.'

'Friendship?'

She winced at his tone, but her voice did not lose its sweetness, its courage.

'Our love, then, since you force me to say it,' she went on. 'I don't think Evelyn needs your love. If she did, we couldn't go on seeing each other every day. But there must be no more of this, Jamie. We must keep everything platonic.'

'Is she too young, too innocent to realize what she is suggesting?' James asked himself. 'Does she realize what torture it is for me, working beside her, wanting her desperately, every minute of the day and night?'

He almost hated Evelyn. He knew it was unjust, unfair to blame her, but he was desperate with lack of sleep, worry, longing, and she was, after all, the barrier that kept him from the girl he loved.

How he loved her! The soft wavy hair, her scent which reminded him of cottage gardens on a summer's night; the dark curling lashes; the little upturned nose and gentle, curved mouth; and most of all he loved her eyes. They were nearly violet, those wide unseeing eyes of hers, yet somehow they seemed to him to reflect the sea, the sky, the wood violets, the lavender, the cornflowers — all that was sweet and beautiful and blue.

Her hands, too, he loved. And her voice, so seldom cross or unkind. And the slim young body with its strong youthful contours. It seemed a tragedy to him that she could not see how beautiful she was.

He put her away from him, unable to bear the strain such thoughts imposed on his nerves, not trusting his self-control.

'Damn it all!' he thought. 'I should have married years ago. But Evelyn put me off time and again. And I've waited faithfully for her, too. There's never been another woman.'

Now the only woman he would ever love, he had ever really desired to possess, must be denied him. He knew it was inevitable, even while he yet fought against it.

Perhaps, when he and Evelyn were married, Margaret would tire of him — want more. It would only be natural. She would have admirers, dozens of them, and perhaps marry some young fellow while he sat back and watched it all happening.

'Jamie!'

With that uncanny sensitiveness of hers which he put down to her blindness, she had followed his train of thought, was saying very tenderly:

'Jamie, there will never be any other man in my life but you. Never, as long as I live.'

He kissed her gently, almost hopelessly. But he was not comforted by her words. She loved him now, but she was young, very young. Everything would be so different when she grew up. It was selfish of him not to want it so.

The same thought was crossing Margaret's mind.

'Jamie's so young,' she was telling

herself. 'He may be a clever doctor, and old in years, but he is still such a little boy at heart. When he marries Evie, it will all be different. He will learn to love her.' How could he fail to love anyone so good, so strong and fine as her darling sister?

A little of her courage failed and she was afraid.

'Jamie!'

He looked at her quickly.

'Please take me home. Now!'

'But darling, we've only been here . . . '

'I know! I know!' she cried. 'But I want to go back. Now! Please, Jamie!'

He shrugged his shoulders and she knew he was hurt. Knew by his silence, by the way he jammed the gears once or twice, muttering under his breath.

'Oh, Jamie! Jamie!' she cried silently. 'I've got to do this. I must hurt you. This is the only way. We mustn't ever come out alone like this again.'

She wished for the first time in her life that she had this sense called sight. People said you could make paper images of yourself. She could not understand how it could be so, not on a flat surface, but Evie had said it *was* so; that you could carry these images with you, knowing they were there. For her, nothing but the person could do — their voice, the feel of their clothes, their smell.

She knew so well what Jamie was like. Rough, curly hair that fell in a lock over his forehead. Smooth cheeks. Long straight nose. Soft, firm lips, and square scratchy chin. She knew his hands, long, slender, surgeon's hands, that smelt like the rest of him of clean antiseptics. She knew how tall he was, head and shoulders above her. She knew the sound of his voice and could recognize his cough, his breathing among a crowd of other people. She knew his footsteps, his laugh, the little trick he had of running his hand down the side of his face when he was thinking. Sometimes she even knew *what* he was thinking. But without him there, in the same room, the same house, she was lost.

'What does he *look* like?' she had once asked Evelyn. 'How do you see him?'

Evelyn had tried to explain.

'Well,' she had said. 'He has sandy, fair hair. Like corn growing in the fields.'

Margaret had understood that. His hair smelt of fresh air and fields.

'And he has blue eyes, the same colour as yours, darling. The same colour as the sky on a windy day when the white clouds are scurrying across it.'

No, she had not understood that. What was the sky? The top of the earth, but not solid like the earth. Coloured air. But eyes *were* solid. Shiny. Wet. How could they resemble air?

Evelyn had given it up.

'Anyway, darling,' she said. 'He's very good-looking.'

Yes, he must be nice to look at. He was so nice to feel, to smell, to hear.

The car pulled up with a jerk, and as James turned towards her, his elbow caught on the horn and it blared out suddenly, breaking the silence of the sleeping village.

'Damn!' said James.

'Oh, I do hope it hasn't woken Evie,' Margaret said. Then, 'Jamie, I'm going now. Don't ask me to stay. We mustn't ever be together like this again. Promise me you won't ask me.'

'All right,' James assented quietly. 'But kiss me before you go. Please, darling.'

She put her arms round his neck and lifted her face for his kiss. The tears were coursing down her cheeks and dropped unheeded on to his coat. This was their goodbye. They would meet again in the morning, he the doctor, she the nurse, but never again — like this.

'Goodnight, my dearest love,' she whispered.

And then she was out of the car, moving as quickly as she could away from him. One step up, the gate, the latch low down, twenty paces along the flagged path, two steps up, the door, handle on the left . . .

James let in the clutch, released the brake and drove fiercely off into the night.

Upstairs in her little room, Evelyn lay wide awake. The horn of James' car had woken her and she had listened for the sound of Margaret's feet on the path. When that sound had not come, she jumped out of bed and went to the window. Was something wrong? But no! She could see two figures, very faintly in the front of the car. She could hear their voices.

The blood rushed to her cheeks, then drained away as a violent fit of shivering overtook her. She stumbled back into bed and lay trembling beneath the bedclothes.

'I must have been mistaken. I must have been mistaken,' she told herself over and over again.

She had seen James take Margaret into his arms. It was such a little way away, near enough to see, also, when the fair head bent over the brown and to know that the only thing he could possibly be doing was kissing her.

'No!' she cried. 'Not Margaret, my sister, and James!'

But she had seen it all so clearly, and she knew without the shadow of a doubt that her eyes had not misled her. It was all horribly true.

18

Evelyn was acutely aware of the sound of Margaret's footsteps approaching her door. Her mind was in a turmoil of indecision but one thing stood out clearly — she could not talk to Margaret now. She must have time to think first — to plan her course of action.

The door opened softly and she heard Margaret's whisper:

'Are you awake, Evie?'

She lay very still, her eyes closed although this deception was hardly necessary since Margaret could not have seen even were they open.

It seemed to the elder girl that her sister stood in the doorway for an incredibly long while. When at last the door closed softly and Margaret's footsteps disappeared along the land-ing, she gave a little sigh of relief and the taut muscles of her body relaxed.

'What am I going to say to her?' she asked herself. 'Is she in love with James? Why hasn't she told me? Why didn't it occur to me before?'

The questions crowded through her distraught mind. Margaret and James! Working together, attracted to each other through their common interests. Her own lack of attention to James. It all made sense! Evelyn couldn't understand why she had not thought of this before. Margaret's unusual pallor, her quietness of late, her many evenings out alone with James. And James — he, too, had changed. No persistent worrying for a date when they could get married; no attempt to kiss her, make love to her.

Poor Margaret! Poor James! But they should have told her. That was what hurt so much — that it had happened behind her back . . .

'Margaret isn't deceitful!' she argued with herself. 'I'm sure she would have told me. Unless . . . ' the thought took shape . . . 'Unless they were afraid of hurting me.'

Now she was sure of her suspicions. Pity for them both engulfed her for a moment, and then, being only human, self-pity overcame her. James and Margaret would get married and she would be alone. She would never get married now; never have children, a husband to take care of her.

'I shall become an embittered old spinster!' she thought, with a hard, painful laugh. 'I've loved two men — and I've lost them both.'

But had she ever loved James? Could her deep affection for him, her respect for him be called love? Was she really heartbroken now she knew she had lost him?

No! She could face life without him, she thought, forcing herself to admit the truth. This feeling was not the same as it had been when she had lost Nicky. But nothing could ever equal that sorrow, that despair, that utter hopelessness.

'But I don't want to be alone!' she cried pitifully. 'I wanted my own home — and children.'

Tears forced their way down her cheeks even while she fought against them. Then she allowed herself to give way to them, knowing she would have to be tearless, strong, diffident when she spoke to Margaret in the morning.

She lay awake till the dawn, thinking what she would say, how she would say it, the way which would be easiest for Margaret whose happiness was more important to her than her own.

Margaret also lay awake. She was desperately concerned, desperately afraid. When she had knocked on Evelyn's door, she had not expected to find her sister awake. But Evelyn was such a light sleeper that it seemed strange she did not stir or turn over when she spoke to her. As she stood in the doorway, listening to her sister's breathing, the suspicion that Evelyn was only pretending to sleep became a conviction. So acute was Margaret's hearing that she could easily distinguish the short, controlled intakes of air from the deep, steady breathing of someone who was unconscious.

Evelyn was only pretending to sleep. Why? she asked herself. There could only be one answer to that question — because she did not wish to speak to her sister — Evelyn who always had a loving word — a warm goodnight embrace awaiting her.

'She must know about James — about us!' she reasoned. 'She may ask me about it. Oh, what am I going to say? How can I pretend that it means nothing when it means so much?'

Deceit would never come easily to this girl who had been honest and truthful all her life. She was by nature so straightforward that any form of acting was impossible for her. Yet she must try! She must succeed for Evie's sake!

When at last she slept, it was to dream fitfully — troubled, muddled dreams about James and Evelyn and herself.

She awoke to the knowledge that Evelyn was standing by her bed. Under the clothes, her hands clasped one another in an effort to steady her nerves. She waited for her sister to speak.

Evelyn sat down on the end of the bed and was glad that Margaret could not see her face. Her sleepless night had left dark circles under her eyes and she was so pale that she looked really ill.

'Margaret, do you love James?'

Now it had come! Margaret sat up in bed, her head turned towards her sister.

'Why, Evie!' she said. 'What a funny question for so early in the morning! Of course I do. Don't you?'

Evelyn had not been prepared for this answer.

'I mean — well, are you *in love* with him?' she faltered.

Margaret gave a little laugh.

'But Evie,' she said. 'I don't understand. James is your fiancé. How could I be in love with him?'

'Love isn't governed by ties!' Evelyn

answered quietly. 'You can love someone who belongs to someone else, although you might never admit it.'

'She's right! So very right!' Margaret was thinking. But aloud she said:

'Well, I suppose you can, Evie! But how could I be in love with James? He's years older than I am. I look on him as an elder brother.'

'Is she speaking the truth?' Evelyn wondered. 'Is she pretending for my sake?' She had to know the truth.

'Margaret, I saw you and James last night . . . in the car. I saw him kissing you!'

'This is worse than I thought it would be,' Margaret told herself. She must be careful — must not spoil it now!

'James always kisses me goodnight,' she said lightly. 'You don't mind, do you, Evie?'

Evelyn turned to her impulsively.

'No, of course not, if it's like that. But I thought . . . I thought . . . ' She could not go on.

'Evie, you didn't think I was trying to steal James's affections from you? Why, it's ridiculous. James still thinks of me as a little girl!'

At last Evelyn was convinced. She flung her arms around the girl's trembling body and hugged her closely, tears and laughter flowing fast one upon the other.

'Oh, Margaret, darling,' she cried. 'It was beastly of me, I know, but I *did* think so. At least, not that you were trying to steal James from me, but that you loved each other and did not want to tell me for fear of hurting me. But I should have known better.'

'How near she is to the truth!' Margaret thought. 'If I hadn't suspected she knew — if I hadn't been to her room last night, I could never have convinced her.'

'You would have told me if there had been anything like that, wouldn't you, darling?' Evelyn was saying.

'Of course I would, Evie!' Margaret lied, hating herself or the necessity. 'We always share secrets, don't we?'

'Always!' said Evelyn with a little sigh of contentment.

'Evelyn, there's something I often wanted to ask you, but of course you don't have to tell me if you don't want to.'

'What is that, darling?'

'It's about that other man!'

She felt Evelyn's body stiffening, but she went on.

'You were in love with him, weren't you?'

'Yes, I was!' Evelyn spoke quietly, her voice carefully controlled.

'Then why didn't you marry him? Wasn't he in love with you?'

'Not sufficiently in love to want to marry me!' Evelyn answered, unable to keep the bitterness from her voice.

'If — if he came back, would you still want to marry James?'

Evelyn hesitated. Only for a fraction of a second but time enough to ask herself: 'Would I?' and to know the answer was in the negative. Then she said lightly:

'Well, darling, I don't know! It was all

such a long time ago, and besides, the question would never arise because it isn't a bit likely he will come back. If he wanted to marry me, he could have done so six years ago.'

'I'm so sorry, Evie!'

Evelyn rose from the bed, frightened of the tears which were threatening her tired eyes, weakening her control.

'There's nothing to be sorry about,' she said lightly. 'I'm perfectly content with my James!'

She did not see the swift stab of pain her words had caused Margaret.

'I'll go and get breakfast!' she went on. 'Would you like yours in bed for a treat, darling?'

Margaret jumped out of bed and flung her arms impulsively round her sister's thin shoulders.

'You're much too nice to me!' she cried. 'I think you're the most wonderful sister one could ever have!'

'What nonsense!' Evelyn countered, as she hugged the girl to her.

'It's true!' cried Margaret.

'Well for that matter, the same applies to you,' Evelyn returned affectionately. 'Now don't catch cold, darling. I'll turn on the bath for you.'

As Evelyn closed the door behind her, Margaret stood perfectly still, conscious of the cold floorboards against her bare feet, feeling the fresh morning air blowing her thin silk pyjamas about her body.

'Oh, Jamie!' she whispered. 'I've done it. I have succeeded. And now we must never give her reason to suspect again. But Jamie, it's going to be hard. Because I love you so!'

★　★　★

Two days later, Evelyn asked Margaret if she could take a day off from her work with James.

'I hate to have to ask you, darling,' she said. 'But I've got to go to the Food Office this morning and I made another appointment yesterday, forgetting today was Wednesday. There just isn't anyone else available.'

'What is it you want me to do, Evie?'

'Some troops near here want to use our village hall for a dance and I thought you could fix things up for me. The adjutant rang up yesterday and said the officer commanding was arranging things himself and wanted to meet me this morning.'

'I'd love to go, Evie,' Margaret said, welcoming this opportunity gladly. These last few days had been so difficult, working with James, knowing she mustn't touch him, mustn't let him kiss her; both of them struggling so hard to keep to their bargain.

'But do you think I can manage?' she asked doubtfully. 'I mean, won't the officer commanding expect someone older, more efficient?'

'Well, he might expect someone older,' Evelyn answered with a smile. 'But I can't have you trailing round a town by yourself. I shall *have* to go to the Food Office, so you will have to do this for me. Anyway, darling, you will be a nice surprise for him. I don't suppose he will have met such a pretty Woman's Voluntary Service worker for a long time!'

Margaret smiled with her.

'What time did you say you'd meet him?' she asked.

'Ten-thirty at the village hall,' Evelyn replied. 'You know all the details, don't you? Prices and so on?'

Margaret nodded her head.

'See you lunchtime then, darling. Now I must rush!' And she hurried away to catch the morning bus into town.

Margaret had no difficulty finding her way to the village hall. She had spent so many years in this place that she knew every inch of it as well as she knew their own cottage. Her blindness was no handicap to her here.

She arrived punctually at ten-thirty having first telephoned James to say she would not be arriving until after lunch. She was still thinking about him when she heard a car draw up, the driver opening the door for the officer and the click of his heels which must have meant a salute.

'I won't be long,' the officer said, and she heard his footsteps approaching. Then they faltered, stopped just a little way in front of her, near enough to hear his muttered exclamation.

'No! Damn it! It can't be!'

'Are you the Commanding Officer?' Margaret asked, holding out her hand.

She felt the strong grip of his fingers, realized a few seconds later that he had not freed her hand.

'Excuse me,' he said, stumbling over his words. 'I must apologize — but you are so very like . . . so like someone I used to know. Only the eyes are different!'

'I'm blind, you know!' Margaret said softly, not wishing to embarrass him. She was so used to explaining; so used to the awkward silence that followed and the inevitable expressions of sympathy. But this time, the man beside her did not offer any such words.

'Then you — you *must* be Margaret!' he said.

'Why, yes! That's right!' the girl said, his voice suddenly sounding familiar to her. 'I seem to know you, too. But I can't remember . . . '

'I'm Major March,' the man broke in eagerly. 'Nicholas March. I used to know you when you were a little girl. We went on a picnic together once. Do you remember? You said I looked like a goat. At least you said the God Pan, but you meant a goat, didn't you?'

His voice was gay, happily reminiscent, boyishly eager. But she did not answer him.

'Nicholas March!' she said slowly.

He did not notice the tone of her voice.

'Tell me,' he said, still holding her hand in a firm unconscious grip. 'How is your mother?'

'My mother?'

'Yes, Evelyn! How is she? Is she here with you? In this village?'

He could not restrain the flood of

questions, disguise the eagerness with which he awaited her answer.

'My mother died soon after I was born,' Margaret said coldly. 'Evelyn is my sister. Have you forgotten?'

Her voice was scornful, remembering that this was the man who had thought himself too good for Evelyn.

Nicholas March was as white as a ghost and Margaret could feel his hands trembling. He loosened his grasp and said in a hard, controlled voice:

'Can we go indoors — somewhere alone? I must speak to you.'

Margaret unlocked the doors of the village hall and he followed her inside. The chairs were stacked in twos, one upon the other, round the wall. The stage was bare except for one curtain which hung in an absurd loop of tattered velvet.

Nicky guided her across the room and placed two chairs upright for them to sit in. As he was doing this, his mind was working furiously.

Suppose Evelyn had told this child

they were sisters? Had thought it best to leave her ignorant of her Italian father? He must find out somehow — without giving the show away.

'Margaret,' he said carefully. 'Is Evelyn married?'

'Not yet!' the girl answered quietly. 'She is engaged to marry Doctor Cathy.'

This news stunned him for a moment.

'Then — then she is free to marry if she wishes?'

There was surprise in Margaret's voice as she said:

'Well, of course!'

'Does she love this doctor?'

Margaret turned on him, her usual gentleness stirred into anger.

'Is that any business of yours?'

'Yes!' said Nicholas March without hesitation. 'You see, I'm in love with her myself. Always have been.'

'You . . . you . . . I don't understand. Of course I knew — that is, Evelyn told me that at one time you were in love with each other. But that you — you wouldn't marry her.'

'Good God!' the exclamation was forced from him. '*Wouldn't* marry her! Couldn't, you mean.'

'Why not?'

'She was already married!' Nicky said bitterly, forgetting his resolve to keep this from Evelyn's sister.

'Already married?' Margaret echoed. 'But that's absurd. Evie's never married anyone in her life. Did she tell you that herself?'

'Well, now I come to think of it, she didn't!' Nicholas March said, suspicion growing with every word. 'It was your other sister . . . '

'Gay?'

'Yes, Gay! She told me Evelyn had asked her to inform me she didn't wish to see me again because she was already married.'

'But that's not true. Evelyn told me only the other day that you — you hadn't loved her enough to want to marry her. I *know* she wouldn't have lied to me.'

'Somehow I think you're right,' Nicky said with a hard laugh. 'And I'm going to find out. Something makes me think Miss Gay Challis has been making a fool of me. If she has, I'll . . .'

'Please, Major March!'

He turned to face her and she sensed his change of attitude even before he spoke.

'I'm sorry, my dear,' he said gently. 'But you see, I've never loved anyone but Evelyn. Never could! And if we were parted through some silly prank of your sister's, I'll beat the daylight out of her. It's six years since I saw Evelyn — six long years . . . But I can't expect you to understand. You've never been in love.'

She gave a short, bitter laugh that drew his attention.

'Oh, but I do understand — perfectly,' she said. 'You see, I too have been parted from the person I love.'

He was immediately contrite, instantly sympathetic.

'I'm so sorry, Margaret,' he said gently. 'I never realized you were so — so grown up. You were only a little girl when I last saw you. You have grown very beautiful — exactly like — like your sister!'

'Am I really like her?' Margaret asked eagerly. 'That's what James said!'

'James?'

She hesitated, but only for a moment. The longing to confide in someone had been so acute, and now this strange man, who was not really a stranger, had confided in her. Why not?

'James is Evelyn's fiancé — Doctor Cathy.'

'Is he the man you're in love with?'

He saw the tell-tale colour mount her cheeks as she nodded her head.

'But you must never tell a soul!' she cried. 'You'll promise me, won't you? If Evelyn ever found out . . .'

'Would she mind so much?'

His tone was very bitter and she was aware that she had hurt him.

'I don't know!' she answered truthfully. 'Sometimes I think she still loves you!'

She heard his quick intake of breath.

'But the other night, when she had reason to suspect . . . about James and me . . . she was so upset. Oh, I don't know. I don't really believe she loves him — not as I do. But she needs him.'

His heart filled with hope. It was as if that heart had been a dark, closed room and this girl had suddenly drawn the curtains and let in a flood of sunshine.

'Margaret,' he said, 'do you realize what this is all going to mean? I must find out if Gay was ly . . . was fooling me. I must find that out first. Then I shall see Evelyn and ask her to marry me. If . . . if she still cares, then you and your James will have nothing further to keep you apart.'

'Oh!'

He saw her face light up and knew that her heart, too, must be filled with that same radiance of hope.

'Tell me, Margaret!' he said quietly. 'Where can I find Gay?'

'Well, she may be at the camp!' Margaret said. 'But I think she told

Evie in a letter yesterday . . . yes, that's right. She's going to her flat in town for a few days' sick leave. That's in Chelsea. Major March . . . '

'Yes?'

'Don't — don't be too hard on her. If she was, well, if she wasn't speaking the truth. She couldn't have realized what she was doing. Gay is different from most people. She doesn't mean to do wrong.'

'And you're so like Evelyn it just isn't true,' said Nicky with a rough tenderness. 'I think you would both allow that sister of yours to get away with murder! Now let's get this wretched business of the hall finished. Then I can go to London.'

'Will you go right away? This afternoon?'

He nodded his head.

'Yes!' he said. 'And in the meantime, Margaret, not a word to Evelyn. I want to surprise her — find out how she really feels. She might pretend she doesn't care because she's afraid of hurting James, or something. One never knows with you two girls. You're so confoundedly good! But I shall know — by her face, her eyes, her voice, when I just walk in unexpectedly.'

'I won't say a word!' Margaret assented.

They stood up and said together:

'Well, about the hall . . . '

They broke off laughing, then Nicky caught her in his arms and gave her a hug that would have shaken the army driver to the core had he been there to witness it.

'Oh, Margaret!' he said. 'It must have been Fate that sent you here today. And I so nearly let my adjutant come this morning!'

'Yes!' said the girl simply. 'I think it was Fate. And — oh, Major March, I do *hope* it will all turn out right!'

'So do I!' said Nicky fervently.

And he meant it with his whole heart.

19

Nicholas March rang the bell outside Gay's flat three times before the door was opened.

'Is Miss Gay Challis . . . ' he began, but his voice stopped short.

It was unbelievable but true enough that the pale, unhappy-looking girl standing facing him, staring at him from red-rimmed eyes, was really Gay. She was scarcely recognizable as the bright, pretty girl he had seen in that fashionable restaurant only two months back.

'Oh! So it's you!' she said, in a dull lifeless voice.

'Yes! I . . . could I come in for a minute or aren't you well enough?'

Although she obviously enough was feeling ill, she said with a shrug of her shoulders:

'Oh, what the hell! You might as well

come in and get it over!'

How he disliked women who swore, he thought as he followed her through the little hall into the sitting-room. He was feeling distinctly uneasy. All the way up in the train he had been thinking of the things he would say to her; the thrashing he would give her (and with his own hands, too!) when he had forced the truth from her. Now everything would be different. She wasn't well. She wasn't happy either. He had expected to meet the 'bright young thing' he had seen in the restaurant — not this pale, wretched-looking girl in an untidy pair of navy blue slacks and equally disreputable red sweater.

'Well, what is it?' Gay asked in that same dull tone.

He drew out his cigarette-case, playing for time.

'Like one?' he asked, keeping his voice casual.

She shook her head and he lit one for himself, wondering how he could start this interview. In the end, it was Gay who brought up the subject first.

'I suppose it's about Evelyn,' she said.

(After all, what did it matter now? What did anything matter?)

'Yes, it is!' answered Nicky, all the old anger and determination returning. 'I want the truth, Gay, and God help you if you don't tell me. I want a straight answer to my questions, please.'

'O.K. Shoot!' she said, her eyebrows raised in a supercilious curve which irritated him to the pitch of wanting to hit her. And it wasn't often he felt that way about a woman.

'Is Evelyn married, or isn't she?' he asked.

Again that casual shrug of her shoulders.

'Not that I know of,' she answered him.

He was sufficiently annoyed now to lean forward and catch hold of her arm in a brutally strong grip. But Gay did not even appear to notice it.

413

'Apparently I don't make myself clear,' Nicky said, his voice dangerously quiet. 'Suppose I put it this way — *was she ever married?*'

She flashed back at him defiantly:

'No, she wasn't!'

So he was right! Gay had been lying! His grip tightened unconsciously and a little afraid of him now, she tried to free herself.

'Let me go, damn you!' she cried fiercely.

'Not until you have explained first!' Nicky replied coolly. 'I want the truth, mind.'

'Well, let me go and I'll tell you!'

He released her arm, a little ashamed of himself when he saw the red marks of his fingers on her bare flesh. She walked over to the window and he sat watching her, unable to make up his mind whether he was more sorry for her than angry with her. She looked so young, so forlorn and helpless now that the defiance had gone out of her.

'I mustn't weaken!' he told himself.

'Remember what she has done to you and Evelyn.' Aloud he said:

'Well, Gay, why did you lie to me?'

'I didn't think it made all that difference to you — or to Evelyn,' the girl answered quietly.

'Then it was just spite? Because you didn't want your sister to have a boyfriend of her own?'

She flared up at him, her eyes bright and angry.

'Oh, don't be so damn silly!' she said. 'Do you suppose I was jealous of her? What could it matter to me how many boyfriends Evie had?'

'No, you've always been so self-centred I don't suppose it *did* matter to you,' Nicky said sarcastically. 'So why the lies, Gay? What could it profit you to break things up between Evelyn and myself? You must have had some reason.'

She faced him, her cheeks flushed, almost feverish in colour.

'Because I wanted to marry Gordon de Verriland,' she retorted. 'Because I found out you knew him and because I was so afraid you'd tell Gordon about Margaret! Now are you satisfied?'

He ignored her last question.

'About Margaret?' he repeated. 'I don't understand!'

'No, I don't suppose you do!' Gay said bitterly. 'But you once knew Gordon, didn't you?'

'Yes! But why should that . . . '

'Well, perhaps you also knew Gordon's mother,' she broke in. 'She's a . . . '

'There's no need to swear,' Nicky said quickly.

'Well, she is anyway! And if she had ever thought her wonderful son and heir was intending to marry a girl with a family like mine, she would have put that revolting de Verriland foot down. Firmly, too! And yours truly would have been out on her ear.'

'What's the matter with your family, Gay?'

She looked at him for a moment, weighing up his words. Then she gave a short, bitter laugh.

'It's really rather funny!' she said. 'I took all that trouble to keep you away from Gordon and I don't believe you even know about the black sheep in the family tree.'

'I certainly don't,' Nicky said, suddenly remembering a certain conversation he had had with his mother the night he first met Evelyn.

'I never liked Lionel Challis' wife,' she had said. 'Hard, selfish woman . . . killed in a car crash while you were studying in Munich.'

Himself, asking:

'Wasn't there some scandal attached?'

And his mother's reply:

'They thought she had been drinking . . . But it was all hushed up . . . '

Strange how well he could remember that talk after all these years! But then he could remember most things that had to do with Evelyn.

'I think, if you will tell me, that I have a right to know — about this black sheep,' he said to Gay.

'Why not?' she answered, shrugging her shoulders again — a gesture which was fast becoming a habit. 'My revered mother was a drunkard! Isn't that a charming background for a girl who wants to marry into the aristocracy?'

He ignored her sarcasm, remaining silent because he could think of nothing appropriate to say.

'*Surely* you heard about her,' Gay went on in that same voice.

'Or if you didn't, surely you wondered somewhere up in that Sherlock Holmes brain of yours why dear sister Margaret was born blind?'

Again he did not speak. He was knocked backwards by this girl's words; trying to sort things out in his mind and piece them together.

'Since you don't know, I'll tell you,' Gay went on, her voice coaxing and gentle as if she were talking to a backward child. 'Dear sister Margaret was born blind because dear Mamma did not want her and did everything she could to injure herself (and of course the baby) during her confinement. Believe me, Major March, I ought to know. I had the misfortune to be mother's little favourite during those months and I shared her room. So I ought to know, don't you agree?'

She was watching his face, seeing the effect her words had on him — even enjoying the scene and actress enough to appreciate that she held the stage.

'So that shocks you, does it?' she went on. 'Well, listen to this! After Margaret was born — like she is — Mother tried to drown her conscience in drink. That's how she killed herself. She probably saw two trees instead of one and missed the wrong one . . . '

Her voice had been rising steadily and now she laughed, a high-pitched laugh with a sob in it, a hysterical note that roused Nicky from his thoughts.

'Stop that!' he said, using his parade-ground voice.

But Gay was past hearing him, past anything but the desire to laugh and laugh and cry at the same time.

Nicky stood up and slapped her on the face; saw her stare at him in surprise as the laugh broke off, then sink into the armchair and bury her face in her hands.

'Oh, God!' she whispered, sobbing quietly now. 'Oh, God! Oh, God!'

He had been prepared for tears, expecting Gay to use this form of appeal if she had to. But he had not been prepared for these deep, rasping sobs that shook her whole body.

Like all men, he was embarrassed seeing a woman cry, and he stood awkwardly in the centre of the room, watching her. It felt indecent, almost callous standing there, staring at her, so he said:

'Look here, Gay, don't cry like that! I never realized . . . I mean, I never knew . . . about your family, that is. I say, please don't cry!'

She recovered her self-control and blew noisily into the handkerchief he held out to her. Her eyes were swollen with weeping and her nose red and shiny, but for once she didn't care what she looked like.

'Throw me a cigarette!' she said, her voice still husky from the tears.

He produced his case, lit her cigarette and one for himself.

'Sorry!' she said, attempting a smile. 'Damn silly of me!'

'That's all right!' Nicky said awkwardly.

'Of course, I never realized you and Evelyn were really in love,' Gay said suddenly. 'You'd only just met and I didn't think Evelyn would mind until after I'd — I'd told you that story. She was awfully cut up but I thought she'd get over it. She never spoke about you, and there was the doctor chap. I suppose I never stopped to think about it very seriously. I was so afraid you would tell Gordon. He didn't know about Margaret then. In fact he didn't know she was blind until — the other day.'

'So you did marry him?'

'Didn't you know? Still, it didn't do me much good. I seem to have mucked up four lives, including my own!'

'You aren't happy with him?'

He saw her hands clench, the knuckles showing white against the brown skin.

'We're separated!' she said shortly. 'Except when Gordon turns up suddenly to demand his conjugal rights. Now I'm going to have a baby. Isn't that funny?'

'Good lord!' Nicky exclaimed boyishly. 'Are you sure?'

'Yes!' she said, and added with a half-smile: 'The M.O. says I have all the symptoms! I am on indefinite sick leave until my discharge comes through. Flying isn't supposed to be good for the dear little mite!'

'Does — does de Verriland know?'

She shook her head, her eyes darkening into deep, indecipherable pools.

'He came to see me when he was on embarkation leave. That was over two months ago and I haven't heard or seen of him since.'

Something in her wistful tone struck pity in his heart.

'You're still in love with him?'

She bit her lips and nodded her fair head.

'Well, you never know,' he said, trying to comfort her. 'If he's on this invasion racket, you probably won't get news for a bit.'

'I don't think he'll write,' Gay said, almost to herself. 'I — I was a bit of a pig, really. He . . . he doesn't know I care.'

'What about the baby?'

'Oh, well that's something, I suppose. But can't see myself as a mother, can you?'

'Do her all the good in the world,' Nicky thought. But aloud he said:

'Does Evelyn know?'

'Nope!'

'Then you must tell her. She'll want to look after you. You must go down there and stay with her.'

'I don't want her pity!' Gay cried fiercely. 'I can look after myself.'

'Gay, Evelyn loves you. She's got more faith in you than anyone else on earth will ever have from what I remember.'

'Well, she won't give two twopenny damns about me when she hears about . . . about you . . . and what I did!'

Nicky leant across to her and said in a low, urgent voice:

'Look, Gay, Evelyn doesn't know yet! I haven't even been to see her yet. I had to find out first what had happened. I met Margaret by accident in the village where we are stationed and that's how I heard that Evelyn wasn't married. But listen, Gay, Evelyn has always believed in you. Even when you were the spoilt pampered girl straight out of school that I once knew, she still thought you were marvellous. Used to tell me about you. I think it would break her heart if she ever found out — the truth.'

'You mean you won't tell her?'

'That depends on you!' Nicky said.

'We can easily think up some story —
say Gordon told you I was married and
you thought it the kindest way of fixing
things for her. Evelyn will believe us.
She never could see any wrong in
anyone.'

'And what do you get out of this?'

'Your promise to go down to her —
to look after her for me while I am
abroad. And to look after yourself and
that baby. If Evelyn — will marry me,
that little blighter is going to be my
nephew.'

'Or niece,' Gay said with a smile that
held a hint of tears in it. 'Honestly, I
can't think why you should be so
decent to me . . . when I'm responsible
for keeping you and Evie apart all these
years.'

'Damned if I know the reason
myself,' Nicky thought. Unless it was
because Gay was Evelyn's sister — even
looked a little like her at times. And he
felt sorry for her, too. Obviously her
mother's influence had a bad effect and
she had only been a kid when she

separated him from Evelyn.

'Never realized the harm she was doing us both,' he thought. 'When are you going to see Evelyn?' Gay was asking him.

'I'm going back now!'

Suddenly excitement took hold of him — anticipation tinged with apprehension. Suppose Evelyn did not care. Suppose after all this, she was in love with that doctor . . .

'I think you had better come back with me,' he told Gay suddenly. 'Might as well have the whole bang shoot of us there while we're about it.'

'I must say I'd rather like to be out of town while these odd bombs are floating about,' Gay said. 'I don't feel too hot, either.'

'Then that's arranged,' Nicky said. 'I'll give you an hour or so to pack, then I'll call back for you in a taxi. We can catch that five-something train. I've got one or two things to do while I'm in London. Can you manage your packing by yourself?'

Gay laughed, that sudden spontaneous natural laugh which had endeared her to Gordon.

'I may be a prospective mother,' she said, 'but I'm not an invalid — yet!'

And she showed him to the door.

There were four things Nicky wanted to do. Three for himself and one for Gay. He decided to tackle Gay's problem first.

A taxi took him to the club which he knew de Verriland used to frequent. In fact he had had lunch with him there once, ages ago. A hasty word and a tip to the hall porter reassured him that Gordon was still a member, and procured for him the forwarding address he had left in case of odd letters.

'A.P.O. number!' he thought, and automatically, 'That means he's on this invasion racket, I expect.'

Nevertheless he despatched a telegram, sending it priority, saying:

'*Gay expecting son and heir. Address*

*Cherrytree Cottage, Inglewhite, Sussex.
Come if possible.'*

The signature he omitted.

'If de Verriland is still in this country, he'll turn up,' Nicky told himself confidently. 'So that's that!'

Another taxi took him to Hawkes in Walton Street where he purchased a beautiful ruby, set in diamonds, and a plain gold wedding ring. His last trip took him to Doctors' Commons where he put in an application to the Archbishop of Canterbury for a special wedding licence.

'I'm stark staring crazy!' he told himself. 'Supposing she won't have me!'

But something deep down in his heart was trying to reassure him that his purchases — and his hopes — would not be in vain.

'If she still loves me,' he thought, 'these last six years won't matter. Nothing will matter if she will only marry me!'

Afterwards, soon probably, there was the war to fight and win. But he'd come through it. He'd come through anything if he knew Evelyn was waiting for him.

'Funny how this afternoon has turned out,' he meditated. 'Never thought I would be feeling sorry for Gay. But she's not really bad. Only thoughtless. Hope de Verriland turns up. Didn't much care for him, if I remember right, but this war may have changed him. It's changed most of us, come to think of it.'

And automatically followed the thought: 'Will *she* have changed?'

His mind wandered back to the last time he had seen her. In that wretched little ski-hut, it had been.

'Wonder if Hans — or was the boy Peter?' he couldn't remember now — 'is fighting for the Huns! The whole family was very anti-Nazi. At least, when I last knew them. One couldn't be sure, now. Rotten race. Always fighting.'

But he could not believe those simple Bavarian peasants were pro-Hitler.

'Mustn't think like that!' he told himself firmly. 'The only good German is a dead one!'

He could remember his father saying that when he was still a kid at prep school — just before the Pater died. Funny to think they were fighting the same war all over again! Only it wasn't so funny, really. Not the way the Hun fought it — bombing innocent children and helpless civilians, and torturing prisoners . . .

A quick glance at his watch told him it was time to return for Gay. He was a bit late, actually.

'I've got a train to catch,' he told the driver of his taxi. 'So hurry if you can, will you?'

'There's-a-war-on, y'know!' grumbled the driver.

'Don't I know it!' Nicky thought with a smile. But he didn't mind. Only one thing could matter to him now.

'If only she still cares!' he thought for

the hundredth time.

Then the taxi stopped and Gay was waiting for him in the hall, saying:

'I was beginning to get anxious. Decided you must have thought better of your generosity!'

'What nonsense!' he said as he helped the driver with the luggage.

Excitement was mounting inside him again and he felt restless, nervous, happy, afraid.

'Hurry!' he told the driver. 'The train goes in twenty minutes.'

'Always in a hurry!' mumbled the old man as he drove his ramshackle old taxi towards the station. 'Hurry to your own funeral, you would!'

But Nicky could not be annoyed. Only anxious and nervous and happy and afraid.

'I'll know soon,' he told himself. 'Another hour and I shall see her. Oh, Evelyn, Evelyn, I don't think I can bear it if you don't still care.'

And all the way down in the train his fingers played nervously with the little square boxes in his coat pocket.

'You're much too old for this sort of behaviour,' he reproached himself. 'You're not in your twenties now!'

But couldn't he — at thirty-four — give her a finer, truer and deeper love that had grown from these six interminable years of separation?

'Yes!' he thought. 'Yes! If only she still cares!'

20

It was past six-thirty and Evelyn was preparing the vegetables for their evening meal. Evelyn always had sandwiches and coffee at the canteen at midday and Margaret had a light lunch with James, so they had their big meal at night.

Margaret was laying the table, conscious of the light scratching of Evelyn's knife on the potatoes, but not really hearing it. She was waiting for the sound of a car and footsteps on the flagged path.

For once she was not listening for Jamie, but for another man. For Nicholas March.

'Surely he should be back by now?' she thought. 'Unless something has gone wrong.'

She asked Evelyn the time and her sister looked up in surprise.

'What is the matter with you tonight, darling?' she said. 'That's the third time you've asked the same question in about half an hour!'

'Oh, I just wondered!' Margaret said nervously.

'Well, it's nearly twenty minutes to seven,' Evelyn stated, still wondering about Margaret. She seemed a bundle of nerves this evening. One plate had been broken and a spoon dropped as well, and Margaret was usually so careful.

She pushed her hair from her eyes, straightened the printed overall and resumed her work. For a few minutes there was no sound but the scratching of her knife and the steady tick-tick of the kitchen alarm clock.

Suddenly Margaret rushed to the door and opened it.

'There's a car coming,' she called over her shoulder.

A full minute later, Evelyn heard it and Margaret was hurrying down the flagged path to the gate.

'Perhaps she is expecting someone,' Evelyn thought. 'She has been so on edge. Maybe . . . James!' But she pushed the thought quickly from her. Ever since that night when she had suspected so unjustly that there was something between the two, Margaret had shown no interest in James at all. 'No, it must be someone else,' she told herself.

Then she heard Gay's voice.

'Well, Margaret! How's things?'

'Gay!' Margaret was shouting. 'Oh, it *is* nice to see you. Have you come to stay?'

'If Evie will put up with me,' Gay answered.

'Put up with you!' Evelyn cried as she hurried to the door to welcome her. 'Why, Gay! What a lovely surprise!'

Gay bent and kissed Evelyn's cheek, a demonstration of affection that was so unexpected coming from Gay that Evelyn was as much surprised as she was pleased.

'You can have the spare room,' she

said, drawing Gay inside. 'I'll take you upstairs . . . '

'It's all right, I can find my way up,' Gay broke in, and then casually:

'Oh, by the way, I brought an old friend down with me. When he comes in with the luggage, perhaps you will give him a drink?'

'Of course,' Evelyn answered. 'Will he be staying to supper?'

'I don't know,' Gay returned quietly. 'It's up to you!'

And she hurried away leaving Evelyn staring after her in amazement. Margaret came running in, carrying a small suitcase, but before Evelyn could speak, she was up the stairs, calling to Gay to wait for her.

'What *is* going on?' she said aloud. There was something mysterious afoot, she was certain. Margaret's nerves, Gay's unexpected arrival . . . her mysterious answer, 'It's up to you!'

As she went to the door, she saw a tall, dark man in the uniform of an army major come striding down the path towards her. For one breathless second, she thought it was Nicky. It was so like him — so incredibly like him that all the strength seemed to leave her legs.

He dropped the suitcases and only two steps separated them, leaving Evelyn no longer in doubt.

'Nicky!' she whispered and unknowingly she reached out her hands to him in an instinctive welcome. That automatic gesture answered all the uncertainty in Nicky's mind. He cleared the steps in one bound and she was in his arms, held so tightly that they were almost one.

'Evelyn!' he said, 'Evelyn, my darling girl!'

She was half laughing, half crying as he released her. All she could say was:

'Nicky, Nicky, is it really you?'

He gathered her into his arms again, crushing her against him so that the buttons of his tunic pressed against her soft flesh. But she was not conscious of any pain. Very gently he lifted the soft brown head from his shoulder and turned the tear-wet face towards him.

'Evelyn, you're more beautiful than ever,' he said huskily, and his lips came down to hers, relentless, demanding, with all the passion of his love for her consuming them both in that swift embrace.

'I love you!' he said against her mouth. 'I love you, Evelyn! Will you be my wife?'

His words brought her back with a jolt to the present. She was suddenly aware of the fact that they were standing in full view of the village, behaving like — like a pair of young lovers.

She drew him inside and closed the door, but she did not allow him to take her in his arms again.

She saw a shadow of fear cross his eyes.

'What is it, Evelyn?' he asked her. 'Tell me, please!'

'Nicky, I'm engaged to be married,' she said slowly. 'I — I can't let him down!'

Nicky breathed a sigh of relief.

'Let's sit down, shall we?' he said quietly. 'There are several things I should have told you about before — before asking you to marry me. I'll start at the beginning, shall I?'

She nodded her head, and listened without speaking while he told her of his conversation with Gay over the telephone seven years ago. He told her that Gay had been misinformed that he, Nicky, was married, and had thought her way the kindest way of fixing things for Evelyn.

'It certainly fixed things for me, too!' Nicky said with a short laugh. 'When I heard you had a husband and a child, I cut out right away. I had wanted to marry you and it came as a dreadful shock to me to know that you had only been fooling around with me. I thought you were different. Evelyn, I know now how silly I was ever to believe Gay's story. If only I had stopped to think I should have *known* it couldn't be true. You were so obviously not an experienced young married woman, not the type to lead a man up the garden path. But I was so hurt, so shocked, that I lost my head. I just ran as fast as I could and as far as I could, hoping I would never see you again. But Fate brought us together again in Germany.'

'It's incredible, unbelievable,' Evelyn said, feeling dazed and stunned by this revelation. 'I thought you had found out . . . about the family . . . that you didn't love me enough to want to marry into that strain . . . '

'Oh, Evelyn, my darling!' he said, holding her hand tightly in his own. 'Do you think that *that* would have made any difference? Gay has told me the whole story. You don't think it makes any difference now, do you?'

She met his gaze, and her eyes softened into a smile.

'I should have had more confidence in you,' she said gently. 'If only we'd talked it over, Nicky, up there in the ski-hut. You wanted to, I know, but I was afraid to let you. I was afraid of hearing you tell me in your own voice, that you couldn't go through with it. When you left me that night, I wanted to die.'

'I did not want to go on living either,' Nicky said quietly. 'I have only been existing all these years, Evelyn. Not really living. Once, not very long ago, I saw Gay in a restaurant in London. I wanted to ask her about you — thinking perhaps that this 'husband' of yours might have been killed. But I decided you would have found some way of letting me know — if you had cared. I did not dare to hope you could still be caring for me after all this while. I felt sure you would have married again, for your child's sake, if not for your own.'

'My child!' Evelyn echoed. 'I can't believe it. It's incredible.'

'Yes, to you!' Nicky said. 'But to me it made sense. Margaret is so like you and you were so very, very fond of her. It was more of a mother's protection you gave her than a sister's affection.

But I see now that it was only natural — there being such a difference in your ages and Margaret having no mother. It was through Margaret that I found out the truth. When I met her in the village to discuss the hall for our troops' dance, I recognized her immediately, and I asked after her mother. A word or two and I knew for a certainty that Gay must have made up the whole ghastly story. I went to see her right away to confirm my suspicions and of course she was terribly cut up when she realized what she had done.'

'Oh, but it wasn't her fault,' Evelyn broke in. 'She thought she was doing the best thing for me. We mustn't blame her at all.'

'No, darling!' said Nicky very, very tenderly.

'Then . . . then you're not married and . . . and nor am I!' Evelyn said shyly, a delicate colour stealing into her cheeks.

Nicky was already on his feet, his

arms lifting her from her chair, drawing her close to him again.

'I hope we will both be married — very soon,' he said breathlessly. 'Will you be my wife, Evelyn?'

He thought he had never seen anything more beautiful than the eyes which looked into his. The shining radiance in them blinded him so that for a moment he could see nothing, hear nothing but the loud, hard beating of his heart.

Then he felt her lips pressing softly against his mouth and heard her voice saying:

'There has never been anyone else but you, Nicky! But what am I going to do about James? Nicky, I owe my life to him. When I had pneumonia after you left me, he saved my life. He's been so good to me, so kind and understanding. Nicky, what am I going to do?'

'I think I can settle that problem for you, Evie,' said a quiet voice from the stairs.

Evelyn and Nicky turned to face the

girl, seeing instantly the radiant happiness shining in her face.

'James and I have been in love quite a long time,' Margaret said slowly. 'It was just as you thought, Evelyn, but I had to lie. I *had* to! We were so afraid of hurting you!'

'Oh, Margaret, darling,' Evelyn cried, breaking away from Nicky and running towards the slight figure standing upright on the stairs. 'You should have told me, you silly, silly, little goose. It hurts me far more to know how unhappy you must have been all these months.'

'Well, it's all right now, isn't it?' Margaret said, her voice suspiciously near tears. 'I thought . . . that is if you don't mind . . . I would ring James and ask him to come round — so that we can tell him.'

'Oh, *of course!*' cried Evelyn. 'We'll have a big dinner party. It will have to be an omelette or something from that powdered egg, but we'll cut the meat up and put it inside. And there's lots of fruit which we bottled last year . . . and we have got that bottle of champagne we were saving for the end of the war, but I think this is just as important an occasion . . . '

She stopped short, suddenly remembering Gay.

'Oh, how could I have forgotten her!' she reproached herself. 'How selfish I am. I'll go up to her while you're telephoning, Margaret.'

'Just a minute, darling,' Nicky said, smiling tenderly at the flushed, excited face of the girl he loved. 'Gay asked me to tell you that she's hoping to produce a son and heir for the de Verrilands.'

'A baby!' Margaret cried. 'Oh, how wonderful!'

But Evelyn stood perfectly still, the light dying from her eyes and a worried little frown creasing her smooth forehead.

'Where's Gordon?' she asked Nicky abruptly.

'I don't know,' Nicky answered thoughtfully. 'There was a slight row, I think, and Gay hasn't heard from him since he was on embarkation leave. But I have sent him a telegram and if he is still in this country, I feel certain he will come. Gay doesn't know about the wire, of course. I didn't want her to be disappointed in case he couldn't come.'

'Poor little Gay,' Evelyn cried. 'But I shall look after her. She will be quite happy here with us. I'm going up to her now!'

But before she went, she allowed Nicky to take her in his arms again and gave him back kiss for kiss.

Twenty minutes later, James walked into the room.

'What's all the excitement about?' he asked. Then he saw Nicky.

'This is Major March!' Margaret said, introducing them. 'And this is James — I mean Dr. Cathy. Oh, Jamie, Gay is going to have a baby and she's staying here, and Evelyn is going to marry Major March, so . . . so . . .'

Nicky, watching the two of them, judged it his turn to be tactful.

'Think I'd better see to the rest of that luggage,' he murmured and left them alone.

As the door closed behind Nicky, James strode forward and took Margaret in his arms.

'Margie, this isn't a joke, is it?' he said roughly. 'I couldn't bear it if . . . if . . . '

'No, Jamie! It's true, wonderfully true!'

'And that army chap was the fellow Evelyn broke her heart over in Germany! What's made him change his mind?'

'Oh, Jamie, don't be so cynical!' Margaret reproached him, laughing. 'He's always been in love with her but he thought she was married!'

James thought this over for a minute, then he shrugged his shoulders.

'All I can say is he couldn't have chosen a better time to return,' he said. 'Margie?'

'Yes, James?'

'There's no need for me to say it, is

there? But now I'm free, I'd like to ask you to marry me. You will, won't you?'

'Jamie, you silly darling,' the girl said very tenderly. 'Of course I will!'

Then the clean fresh smell of antiseptic came closer to her and she felt his arms round her tightening, crushing her against his heart.

'Jamie, oh, Jamie!' she whispered, and lifted her face for his kiss.

★ ★ ★

'Better late than never!' Gay said in reply to Evelyn's apologies for the lateness of the meal.

'You're a really good cook, darling,' Nicky teased her. 'It was worth waiting for!'

Evelyn, seated at the head of the table, Gay and Nicky on her right, Margaret and James on her left, felt that her cup of happiness was full.

'Never, never again shall I be so happy!' she thought.

'I'd like to propose a toast!' Gay said suddenly.

She stood up, raising her glass which brimmed with the crystal loveliness of the champagne.

'To . . . ' She broke off suddenly as Margaret interrupted her with a little cry.

'There's someone opening our gate,' she cried. 'They're coming up the path . . . '

Nicky left the table and went towards the door, his eyes meeting Evelyn's across the room. He saw that she, too, was praying for this late visitor to be Gay's husband.

As Gordon de Verriland came through the open door, his eyes searched the room and came to rest on the pale, unbelieving face of his wife.

'Gay!' he cried.

The glass slipped from her fingers and crashed into a hundred little fragments on the stone-flagged floor. Champagne stained the tablecloth, her dress, the chintz covering of her chair. But she did not notice it.

'Gordon!' she whispered, and as he strode forward she slipped into his arms and he held her dead weight against him.

He stared at that pale face, those closed lids with the lashes curling softly on to her cheeks, and he was so frightened that she was dead that for a moment he could not speak. Then he felt the irregular beat of her heart beneath his hand and knew that she had only fainted.

'She'll be all right in a minute,' James said, coming round the table to him. 'It's quite customary in her condition to faint like that . . . a slight shock. You'd better take her to her room.'

'I'll show you the way,' Evelyn said, and still oblivious to anyone else in the room, Gordon turned and followed Evelyn up the stairs.

'Well!' said Nicky. 'We only want a few bombs and an announcement that the war is over and the curtain can come down. In the meantime, I'm going to finish my supper!'

The tension immediately relaxed into laughter which greeted Evelyn like a warm ray of sunshine as she came back into the room.

Upstairs, Gordon sat by the side of Gay's bed, her hand cool and soft in his grasp.

'I'm so sorry, Gordon!' she said. 'I didn't mean to frighten you!'

'Frighten me!' he said. 'Gay, I thought . . . I was afraid . . . '

'Would you have minded so much then?'

He saw the smile in her eyes, but he still could not joke about it. His fear had been so real.

'You mean everything in the world to me,' he said huskily. 'I wanted to tell you so that . . . that last night we spent in your flat. But I wasn't sure you cared. I wanted to make you love me — as much as I love you.'

They were silent for a minute, then Gay said softly:

'Are you pleased about the baby, darling?'

'Pleased! I'm so happy I shouldn't even mind if it were twins! But Gay, darling, I'm worried. I can't bear to think of you having to go through it all by yourself.'

'Evie will take care of me!' Gay said gently. 'I shall be quite all right.'

'Goodness only knows when I'll be back,' Gordon said miserably. 'Having to say goodbye to you now is going to be hell!'

'We'll be waiting for you!' Gay whispered. 'Both of us. And as long as you come back, we won't mind how long we have to wait.'

'Oh, Gay, Gay, I love you!' he said. 'More than anything in the whole world.'

'When do you have to go?' Gay asked, her voice betraying her fear for him, her anxiety.

'Not until tomorrow,' he told her.

'Then we'll be together tonight?'

'Tonight and in my heart until the end of the world!' he said, and gathered her into his arms.

★ ★ ★

It was very quiet in the little sitting-room. Margaret and James had gone out in the car and Gordon was upstairs with Gay. Nicky sat on the stool at Evelyn's feet, his head resting against her knees.

'It's so peaceful,' she said, breaking the silence that had held them captive for the last ten minutes. 'And yet this is really only the quiet before the storm!'

He knew she was thinking of the invasion and for a moment his own courage failed. Then he said:

'Will you marry me tomorrow, Evelyn? Before I have to go?'

'Yes!' she answered quietly. 'If it can be arranged.'

'I've got a special licence,' Nicky said with a smile. 'Just in case! And Evelyn?'

'Yes, darling?'

'I bought this for you in town today — also just in case!'

He slipped the sparkling ruby ring on to the finger where so short a time ago

James' sapphire had been, but she had no thought for that other ring — that other man.

'Nicky, come back to me!' she said very softly.

'I will!' he answered as he lifted the hand that now wore his ring and rested his cheek against the soft white palm. 'I will, my darling!'

And some inner faith brought the warmth of certainty into her heart. She knew now that however long the war might last, Nicky would come home to her. She knew it as surely as she knew the night must end and another new day would shine forth to offer its golden promise of love and happiness, truth and goodness to the peoples of the world.

THE END

THE WAYWARD HEART

Stella Kent

Francesca had loved her unruffled way of life, working in the Lynford bookshop with fatherly Mr. Pinkerton. But it had all come to an abrupt end when the shop was sold over Mr. Pinkerton's head, by his nephew Adam. The news caused the old man's death, and fury overwhelmed Francesca. But when Adam offered her a job in the Paris bookshop, she accepted. Here was a chance to get all she could out of a particularly heartless man . . .